The Kidnapping of Crystal Covington

Tighe Taylor, JD

Black Cat Publishing—Sherman Oaks, CA
Paperback ISBN: 979-8-218-30776-9
Library of Congress Control Number: pending
Title: *The Kidnapping of Crystal Covington*
Author: Tighe Taylor
Digital distribution | 2023
Paperback | 2023

This is a work of fiction. The characters, names, incidents, places, and dialogue are products of the author's imagination, and are not to be construed as real.

Previous Books by Tighe Taylor

The Tragic Death of Marina Habe
The Kidnapping of Tammy Fitzgerald
The Kidnapping of Taylor Shaw
The Kidnapping of Isabel Miller

Dedication

Dedicated to

Yuki Terayama,

for her hours of listening and contributing.

Savages we call them,

because their manners differ from ours,
which we think the perfection of civility;

they think the same of theirs.

Benjamin Franklin
From "Remarks Concerning the
Savages of North America" (1784)

Chapter 1
The Miller Family

I was looking out over the desert and could see her coming on horseback from far away. She looked so cute directing the horse. She had been out on a ride with Chuck, the Chief's nephew, who has done such a great job teaching her over the past years. And she was getting pretty good.

My name is Taylor Shaw. This advanced rider we are watching is Isabel Miller, my 10-year old daughter. Her father, my husband, is Rick Miller. He is, of course, standing right next to me, as he has for the past 12 years since we got married and began sharing our most beautiful life together. We have the same enthusiasm for Isabel and her accomplishments. Are not Isabel and I the two luckiest girls in the world?

I was born poor on an orange farm. My father left us when I was 10. My mother was a raging alcoholic. When I was a teenager, a little girl for whom I babysat was kidnapped. The police were unable to solve the crime, so I decided to mount my own investigation. I ultimately enlisted the help of my junior college history professor, Rick Miller. Together we found the kidnapped child and returned her home.

I continued my college and law school education, and after passing the bar, I went to work for the State Attorney General initially in elder abuse. Rick and I were out of touch. I think that he thought that he wanted more for me than he could offer. Thank goodness, he finally came to his senses and called, and we started dating.

He arranged for me to meet him at a fancy restaurant. I made my way across a crowded room to his table. After I sat, he got up. I thought that maybe he was leaving. I was wrong. He came over to my chair, got down on one knee, and asked me to marry him, while showing me a beautiful diamond ring that he got for me. I almost passed out.

I said yes, and our life together began.

I remained in the State Attorney General's Office for two years when I was kidnapped because I witnessed a death which occurred during a toxic waste dump. I was taken to the 15-story office building of the kidnapper and was thrown off. Rick scaled the outside of the building, ran across the roof, and dove over the side to save me tied to nothing but a bungee cord. He was able to catch me and return me safely to the ground.

I was promoted to the United States Attorney's Office. My first assignment was as part of the Native American Task Force. The Native Americans complained that they were not receiving the representation they thought that they deserved from the government. They were probably correct.

Much of the interaction between the Native Americans and the U S government centers around criminal law. Of the first four task force members, three would be criminal law specialists, and one, me, would be an environmental law specialist.

Around this time, Isabel, or "Izzy" as we called her, was born.

One very significant case we had in the office concerned water rights on a nearby Indian Reservation. As the task force member hired to concentrate on environmental law, it became necessary for me to be assigned to the case. However, this was exactly what my bosses, the heads of the two water companies, and the primary bad guy did not want.

Under the Coachella Valley, the valley in which Palm Springs, Palm Desert, and the Tribe's Reservation are located, there is an aquafer, or a natural underground spring. For thousands of years, the Native Americans used this water for their activities in the valley and in the foothills south of the valley where they settled.

The primary bad guy had an arrangement with the water companies to obtain more than his allotted share of water for less than its actual value.

The Indians' lawsuit, heard in the United States District Court in Riverside, found that the Indians had historical water rights but lacked standing to quantify the amount of water to which they were entitled or to challenge the quality of the water that they would receive because the tribe could not show an injury. It was given all of the water it needed for "reservation purposes."

The primary bad guy disguised himself as a food grower; however, he was actually a drug smuggler. He stored his drugs in a compound in the mountains south of the highway.

As I moved closer to interfering with his water rights, he found it necessary to devise a plan to slow me down. What was this plan you ask? Simple, instead of kidnapping me, he would kidnap my daughter. Bad move on his part.

When Isabel was kidnapped, she was taken to the bad guy's compound in the mountains.

Rather than working with law enforcement, I enlisted my Indian friends. The Chief came up with a plan in which I would be dropped down into the compound, find Izzy, and escape on the back of a huge black stallion.

The plan went well. Izzy and I made it out of the compound, and the rock walls were blown, sealing the compound and everyone in it closed. Through a wire-tap, sufficient evidence was gathered to lock up all of the bad guys for a very long time.

Over the next years, Izzy would go to school, grow, play with her friends, and come to the Reservation with me and her father.

Of all of the many activities in which we engaged, the thing we loved most was going to the Reservation. We went several times a month and continued perfecting our riding and weapons skills. We also spent time learning about their wonderful culture.

Since Rick and I met, I finished school, solved a kidnapping, was kidnapped myself, and had my daughter kidnapped. Needless to say, we were too busy for socializing. After Izzy's return, things began to settle down, at least a little.

We decided that we would double date and try our best to make new friends. Many of my single female friends looked to me and Rick as a way to meet people of the opposite sex, as they figured that people we might know would be a better bet than people they might meet in a public place.

We took several of our friends to the Reservation. It made a great day trip and allowed our friends to see the animals, meet the people, and try to understand the culture. Some of my female friends even asked about Chuck, Michael, and Roger. They were nice young fellows who worked at the Reservation. I didn't see a problem with them intermingling with my friends. All three were also pretty good looking.

So, things went along swimmingly.

Chapter 2
Next Years

Examining the pool of candidates for socializing it appears as if the U S Attorney's Office was deep. It seemed as if young, good-looking, rich or at least semi-rich kids gravitated towards the assistant U S Attorney job.

It stood to reason. The U S Attorney's Office was prestigious, but did not require an abundance of experience. The Office itself was set up to act as a training ground for new recruits. Because of their economic background, most would not be staying for the rest of their careers. They would learn what they could and jump over to a large law firm, where the money was better.

I came into the Office with three other new hires for the Indian Task Force, John Jacobs, Claire Fielding, and Chris Lightfoot. Several new people had come aboard recently, Pamela Key, Micki Shapiro, Matt Witt, Bill Small, and Janet Halperin, to name a few.

There were some minor changes in the office. The task force was changed to the Indian Division. I went into sex crimes. John and Claire went into the Criminal Division. Chris Lightfoot stayed with the Native Americans. He was a great guy who really cared about the Indians. His parents lived on a reservation. I was glad that he would stay with them, as they needed someone, such as he, who really cared.

Pamela and Micki were new, though Micki had some experience. Micki came to work with me in sex trafficking. They were both great people. Micki was happily married and just had her first child. Pamela was not married and seemed a good candidate to meet someone. She was also very good looking.

I thought that John or Chris would be a good fit for her. My plan was to ask her to meet me for a drink at the bar across the street. I could feel her out and see if she was even interested in meeting anyone.

That evening I spoke with Rick about it. He met Chris once and liked him. He never met Pamela. His opinion was that if I asked her first, that it should be alright.

The next day at the office I asked Pamela if she wanted to have a drink at the bar across the street. The name of the bar is the Service of Process. She said yes, and we arranged to meet at 5.

5 came around, and I headed first to the bathroom to freshen up a bit and then to the bar. Pamela and I arrived at about the same time. We were shown to a table. We sat. We each ordered a Greyhound. We nursed our drinks for a couple of minutes.

I asked, "I guess you are wondering why I invited you here. Rick, my husband, and I wanted to know if you and Chris would like to have dinner with us or go out to the Indian Reservation for a day trip?"

Pamela answered, "That sounds like fun, but I am not really dating right now."

Taylor replied, "I would think that a beautiful girl such as you would have no trouble getting a date."

Pamela answered, "That's not it; it's just that I have not found anyone interesting."

Taylor replied, "I can understand that."

Pamela is really cute. She is 25 years old, but she looks like a teenager. She is always dressed nicely with her skirt above the knee, tinted nylons, low heals, blouse, and jacket. She is generally accessorized with rings, bracelets, pins, etc.

It is presumed around the office that she must have several guys trying to date her, because she is so beautiful, but no one has ever seen her with anyone.

Pamela asked, "What do you think of being married?"

Taylor asked, "It's really all I've ever known. I met Rick when I was only 19, and for the first several years I was involved in solving a kidnapping case, returning the child to her mother, getting into college and law school, and getting a job. Rick was older, and he always knew what he wanted. I came to understand ultimately that Rick was what I wanted, but it still didn't leave me without questions."

Pamela said, "Those questions my dear are asked by everyone. By all accounts, you have a great husband, a beautiful child, and a good job. It would be hard to ask for more, but the human condition is such that there is always something just around that proverbial corner."

Taylor said, "When Rick and I talked about doing some more socializing, I don't think that either one of us thought it might create problems in our relationship. I think we both thought that we would just keep on going the way we were, and we could introduce our friends to one another."

Pamela said, "In life, things don't always work out as we think. But I believe that your hearts were in the right place."

Taylor said, "Well, how about the guys at the office?"

Pamela said, "Most of the guys are either young and appear inexperienced or are older and married. Married is just out for me."

Taylor said, "I thought that John or Chris might be a fit. They both came in with me to be on the Native American Task Force. This implies, at least to me, that they are compassionate about something."

Pamela asked, "What about Chuck?"

Taylor replied, "Chuck? Do you mean the Chief's nephew? I didn't know you even knew him."

Pamela said, "I don't, but I have heard you mention him a couple of times, and it seems as if you think that he is attractive in addition to being well versed in all of those guy things, you know, weapons, riding, and so on."

Taylor, a little taken aback, asked, "Do you think you would have much to talk about?"

Pamela said, "Sweetie, talking is over-rated, if the guy is good looking enough."

Pamela sensed that Taylor's feeling about Chuck might be a little bit more complicated than she thought.

Pamela went on, "If I've hit a nerve with Chuck, I can pass."

Taylor, now a little defensive, "Don't be silly. I'm happy to introduce you to Chuck. My relationship with him is strictly Platonic. He's like a brother."

Pamela was thinking to herself that she felt bad for Taylor. It appears as if with Chuck, she has met someone that she actually likes but cannot do anything about because she's married and has a child.

Pamela decided to change course completely.

Pamela said, "I don't know about meeting people at the Reservation. That might not be a great idea."

Taylor was relieved more than Pamela knew.

Pamela replied, "Maybe I will give Chris a shot and see how that goes."

A little relieved, Taylor replied, "Sounds like a good idea. I really like him. He's solid. Even Rick likes him."

Pamela replied, "It's getting late; perhaps we should wrap this up. We both have to be up early tomorrow for work."

The next day was business as usual for both Taylor and Pamela. Oddly, Taylor felt a little uncomfortable having revealed some of her secrets to a virtual stranger. She really was not used to having relationships of any depth at all, except with Rick, and it made her feel a little vulnerable.

That evening she spoke with Rick after dinner and after Izzy was in bed. She related much of that which she and Pamela spoke, leaving out the part about Chuck. Her relationship with Rick was so long-standing that she did not realize that there might be room in there for someone else.

She resolved that she would maintain her marriage not only because she loved and cared for Rick, but also because she desperately wanted Izzy to have an intact family in which male and female role models would work together to make something beautiful. Running off with someone else involved more than her own feelings. They involved Izzy's feelings, the most important person in her life.

On the second day after drinks with Pamela, she figured that she would re-visit the Pamela situation. So, she arranged to meet her again at 5 at the Service of Process bar.

After being seated and ordering the obligatory mixed drink, Taylor started, "I had a great time with you the other night. I'm glad we can do it again."

Taylor was a terrible liar. It's amazing that she has been successful in the law business at all, as bad as she is at lying. The only thing that saves her is that her cases are primarily government prosecutions, and most of the evidence has been neatly laid out to the point where a first-year law student could get a conviction.

Taylor was willing to step back into the breech. At this point, it is difficult to evaluate her motivation. Was she actually trying to help Pamela get a date? Was she actually trying to hook up Chris or John with a very attractive girl? Or was she really interested in learning more about herself?

Pamela said, "It's really nice that you are thinking about me and introducing me to a couple of the guys around the office. Chris seems like such a nice guy. Also, he's a couple of years older. I generally prefer guys 5 to 10 years older, like you and Rick. Guys seem to need a little seasoning before they become interesting."

Taylor replied, "I agree, but we don't have much to work with at the office. Most of the guys are from rich families and are pretty sheltered."

She continued, "I was giving a little more thought to the Reservation. I know that you initially wanted to pass, which I understand. You might not be all that outdoorsy, and meeting someone new in a place where you are not that comfortable might just make matters worse.

"But I think that you would enjoy the Reservation.

"Our plan is to go up Saturday, and I would like to re-new my invitation to you to join us. I thought that I would invite Chris. This will give you guys a chance to meet each other doing something at which neither of you is completely comfortable."

Pamela answered, "I have always been someone who is up for a challenge, and this might be a good opportunity to learn about the Reservation and other people at the same time. I'm in for Saturday, if you still want me."

Taylor replied, "Of course we want you. Perhaps you could drive over to our house at around 8 a.m. You can leave your car there, and we can all go up together. Just so there are no surprises, I already asked Chris, and he said yes. Confidentially, when I told him that you might be coming he remarked, 'Oh, you mean the hot one that just started working in the office.' To which I replied, 'Yes. Her.'"

Taylor continued, "I am going to ask Claire to come also. She visited the Reservation with the Indian Task Force along with me, Chris, and John. She's nice, and it will look like less of a set-up if we have another single woman."

Later, Taylor asked Claire to come with them, but she politely declined. Her one day at the Reservation appears to have been enough.

After Taylor and Pamela settled the Reservation trip, Pamela still had a few questions for Taylor about their work. These questions were unrelated to the Reservation, Chris, or Chuck.

Pamela asked Taylor how she wound up in sex trafficking. In response, Taylor decided to explain her entire working life. Taylor said that she started out in the State AGs Office in elder abuse. She figured that her bosses felt that she could not do much damage there.

She quickly proved to be too valuable to be tied down in elder abuse and was promoted to environmental law and white-collar crime. There she really made her mark. She went after corporate higher-ups with abandon, landing a few in jail. This provoked most of them to be critical of her and a few of them to seek retribution against her. One went so far as to throw her off of the roof of his 15 story corporate headquarters building which she barely survived with her husband's help.

She was then promoted to the U S Attorney's Office. Initially, she was to serve in the Native American Task Force along with Claire, John, and Chris. As part of their training, they were required to spend a full day at the Reservation.

She spent the day and then received permission to return for the rest of the week. She was so enthralled with the Indians and their culture that she wound up going to the Reservation as often as she could. She learned how to fight, throw knives, shoot arrows, and ride horses, some of which she already knew, having been raised on a farm.

Her daughter was kidnapped, and the Indians helped her extricate her from the kidnapper's people. After that, she went into sex trafficking.

Taylor had a sorted history with her bosses. Of course, the crooked ones hated her. She had a couple of bad ones at the Attorney General's Office and at the U S Attorney's Office. Most of the bad ones were guys who were dissatisfied with the amount of money that they could make from their jobs so they started selling confidential information to their clients, who were rich criminals.

Her honest bosses loved her and lauded her performance every chance they had. These people appreciated her honesty and hard work, as her performance reflected on them.

Her co-workers were a mixed bag. They were either jealous and not friendly, or they were interested in doing a good job and wanted to learn from her.

To her credit, most of the hatred coming her way came from the crooks and gangsters whose enterprises she took great pleasure in dismantling.

She destroyed the empires of the gangster who kidnapped her babysitting charge and the drug dealer who made the fatal mistake of kidnapping her daughter.

In her mind, these were her greatest achievements, but surprisingly enough, she was not as exalted by the beneficiaries of these incredible achievements as one might think. Perhaps in their way of thinking her tactics were too draconian. In her way of thinking, taking down rich people rubbed even poor people the wrong way. People with money were seen as necessary. It appears as if for some reason being financially successful is more important than bringing bad people to justice.

Fortunately for her, she did not care. Whether people in general thought she was being too tough meant nothing to her. Instead, she put her faith in the Latin pickers, the motorcycle club vets, and the Indians. In other words, in the people who actually show up when things get tough.

Pamela said, "I see the course you took to get to where you are now, but I still have questions about sex trafficking. As you know, if hired, I would be the most recent hire in the sex trafficking division. I was told that my consideration, at least in part, was due to the fact that I am a woman, and women are needed in the department.

"No one I know loves sex as much as I do. I am downright promiscuous. I'm ready to go all of the time at the drop of a hat. Am I the type of person who should be in sex trafficking?"

Taylor responded, "I wouldn't worry about it. The division is full of men. And men are wired just as you describe, ready to go all of the time. And men excel in sex trafficking. However, men, particularly white men, have one significant advantage. They have the uncanny ability to practice self-justification.

"A white man could get a woman drunk and technically rape her and come back the next day and prosecute a rapist, giving an impassioned speech to the jury about how far outside of the bounds of decency the rapist acted. The white man's ability to self-justify is downright legendary and has been spread around the world many times over.

"With as beautiful as you are, I am certain that your encounters are consensual. If you want to stay in sex trafficking, you might want to think of your encounters as something of mutual benefit to both you and your partner and not as something that was done to you.

"However, in the sex trafficking business, the place where we as women have an opportunity to excel is helping the women for whom the act was anything but consensual. Those are the people who need us. It's very rewarding to break up a prostitution ring or sweat shop and work with social services to re-integrate the abused women back into productive society.

"Believe it or not, I like sex too. But before Rick, sex for me was just rough, fast, and mostly painful. It wasn't until I met Rick that I learned that sex could be a gentle, mutual, and loving act between two people who really cared about one another. The rough stuff I can live without, and have lived without it for the past many years.

"So, if you feel that you cannot be true to yourself and your own feelings, you might consider another specialty. But if your beef is with people taking advantage of nonconsensual sex, this might be the place for you."

Pamela said, "Thank you. You really opened my eyes to a few things. I guess with my vast knowledge of sex, I will know when it's wanted or not, which should help me."

Taylor replied, "At least think about it. This is our top department and could lead you to bigger and better things in your practice.

"Also, I promise to never tell anyone about your fascination with sex. If people find out, we will have so many guys lined up that our office will look like the opening night of Star Wars."

Pamela replied, "Very funny. I will consider everything. And I cannot thank you enough."

They decided that it was late. They would complete the work week and meet at Taylor's to go to the Reservation on Saturday at 8 a.m.

Chapter 3
Taylor, Rick, Izzy, Pamela, and Chris
At the Reservation

8 a.m. Saturday came, and Pamela and Chris, in separate cars, arrived at the Miller house to meet Taylor, Rick, and Izzy for their trip to the Reservation.

Rick and Taylor were wearing boots and jeans with shirts with snaps. Izzy was wearing her Reservation outfit which included chaps over her jeans and boots. Chris was dressed similarly to Rick and Taylor, jeans and boots. Pamela was a little more-dressy. She was wearing tight jeans and boots. Her shirt was more ornate with snaps and buttons all around. Everyone had a hat, which was necessary with the weather.

Rick was loading the car in the driveway of their new house. It occurred to them that their friends had never seen their house, as they entertained infrequently at home.

Chris parked across the street and walked towards Rick's driveway. Pamela also parked across the street and walked over. At this point, Rick, Taylor, Chris, and Pamela were all gathered in Rick's driveway in front of his house.

Rick greeted the group, "Hi, I'm Rick, Taylor's husband. I haven't met either Chris or Pamela."

Chris said, "Hi Rick, I'm Chris. Good to meet you." Chris brought a small bag with a couple of things he thought he might need for the day. He gave the bag to Rick who packed it in the back with the things that Rick brought.

When Rick and Taylor go to the Reservation, they typically bring food not only for themselves but also for other members of the tribe who often join them to eat because the food is different than the food they usually receive. Sometimes Taylor will bring clothes out of which Isabel has grown for the children at the Reservation. As is typical of Taylor and Rick, their offerings are done casually with no expectation of remuneration. A thank you is more than they expect or need. They operate from the heart.

Pamela came over with her bag and handed it to Rick. She said, "Hi, I'm Pamela. I work with Taylor in the U S Attorney's Office."

Rick replied, "Yes, she has told me about you. She says that she really enjoys the time that she gets to spend talking to you. She doesn't get as much female company away from the office as she appears to want."

Pamela said, "She goes on and on about you and what a great husband and father you are. You should be happy."

Rick responded, "Oh, I am. But thank you for letting me know. It's always nice to hear."

After loading up the car, they all got in and took their seats. Rick was driving. Isabel sat next to him, as she often did. Taylor rounded out the front seat. Pamela and Chris were in the back seat. The far back was filled with food and bags.

They drove back to the highway and then east across the floor of the valley. They turned south and headed towards the south mountains. The road passed under a semi-circular sign which read that they were entering the Reservation of the Tribe Indians. After passing under the sign, the road connects to a large dirt infield. On the far side of the infield, there is the main building. The main building houses a gift shop and the Chief's private office and secretary.

To the left side of the main building, there is a mess hall. To the right side of the main building, there are sleeping quarters.

The main building is near the base of the mountains. In the opposite direction, there are hot springs, popular with the tourists.

This settlement on the Reservation acts as sort of a dude ranch for tourists who wish a taste of the old west.

As we drove towards the Reservation, Rick recounted a little of its history. Rick said, "In 1876, Ulysses S. Grant transferred approximately 900 acres to the Tribe. A year later, in 1877, Rutherford B. Hayes transferred another 30,000 acres to the Tribe. Every other section of land was transferred to the railroad. The Tribe received the even numbered sections, and the railroad the odd numbered. The Tribe has 6,700 acres in Palm Springs, and is its largest land owner.

"A valuable piece of land was Section 14. It contained a large portion of the hot springs. Because Section 14 was federal land, the City of Palm Springs grew up around it. It was not zoned, and the City offered no services to its inhabitants. Because the land was less expensive, the low-income employees and laborers settled it.

"As growth continued into the 20th century, the City tried to wrestle Section 14 back from the Indians. It did this by attempting to enforce zoning regulations and building codes. It even bulldozed or burned out homes when the owners were at work.

"By the 1950s and 1960s, the Tribe began to pursue its treaty rights in court. Eventually the City began to work with the Tribe. By 1977, the City and the Tribe worked together under a land-use contract.

"So, it only took from 1877 to 1977 for the City and Tribe to work together, 100 years of treaty fights and court battles. Silly waste of time, in my opinion."

Chris added, "Such interesting history. We went over some of this with the Chief when we came out here for the Indian Task Force."

Taylor said, "Pretty good memory. That was quite a while ago."

The drive to the Reservation was not long. They all got out of the car to stretch their legs, parking the car in front of the main building, at least temporarily.

The Chief and Chuck came out onto the elevated sidewalk outside of the main building to greet their guests. They both looked very dashing in jeans, boots, shirt, and hat.

The Chief started, "Hello everyone. It's nice to have visitors. Of course, we see Taylor, Rick, and Izzy all of the time, but the other two we have not seen as often, if at all. As I recall, the gentleman came with Taylor and two other new hires back when she first started with the U S Attorney. I believe his name is Chris. As I recall, his parents lived on a reservation for a short time."

Chris was startled that the Chief could remember him. He said, "You have an excellent memory sir."

"This gentleman to my right is Chuck. He is my nephew, and we work together here at the Reservation. Any questions you have for me may be addressed to either me or him, as he is quite familiar with the operation.

"In addition to Chuck, Michael works here often. Roger works here too, but not as often. I will introduce you to both of them when I find them.

"I thought that we could adjourn to the mess hall and make sandwiches for lunch. As it is a little before lunch time now, I thought we could pack up the sandwiches and take them with us on our ride.

My plan is to divide everybody into two groups. One group will go with Chuck, and the other with Michael. If it is okay with all of you, I would ask Rick and Izzy to go with Michael, and Taylor, Pamela, and Chris to go with Chuck."

There were no objections. They all dispersed to the mess hall.

Sandwiches were made and packed along with water and some crackers. Treats were included for the horses, of course.

Before heading out, the group excused itself to use the restroom. Taylor and Pamela headed out to the ladies' room together. This gave Pamela a chance to speak with Taylor privately.

Pamela said, in faux anger, "You've really been holding out on me. I don't know whether to be mad as hell or amused."

Taylor responded, "And why's that?"

Pamela said, "You didn't tell me just how good-looking Chuck is. I presume that this was just an oversight?"

Taylor said, "Sometimes people have a different idea as to what is good-looking?"

Pamela replied, "Yeah, right. 6 foot, two inches of solid muscle with black hair and dark features, that never works."

Taylor replied sheepishly, "I didn't know."

Pamela said, "Are you interested in this guy. Like should I stay away from him so he can be saved for you exclusively? I see the way he looks at you; it even makes me a little uncomfortable."

Taylor replied, "No. Nothing like that. I am not interested in him in that way. He's on the open market as far as I know."

Pamela, amused, said, "Wow, you're a horrible liar. I don't know how you got so far in the law business. Maybe it's because you're a government lawyer, and all of the people that you prosecute are already known to be guilty so you don't need to manufacture evidence like the rest of us.

"Anyway, I guess I will take you at your word that Chuck is available, if you don't mind?"

Taylor replied, "I don't mind."

The girls finished with the restroom and joined the group outside of the mess hall. Taylor went to the barn to get horses for her, Pamela, and Chris. She brought them over, and they loaded lunch. She was still uncomfortable with having someone else fetch a horse for her.

Rick and Izzy loaded their lunches and met Michael. Though Izzy was becoming a good rider, because of her size and ability to really control a horse, the Chief generally kept her closer to the main building than the adults. He's very careful with her as he considers her to be the granddaughter that he never had.

One of the workers brought out horses for Michael, Rick, and Izzy. They mounted up and headed off in the direction of the mountains. The Chief gave Michael instructions to make their ride easy and safe.

Taylor brought out the four horses for her group. She gave Chuck a large stallion, as he was by far the best rider. She gave Chris a gentle mare as he never rides. She brought the remaining two horses for her and Pamela. Pamela said that she didn't have much experience with horses.

Taylor came to find out much later that Pamela's act as an inexperienced rider was just that, an act. She later learned that Pamela had been riding equestrian since she was 12 and that she even rode in college.

When riding equestrian, she wore stretch pants, high boots, a short jacket, and a hat, all of which was very upper crust looking. After undergraduate school at Amherst College, she moved back to California to attend law school at Stanford University.

As Taylor picked up right away, Pamela was putting on quite a show for Chuck. She pretended to know nothing about riding so Chuck would have to spend more time with her than he might otherwise. With Taylor, on the other hand, the two of them could take horses out for the day and never even talk about riding once.

When Taylor saw the way Pamela was dressed, she knew right away that she meant business. Poor Chuck. He didn't have a chance. Pamela wore boots adorned with just a touch of silver. She wore jeans so tight that they must have been applied with spray paint. The shirt was almost too much. It was cream colored with silver snaps and dark piping. It was open in the front just enough to be sexy without looking cheap, a very neat trick practiced only by the most experienced ladies in the field.

Taylor remembered back to when she was roughly Pamela's age, and Chuck complained about her perfume. She wondered if Chuck would complain about Pamela's perfume, which could be smelled from six horse lengths away.

Whatever was going to happen among the three of them, Taylor, Pamela, and Chuck, it would be of Taylor's doing. She was attracted to Chuck in many ways, including physically, but she was not ready to go off with him and damage her life-long relationship with Rick, a real person, which would include damage to Izzy, as well.

Taylor resigned herself to the fact that maintaining her relationship with Rick and keeping Izzy safe were more important than a tryst with Chuck, as fun as it might be. She decided that she would just watch Pamela in action, treating the experience as a master class in seduction.

The four of them took off towards the mountain. Taylor was not certain what Chuck had planned for them.

They all engaged in some light conversation. Chris, who was part of the original Indian Task Force, relayed that the other two task force members, the two members other than he and Taylor, were kept quite busy with the various criminal violations on the Reservation. He was a nice young man. He was well mannered and polite. However, he wasn't quite enough for Pamela.

Chris and Chuck engaged in a lively conversation about Indian jurisdiction. Taylor thought that Chuck enjoyed these conversations so that he could demonstrate that he was more than just a pretty face (and hot body) but was able to do some thinking too.

Chris and Chuck's conversation centered around the tribe's ability to prosecute crimes on a reservation. The tendency has been to give the reservations more authority to prosecute crimes on their land. However, federal law allows federal jurisdiction when the crimes become more serious.

There is also PL-280 to deal with. This law allows certain States specified by statute to have jurisdiction over crimes committed on reservations in those States, which includes California.

Chuck took the position which opines that one can only hope that the political branches and courts will do their duty to honor America's promise to allow the tribes greater rights to prosecute crimes occurring on tribal land.

Even Chris, when confronted out here in the middle of nowhere, could see the benefit of allowing the tribes more autonomy, treating them as the sovereign nations that they are rather than part of the State in which they just happen to be located.

We reached the rocky foothills and began our ascent. Chuck said that we could have lunch soon, or we could fish first if we wished. Since lunch was already packed and ready to eat, we chose to eat what we had. Fishing could be done another day. As I learned in the past,

17

fishing is fun and provides a nice meal.

We reached a large, rock lined pond with a waterfall pouring down into it. A perfect place for a swim on a hot day. We put out blankets on the ground around the base of the rocks surrounding the pond. We ate lunch on the rocks and blankets. It was most beautiful.

It was now mid-day, and it was getting very hot. Chuck pulled off his shirt and dove into the pond. When Chuck took off his shirt, it was almost too much. We pretended to not look, but he was so ripped that it was hard not to notice.

The rest of us took off our boots and socks, rolled up our pants, and waded in the shallow, cold water. It really felt good. As we all worked together in the same office, we left it at wading.

Everyone was tired, and people began to separate. Chris moved to the far end of the pond where he could sit with his feet in the water and ponder the outdoors.

I looked for a remote spot from where I could see the waterfall clearly. Chuck moved just to the side of the waterfall. This allowed the water to spray towards him.

There was a large rock with its 45-degree face extending out from under the water between Chuck and the rest of us.

Pamela really outdid even herself. Seeing the slanted face of the large rock, she attempted to pass over the rock to reach Chuck. As she passed over the rock, she lost her footing and fell into the water.

This gave Chuck the opportunity to come to her rescue. He waded into the water, which was not very deep, and picked Pamela up in his arms while he stood on the rocky bottom.

While holding her up out of the water, Chuck lost his footing, and both he and Pamela fell into the shallow water, with Pamela still in his arms.

They were both wet, and Pamela was able to use her condition as a way to further unbutton her blouse to exposed her sheer bra and ample and very attractive breasts.

Taylor, witnessing the fall, thought to herself, how truly masterful Chuck's acting ability had become. Chuck was pretending that he was having difficulty holding up a 115-pound girl. Guess he forgot that he has been carrying around 200-pound animals since he was 12.

By this time, Chris heard the commotion and came over to the water's edge. He asked Chuck if he needed help. Chuck declined his offer.

I, on the other hand, already knew that Chuck needed help, just not that kind of help.

Chuck carried Pamela out of the water. I have to admit with her blouse half unbuttoned, her wet hair slicked back, her tight pants soaked, and her makeup partially washed off, she really looked hot, even to me, and I don't even like girls that way.

Pamela said to Chuck, "Thank you. You really saved me from a dousing."

Chuck responded, "No worries. It was my pleasure."

Taylor thought to herself, 'I bet.'

It was now getting on to afternoon, and our group was getting ready to make the ride back to the main building.

We packed up, cleaned up, mounted up, and headed back. We arrived at the main building at around 3 o'clock. Rick, Izzy, and Michael had arrived just ahead of us.

I took our four horses to the barn where I joined one of the workers in rubbing down the seven horses who were out all day. Even after all of these years, from the time I was a little girl, I still did not like someone rubbing down a horse for me after a ride.

While I was working on the horses, Chris, Pamela, Chuck, Rick, Izzy, and Michael had some of the drinks we brought earlier. We packed up the food containers and left-over drinks into the car.

While all of this was going on, Pamela maneuvered Chuck to a quiet location just outside of the bunk house to speak to him privately. She was good. She thanked him again for saving her from the pond. You would have thought that he rescued her from category 5 hurricane. She asked if she could call him to go out and then asked for his number. She was not going to risk giving him her number, as he might not use it. She was too clever for that. He gave her his number. She was now ready to leave the reservation.

As Taylor was joining the group from her work in the barn, she could see that Pamela had succeeded in separating Chuck from the group. She figured that she must have gotten his number.

Taylor and Pamela joined the rest of the group. They said good bye to the Chief, Chuck, and Michael, thanking them for the use of the kitchen and the horses and for supplying two so accomplished guides.

They entered the car and left the reservation for Rick and Taylor's house.

Interestingly enough, Taylor was upset, but she did not show it outwardly to the group, just a little to Pamela.

Though unspoken, Pamela took the position, and perhaps rightly so, that she cleared her intentions with Chuck with Taylor before acting on them. Women are funny in this way. Even though Taylor really had no interest in having an affair with Chuck, she still did not like the idea of him liking someone else.

After they returned to Rick and Taylor's house, the group dispersed to reach their own cars. Taylor trailed Pamela to her car. Away from the others, Taylor said to Pamela, "I hope you had a good time today. It's nice to meet some of the people you work with in an atmosphere outside of the office. Also, if you plan on doing any work with the Indian Task Force, the opportunity to see the Reservation is a good one."

Taylor then continued, "I must say I think that you made a favorable impression on everyone today."

Then Taylor went on, half-jokingly, "Also, you made quite an impression with the outfit you chose to wear."

Pamela replied, "Thank you. It was nice to meet people with whom I work away from work and to see the Reservation."

She then went on, "Oh, and as to your question about my choice of outfits, I have only one thing to say: It costs a lot of money to look this cheap."

They both snickered as Pamela entered her car and drove away.

Chapter 4
Pamela and Chuck

One might think of Pamela and Chuck as an unlikely couple. She went to Amherst and Stanford Law and was used to the finer things. He went to an Indian Boarding School, and after barely making it out of there alive, became used to nothing but hard work on the Reservation.

One would think that a young, attractive woman such as Pamela who graduated from a top law school could write her own ticket anywhere. But she chose the U S Attorney's Office in Riverside, of all places. The U S Attorney's Office is one of the top destinations in government work, and is a nice piece of employment experience for one's resume, but other, more prestigious, firms were well within her reach.

Being able to land a job out of law school in the U S Attorney's Office shows that someone thought that she had great promise. Remember, Taylor cooled her heals in the State Attorney General's Office before being elevated to Assistant U S Attorney, and she was a busy, proven practitioner with some major victories under her belt before she was given a chance.

Pamela is interesting. As beautiful, intelligent, and well-bred as she is, she showed a legitimate interest in Chuck. One would think that she would go for another high-brow lawyer, such as herself, at least to placate her family, who would probably look at Chuck with displeasure, even though it would be misplaced.

Anyone who has followed the story of Chuck including his abilities in the wild, his readiness to help, and his lack of greed or self-interest would be impressed with him. However, his ability to impress might not dove tail into financial success, which didn't seem to bother him but did appear to bother everyone else, at least everyone else in the white world.

Maybe she sees things in Chuck at which most people choose to not look. One would understand Taylor's interest. She has seen Chuck in action and has spent hours talking to him. She knows that of which he is capable and his ability to think deeply. But Pamela's experience is much more limited.

Perhaps both of the ladies are attracted to Chuck on purely a physical level, as he is quite good looking, but one would think that there are many good looking La Crosse players out there too.

Pamela called Chuck and invited him to meet her for dinner at a place she liked in Palm Springs. Palm Springs was very close for him and fairly close for her. It was a country western bar called Carlos and Pepe's which, in addition to alcohol, also served Mexican food.

The plan was to meet there Friday at 9 p.m. It appears as if she chose a country western place so that neither of them would have to get dressed up.

Friday came, and Chuck drove his pick-up truck to the restaurant. He was cleaned up in jeans, a white shirt, and black cowboy boots. His long black hair was pulled back in a pony tail, Indian style. He arrived a little early and decided to wait in an outdoor waiting area. A few minutes later she showed up. She was dressed in fancy cowboy boots, jeans, and a loose-fitting western shirt with snaps and contrasting piping which showed off her assets.

They went inside. Chuck asked the hostess for a table. She showed them to a table in the main dining room. To reach the table, they had to walk past the bar, where several TV sets were set to a baseball game, and where several semi-drunk patrons were playing pool and watching the game. They received a few looks.

They were seated at a nice table in the back of the room where it was quiet enough to talk.

Each was curious about the other. Chuck asked her about her background. She told him that she went to undergraduate school at Amherst College in Massachusetts where she studied history, primarily American history. She mentioned that it was a small liberal arts college in a small town. She withheld the fact that its acceptance rate is only about 9 percent, that most applicants have SAT scores around 1500, and that a grade point average of 4.07 (better than straight A's) is required. She also failed to mention that she rode equestrian competitively. She reasoned that those were her past. This is her present.

Chuck already knew that she was a lawyer. She told him that she

22

went to Stanford Law which allowed her to return to California, which was her long-term plan. He seemed very impressed, as anyone would be.

She asked him about his past. He told her that he went to a special school for Indians where he was required to cut his hair, speak only English, convert to Christianity, renounce his past culture, and learn to work in the fields or on cars. Not exactly the same as her background.

She asked him about his plans for the future. He said that he had what his people would consider a very good job working for his uncle, the Chief, at the Reservation as a sort of tour guide, not unlike a concierge in a hotel. He explained that the Reservation was set up similar to a dude ranch. People would come from the city and stay a few days where they could indulge in frontier life.

They had access to the hot springs, riding lessons, shooting lessons, campfires, and other activities that one might expect if he lived in the old west.

It was Chuck's job to make sure that everyone had a place to sleep, three meals, transportation to the various activities, and were enjoying an authentic western experience.

Same as Taylor, Pamela's first question to him was the obvious: Why, with all of your skills, do you not find something a little more challenging.

And he answered Pamela the same way he answered Taylor. He said: "The Indians are a conquered people. If they want a better way of life, they need to achieve it within the framework of the white world, and they have no family background, generational wealth, connections for a good job, or ability to raise money for one's own business.

"He explained how the Indians used the land and animals they were given by nature, and they used only as much as they needed to survive. If the land became unable to produce, they moved to other land and allowed the non-producing land time to regenerate itself. The same was true of the animals. They killed only enough animals to feed themselves and to provide hides and other body parts necessary to make clothes or implements. An animal was only killed after much soul searching and only with the express understanding that every inch of it would be used to either feed or clothe someone.

"He explained that white people were much more concerned with settlement. They would use the land allotted to them and raise animals to slaughter to feed themselves and to sell to others.

"Because of their settlement culture, white people were much more possessive of their land. They developed a system under which land was actually owned by someone making it possible for the owner to transfer the land by sale or will to the next generation. Over time, the owners of the land felt that they could exclude others from using it.

"The Indians had no such system of land ownership. They felt that the land belonged to everyone. As the whites began to outnumber the Indians, the Indians were shocked to learn that someone owned the land on which they had lived for centuries. They were equally shocked to learn that they were being moved to other land, which was generally of lesser value or use.

"Looking at it historically, white people (known as "English") came to America around 1600. Initially, the Indians helped them survive the harsh winters. By 1650, many of the Indians knew that the white man intended to take over the entire continent, but they failed to take the action necessary to prevent this from happening.

"By the 1700s, the white man already considered the Indians to be savages without the intelligence or industry to improve their condition. In the late 1700s, Benjamin Franklin wrote an interesting essay about the Indians and their habits. Though he personally favored the way the Indians handled many of their situations in terms of self-governance, listening to others speak, and self-policing, he was a realist, and he recognized that white people generally did not hold the Indians in high regard, which was true.

"In the 1770s, 1780s, and 1790s, as George Washington was founding a nation in which it was professed that all men were created equal, he ordered armed troops to exterminate Indians in large numbers.

"By the 1800s, the white man began his push to move the Indians to other lands.

"With the Indian Removal Act of 1830 passed under President Andrew Jackson, the white man removed 60,000 Indians from the east in exchange for territory west of the Mississippi. Many Indians did not wish to make this move, but they were forced by the U S military to do so and were marched 1000 miles to Oklahoma, along the Trail of Tears, where many died.

"The following story shows the attitude white people had about the

Indians. This is not a musing between two buddies sharing a beer in a local bar, but it is a statement made by Andrew Jackson, President of the United States, to Congress. To paraphrase as well as I can, President Jackson, when speaking of the Indians, said that they have neither the intelligence, the industry, the moral habits, nor the desire of improvement essential to any favorable change in their condition and that because they are established in the midst of a superior race, they will have to yield.

"Is this the way that white people honestly felt about the Indians at that time?

"By 1845, white Americans were looking to complete their Manifest Destiny which included taking over the entire continent. By the late 1890s and into the 20th Century, the Indians were all but exterminated or moved onto reservations.

"The movement of the Indians onto reservations was generally accomplished by force, after which the parties entered into reservation contracts (treaties) under which an Indian tribe would be given land for a reservation and excluded from all other land.

"Many of these reservation contracts were breeched when the whites determined that they wanted back some of the land that they had given away. To further complicate things, the reservation system of ownership gave the entire reservation to the tribe. Individual members of the tribe could not transfer a portion of the reservation to anyone else.

"Conversely, white people owned their land in fee simple and could transfer their portion of the land to others either by sale or will.

"With respect to some land, such as Section 14 right here in Palm Springs, when the land became valuable, the City tried to force the Indians out. In the case of Section 14, the whites tried to burn and bulldoze the Indians' property. This fight went on for decades, and it was not until the 1977 that a land use contract could be struck between the whites and the Indians. The Indians wound up as the largest property owners in Palm Springs but not without years of court battles.

"In short, losing the ability to use the vast areas of land previously available, the Indians were relegated to reservations where they were no longer able to take care of themselves but were required to rely on the white government to take care of them.

"Whites were truly the masters of self-justification.

"White people came into a country about which they knew nothing in 1600 and within 100 years treated the indigenous people as savages. They then took the position that these savages lacked the intelligence and industry to govern which justified them in taking over the land for themselves because they were the superior race.

"Taking it one step further, they felt that they were justified in taking the land by force which allowed them to exterminate as much of the indigenous population as they felt necessary.

"They are a smug group.

"So, if an Indian wants to succeed, he needs to do so in the white man's way, and Indians have neither the means nor the capital to do this.

"One would have thought that the Indians could raise capital by leasing out the land given to them under the reservation system. However, the whites got around this by enacting laws limiting the amount of time for which an Indian could lease his land to a term so short that no one would lease.

"It was not until lease terms were extended to 99 years that the Indians could make money leasing out their property.

"I guess the short answer to your question is that though my deal is not perfect, it is not that bad either. If my uncle were interested, we could improve the restaurant and gift shop, add some newer rooms, improve access to the baths, and even build a golf course similar to the ones we already have. I am only 35, so I need to get moving. We now have some access to capital which we did not have when the whites limited our lease terms."

Pamela inquired, "I studied the plight of the Native Americans in college as a history major. I've always thought that the Native Americans and the American Blacks received very harsh treatment."

Chuck replied, "Harsh indeed."

Chuck asked Pamela if she had anything to add about her upbringing. She said that she had an idyllic life with great parents and the chance to get a great education. She already left out her education and horseback-riding experience, so there was not much left to tell.

The food came and went. They each had a glass of wine. The evening was winding down. They decided to leave.

It was now coming up on 11 p.m. As they walked by the bar to their cars; they got a few looks.

Chuck walked Pamela to her car and said, "Thank you for such a nice time and for being such a good listener."

Pamela replied, "No, thank you for inviting me and for having so much knowledge to impart. I'm sorry to cut the evening short, but I am not feeling well and don't feel that I would be very good company."

Chuck said, "No worries. What we had was fine. I'm happy to go on my way, but I would feel better if you would allow me to follow you home to make sure you arrive safely."

Pamela replied, "That is not necessary, but it is a kind and gentlemanly offer. The only reason that I am not inviting you over is that I am not feeling well. It's a girl thing. I'm really attracted to you, and you seem like such a kind and caring person."

Chuck continued, "I don't know about all of that, but your reasons are your own. But I would still feel better if you would allow me to follow you to make certain that you make it home."

Pamela said, "Okay, but I have to stop at the little market by my house to pick something up."

Chuck said, "I understand. You can go in alone, and I will wait for you out in my truck while you get what you need."

Pamela said, "Fair enough."

Pamela took off in her car. Chuck followed in his truck. Pamela was living in a weekend house that her parents purchased in case they wanted to come to the desert. It was not far from Taylor's home.

Chuck followed Pamela. She turned onto the highway and traveled west, towards the store and then her condo.

Chuck missed a traffic light but found the store anyway, as there was not much around. He could see Pamela's car in the lot in front of the store. He chose to hang back and park his truck at the street side of the lot from where he could look through the glass front door and windows to keep an eye on her.

He was feeling good so he kicked back in his seat and listened to the radio. He looked up to see how Pamela was doing, and what he saw terrified him. He saw one of the customers pull a double barrel shotgun from under his long coat and point it at the cashier.

Chuck exited his truck to cross the parking lot to reach the front door. From what he could see from the parking lot, the perpetrator was asking the cashier for the money in the cash register. He could see that the perpetrator saw the cashier press the silent burglar alarm. This made the perpetrator so mad that he shot the cashier with his shotgun at point blank range.

Pamela was standing in line right next to the shooter. The shot scared her, and she fell backwards hitting her head on the corner of a display shelf and then hard on the concrete floor.

The shooter raised his shotgun to shoot Pamela, who was lying on the floor. From nowhere, Chuck's hunting knife cut through the air and struck the perpetrator in the back of the neck. The blow temporarily paralyzed him so that he could not make his shot, and then killed him.

Chuck entered the store and went to Pamela's aid. He looked around the store and found a couple of rolls of paper towels, several boxes of gauze, rubbing alcohol, and three bottles of water.

He carefully straightened Pamela's head and neck, aligning them with her spine. He folded some paper towels and carefully placed them under her skull. He felt blood coming from the back of her head and soaking through her hair. He carefully placed gauze over the area that was bleeding. As the first piece of gauze became saturated, he was careful to not remove it but to only place fresh gauze over it.

He moved out the displays so that her body had sufficient room to lay out perfectly straight without contacting any shelfs.

A Sheriff's car was arriving outside, but he stayed with Pamela to make certain that she did not move. It appeared as if she was unconscious.

Two Sheriff Deputies burst through the front door with guns drawn. He called to them. They came over to him pointing their guns at him. It appeared as if they thought he was the perpetrator.

At this point, the cashier was dead, having been shot with the shotgun held by the perpetrator. The perpetrator was also dead, having received the knife blade thrown by Chuck from the front door, about 30 feet away.

Chuck was on the floor next to Pamela who he had laid out very flat and very straight on the slab.

The two Deputies had their guns pointed at Chuck telling him to get away from the girl.

Chuck said, "I cannot leave the girl at this time. I have her laid out in such a way that I hope to aid her long-term chances of recovery."

The senior Deputy said, "I don't care what you have to say. Just get away from her."

Thankfully, an ambulance arrived, and two EMTs entered the room.

With the EMTs present, Chuck repeated, "I cannot move away from the girl as you wish. If you want me to move, you will have to kill me first. I have her positioned so that her head is straight with her spine."

The senior Deputy repeated, "Get away from the girl."

The senior EMT interrupted the Deputy and said to Chuck, "I see what you have done. I will make sure that when we move her, there will be as little movement of her head and neck relative to her spine as possible. But we need to get her to the hospital right now."

Chuck said, "So long as you understand the need for care, please take her now and quickly. She needs attention."

Chuck moved away from Pamela, and the EMTs began their work. They ultimately loaded her in their ambulance skillfully.

The senior Deputy started to manhandle Chuck. He was put in handcuffs.

Chuck asked, "Why are you doing this. I was here to help her. This white guy with the shotgun came in to hold up the store. The cashier pressed the silent burglar alarm. The white guy got mad and shot him. Pamela, startled by the shot, fell backwards and hit her head on the shelf and then hard on the floor. Just as the white guy was going to shoot her, I was able to throw my knife in the back of his neck to prevent him from doing so. He also died."

The senior Deputy said, "You can tell your story to the Judge. As far as I can tell you were an accomplice in the hold up."

Chuck said, "No. I was out on a date with Pamela, and I was following her home to make sure that she got home safely. She stopped here. I waited outside. I saw the shot. I came over, and I threw my knife before the white guy could shoot her."

The senior Deputy said, "There is no way that this girl would go out with an Indian. I'm taking you in."

They handcuffed Chuck and put him in the squad car.

Chapter 5
Booking, Arraignment, and Bail Hearing

Pamela was taken off to the hospital in the ambulance. The coroner came and took away the two dead bodies. Chuck remained handcuffed in the back of the squad car.

A forensic team arrived and began its investigation. Everything that even looked as if it might be related to the crime was bagged and tagged and made ready for the evidence locker.

An autopsy would be performed by the coroner, but cause of death appeared obvious in both cases, a shotgun blast to the body for the cashier and a knife to the neck for the perpetrator.

A team of doctors would be working on Pamela.

The deputies took Chuck back to the station for booking. Chuck was photographed, fingerprinted, and booked for murder. His clothes were taken as evidence, and he was issued an orange jump suit into which he changed.

By this time, it was fairly late. Chuck and Pamela left the restaurant around 11 p.m. and arrived at the market around 11:30 p.m. The shooting of the cashier and the knife throw at the perpetrator took place around 11:35 p.m. The sheriff and the ambulance arrived some time before midnight. The forensic team arrived around midnight. Chuck was transported to the Station and arrived there around 12:30 a.m.

By the time he was booked and ready for his call, it was almost 1 a.m. Chuck had one call and he chose to call the Chief. He knew him better than Rick and Taylor, and he was more likely to not be disturbed by a call at this late hour. Also, he knows how to reach Taylor and Rick.

Chuck dialed and the Chief answered, "Hello."

Chuck said, "Hello, Chief, it's Chuck. I'm afraid that I have gotten myself into trouble."

As Chuck is a young guy, he has managed to get himself in some minor trouble involving law enforcement before such as, drinking, fighting, and DWI, driving while being an Indian.

The Chief replied, "What kind of trouble?"

Chuck said, "I went out on a date with Taylor's friend Pamela. She was not feeling well, so she was going to drive herself first to a market and then home. I insisted that I follow her to make sure she got home safely. She reached the market before I did. As I watched her inside of the market, I saw a thief shoot the cashier. I saw her fall backwards on her head. I saw the thief level his shotgun to shoot her. When I saw this, I had no option but to throw my knife.

"The knife struck him in the back of the neck. As you know, this stopped him from shooting her, but it also killed him. I had no choice."

The Chief remarked, "You did the right thing. What happed then?"

Chuck continued, "It appears as if the cashier pressed the silent alarm because the police showed up right away, just when things were over. I tried to explain, but they would not listen. They thought that I killed everyone while holding up the store. They took me in and booked me for murder."

"When are you set to go to court?"

"Tomorrow in Department 2 of the Superior Court in Palm Springs at 8:30."

"There's nothing more we can do about this now. I will call Taylor, and we will meet you in court tomorrow."

"Thank you, John. I'm so sorry about this."

"We'll deal with it one step at a time. See you tomorrow."

The Chief then called Taylor and related Chuck's story. She said that she introduced Pamela to Chuck and thought that they liked each other. She was not certain about the date. She told him that she and Rick would see him in the morning.

Rick, who was now awake, asked what happened. She told him the short version and said that they would see John and Chuck in the morning.

The next morning, Taylor and Rick drove to the courthouse together. Upon entering, they saw the Chief in the hallway. They joined him on a bench outside of Department 2. Taylor looked and saw that Chuck was on the docket for this morning. The docket was busy.

At about 8:45 the courtroom doors opened. Various attorneys went up to the clerk's desk to advise her that they would be representing one or more of the defendants. The clerk typically put cases with a private attorney on the top of the pile so they would be the first to finish after which they could leave.

Taylor reported to the clerk that she would be representing Chuck. Rick and the Chief took seats in the first row of the gallery. Taylor joined them in the aisle seat when she was finished with the clerk.

After everyone was finished with his or her business, the clerk called the court to order and announced the entrance of the Judge. The clerk asked everyone to rise. After the Judge entered and seated himself on the bench, the clerk announced that everyone could be seated.

The majority of the cases for this day were there for arraignment. The defendant would enter a plea, and the case would be set for trial, a pre-trial hearing, or a preliminary hearing, if the case was a felony.

Bail was set in most of the cases, or the defendants were already bailed out. Some of the attorneys asked that the bail be reduced. The Judge advised them that they would need to set a bail hearing due to the size of the docket.

Finally, Chuck was brought out. His name was announced, Charles Lightfoot Blackhorse. He was wearing an orange jump suit, and he was handcuffed. The bailiff brought him to counsel table to stand next to Taylor. The Judge read the charges and asked him to plead. He pleaded not guilty.

Taylor asked if she could be heard on the issue of bail. She was hoping that the murder charge would have already been reduced to manslaughter, as intent was weak. Bail for murder might be one million dollars whereas bail for manslaughter might be 100 thousand dollars, a significant difference.

She reminded the court that her client had no prior criminal history, that his release would not pose a threat to others, that he had worked at the Reservation just outside of Palm Springs for 15 years, and that he was not a flight risk. The Judge said that because of his crowded docket, he could not entertain a bail hearing at this time. However, in the interests of justice, he would conduct a bail hearing at the end of the day if the parties would agree to wait until he completed his docket. Taylor agreed. The Assistant DA also agreed. Chuck was returned to holding, and Taylor joined Rick and the Chief in the gallery to wait.

The other cases droned on and on. Finally, they were all finished.

Taylor rose to remind the court about her bail hearing.

At this point, except for the clerk, the bailiff, the court reporter, the assistant DA, and the judge, the courtroom was empty of all civilians except for Taylor, Rick, and the Chief, who were seated in the first row. Taylor, Rick, and The Chief came through the bar and stood behind counsel table.

As the Judge looked around, his gazed fixed on the Chief.

The Judge said to the Chief, "And sir, what is your connection to this matter?"

The Chief replied, "I am the chief of the young man's tribe, and I am his uncle. He is here fighting for his life. So, it is my duty to stand by him."

The Judge said, "And what is the nature of your duty, as you call it?"

The Chief replied, "Your Honor, I am the chief of his tribe. As the chief, it is my duty to look out for each and every person in my tribe."

The Judge asked, "For how long has this been going on?"

The Chief replied, "Approximately 3000 years."

The Judge asked, "And what is your business in Palm Springs?"

The Chief replied, "We own the cemetery, the cultural museum, three casinos, the hot springs, the canyons, two golf courses, and are planning a hockey arena. We have approximately 6,700 acres. I live in the canyon where, with the help of my nephew Chuck, I run a dude ranch operation."

The Judge asked, "Do you know anyone in this courtroom besides your nephew?"

The Chief replied, "Yes, Taylor and her husband Rick are frequent guests at the dude ranch. We have taught their daughter to ride, and other matters of Indian culture and history."

The Judge asked, "So they trust you with their daughter?"

The Chief replied, "Yes your Honor, implicitly."

The Judge asked, "What do you know about this case?"

The Chief replied, "Are you asking me what I saw or what I know?"

The Judge replied, "What you know?"

The Chief replied, "If you wish to know what I know, I will tell you. I know absolutely and positively that if my nephew had not appeared when he did, the young woman currently still alive in a hospital bed would be dead."

The Judge asked, "And how do you know this?"

The Chief replied, "Because even a complete incompetent could have shot the young lady from the distance this man was away from her with the weapon he had. It is only because my nephew is an expert knife thrower that he was able to throw the knife to the precise location necessary to paralyze his ability to complete this very simple shot.

"After the thief shot the cashier, he knew that he was facing murder charges so he had to kill the young lady to keep her from testifying against him. It was during that attempt that he received the much-deserved knife blade from my nephew. The Gods were watching out for her soul.

"You see, there would be no reason for my nephew to be close to the thief and the young lady, as this would have exposed him to being shot by the thief, particularly when he has a knife which allows him to throw from 30 feet away. Besides, if any man in my tribe strikes a woman, he has to answer to me, and that is a place much worse than your white law enforcement."

The Assistant DA entered, "Your Honor, this person is not qualified as a weapons expert."

Taylor said, "As far as I know, it is not our purpose here to litigate guilt or innocence. Guilt is presumed at a bail hearing. It is our purpose here to determine whether there is a substantial likelihood that the prisoner's release would result in great bodily harm to others or that he would carry out a threat if released. Either of these probabilities would need to be shown by clear and convincing evidence to deny bail, and neither has been shown by any evidence.

"Additionally, in fixing bail, the court shall take into consideration the previous criminal record of the defendant and the probability that he will appear at his next hearing. Here, my client has no previous record. As to probability to appear, he has worked at the Reservation for over 15 years under the supervision of the Chief of his tribe and is not likely to be leaving any time soon.

"Parenthetically, Mr. Blackhorse, if tested, would surely be qualified as a weapons expert."

The Assistant DA asked, "Have you ever seen him handle a weapon of any kind."

Taylor replied, "I most certainly have, and I must say it is a sight to behold. I was able to obtain the police report and medical records this morning. There were no fingerprints belonging to the defendant on the gun used to shoot the cashier. The only fingerprints on the gun were those of the thief. The only fingerprints belonging to the defendant were found on the knife, which stands to reason since it is his knife, and he admits throwing it."

The Judge said, "I am going to go way out on a limb here and release the defendant on his own recognizance into the custody of his uncle, the Chief. There is no evidence, clear and convincing or otherwise, to suggest that Mr. Blackhorse is a danger to the public safety or to any person in particular, since the other two people involved are deceased. I am releasing him to the Chief because the Chief acquits himself as a man of his word, and I feel that young Mr. Blackhorse would fear punishment from him more than punishment from me, and for that I must say that I cannot blame him.

"Further, the next hearing would be a preliminary hearing. I am going to set it off for 21 days from today. It is my hope that within this time, Ms. Key will regain consciousness and will be able to tell us what happened from her perspective. I believe that it would be unfair to have Mr. Blackhorse remain in jail while she is recovering.

"Mr. Blackhorse, do you understand that you are being released on your own recognizance to your uncle. This does not mean that you are free of these charges. It only means that you do not have to stay in jail while the charges are sorted out. Do you understand that you must return to court when ordered by me to do so? I trust that you understand that your uncle will be responsible for you so that if you fail to return to court, it will reflect on him and his character.

"From the looks of things, this is not a position that you, or anyone else for that matter, would welcome. Do you understand?"

Chuck replied, "I do understand, and trust me when I say that if I violate my uncle's trust, it would only be because I am dead, because if I were alive, I would be dead soon thereafter."

The Judge said, "Bailiff please process Mr. Blackhorse out. And Mr. Blackhorse, I will see you back here 21 days from today."

Taylor replied, "Thank you your honor."

Taylor, Rick, and the Chief left the courtroom and went to meet Chuck at the release area.

Chapter 6
Taylor and Chuck

A few days later, Taylor contacted the Reservation asking if she could take Izzy there for riding lessons. She arranged for Saturday. Upon her arrival, she went into the barn and selected a horse. She saddled her and walked her out of the barn to where Izzy was waiting.

Chuck came over. He called Michael to walk Izzy around the corral on her horse. He would then take her out on one of the many trails.

This would give Chuck a chance to speak with Taylor. Chuck started, "I wanted to thank you so much for helping me out last week with the whole jail thing. It is really a nightmare when the victim and the perpetrator are dead, and the only remaining witness is in a coma."

Taylor replied, "For all of the help you have given me over the years, it was the least I could do."

Chuck continued, "And I wanted to thank you for introducing me to Pamela."

Taylor was nothing if not honest. She responded to Chuck accordingly. "Oh, about that. I have a confession to make. I really didn't want you to go out with Pamela. You see, I like you too, and I was a little jealous when you asked Pamela out."

Chuck replied, "But you have a husband and a child."

Taylor replied, "I know. It's stupid. Nothing is ever going to come of it. I love my husband, and I would never do anything to hurt Izzy. It's just one of those stupid things that sometimes happens. But it's over now. Besides, Pamela is very head strong and goes after what she wants. Even if she thought that you were my soul mate and that I would leave Rick and Izzy to be with you, it would not stop her. She would continue to come after you come hell or high water.

"But as I said, I'm over it now, and I can wish you and Pamela the best with all sincerity."

Chuck said, "That's good, because I really like her and hope to see her when she wakes up. I tried to see her yesterday but was told that I could not visit her in the hospital. They said that it might prejudice my case, but what I really thought they meant was that it might damage their case. They might think that if I saw her I might pressure her to testifying in my favor."

Taylor said, "I would not take it personally. They really have to prevent you from seeing her now."

Taylor went to watch Izzy finish her lesson. She helped her dismount and walked the horse into the barn for a rubdown. She and Izzy then drove home.

Chapter 7
The Preliminary Hearing

It was coming up on time for the preliminary hearing. The preliminary hearing is a short trial to determine whether there is enough evidence to hold the defendant over for a full trial.

Taylor found out that though she was still in the hospital, Pamela had made a full recovery and was talking and eating normally. Her first outing would be to the preliminary hearing.

Since the bail hearing, Taylor officially resigned as Chuck's attorney. It was reasoned that she could be called as a witness for Chuck to help explain his relationship with Pamela, to the extent she knew. As Rick was with the DA, they hired Frank Sherman, a criminal specialist who Rick new.

Taylor would leave it up to Frank how preparations for the hearing would be made. He had a meeting with Chuck. He favored Chuck not testifying as was his right under the 5th Amendment. Chuck was, of course, anxious to tell his story.

On the appointed date, Taylor, Rick, Chuck, Pamela, the Chief, Mr. Sherman, Anne Sullivan, a waitress from Carlos and Pepe's, and Dr. Charles W. Adams, a forensic pathologist, met in the hallway outside of the courthouse. The hearing was set for 10:30 a.m., to allow the court to complete its morning docket. At around 10:40 a.m., they were called to enter the courtroom.

Already in the courtroom, there was the DA, the clerk, the court reporter, the bailiff, and a Sheriff's deputy who appeared to be a witness for the prosecution. To handle the trial, the DA selected Jeri Ryan, an assistant DA known for being aggressive. She was reasonably young and attractive, and Taylor presumed that she was selected in an effort to rattle Chuck.

Mr. Sherman and Chuck went to the side of the counsel table reserved for the defendant. Ms. Ryan occupied the other side with one assistant.

The Judge entered. Everyone stood up, and when the Judge sat down, everyone was asked to be seated.

The case was introduced. The Judge asked the DA to call her first witness. She called Deputy O'Grady, the deputy who came to the crime scene and arrested Chuck.

DA Ryan: "Deputy O'Grady, how are you employed?"

Deputy O'Grady: "I am a Deputy Sheriff for Riverside County."

DA Ryan: "How long have you been so employed?"

Deputy O'Grady: "Six years."

DA Ryan: "On the night in question, did you receive a call from the Circle W Market regarding the commission of a crime?"

Deputy O'Grady: "Not exactly. We received word from headquarters that the silent alarm at the market went off and that we were to go there immediately."

DA Ryan: "Sorry. You responded to a silent alarm. How long did it take you to reach the market?

Deputy O'Grady: "Approximately 7 to 10 minutes."

DA Ryan: "What did you see when you arrived?"

Deputy O'Grady: "We saw that the market was lite up as usual and that there were three cars in the parking lot."

DA Ryan: "Can you describe those cars?"

Deputy O'Grady: "Yes. There was a near-new BMW, silver in color. There was an old green pickup truck. Looked like a Chevrolet. And there was a black cargo van. Looked like a Ford."

DA Ryan: "What did you do then?"

Deputy O'Grady: "We looked in the window and saw what appeared to be the aftermath of a fight or holdup."

DA Ryan: "What specifically did you see?"

Deputy O'Grady: "We saw a young lady lying on the floor who appeared to be unconscious. We saw a roughly 5 foot, 10-inch tall white guy on the customer side of the counter who appeared to have been hit in the neck with a long hunting knife. He was holding a shotgun. We saw a roughly 5 foot, 7-inch male of apparently Asian descent lying on the floor behind the counter. He appeared to have been shot, and he was also holding a shotgun. We also saw a roughly 6 foot, 2-inch Indian man sitting on the floor near the female victim."

Mr. Sherman: "Objection your Honor. I object to the Deputy referring to my client as an Indian as it appears to be done in an effort to disparage him."

The Judge: "Your objection is noted. Deputy O'Grady please refer to the defendant either by his name or as the defendant and not as an Indian."

Deputy O'Grady: "Sorry your Honor. But it looked like the defendant killed the two men and knocked out the girl."

DA Ryan: "And on what do you base that opinion?"

Deputy O'Grady: "He was alive and the other two men were dead. One of the men was killed with a knife, the type of knife an Indian would use."

Mr. Sherman: "Objection. Calls for a conclusion."

The Judge: "Objection sustained."

DA Ryan: "I have nothing further for this witness."

The Judge: "Mr. Sherman, do you have any questions?"

Mr. Sherman: "Yes. Thank you, your Honor. Deputy O'Grady, did Mr. Blackhorse attempt to flee the scene when you and your partner arrived?"

Deputy O'Grady: "No. He was just sitting there."

Mr. Sherman: "Were there not three cars available to him in the parking lot?"

Deputy O'Grady: "I guess. I didn't know at the time if any of the cars were his."

Mr. Sherman: "But you have learned that in fact the green pickup belonged to him, is that correct?"

Deputy O'Grady: "Yes."

Mr. Sherman: "You testified that the defendant was sitting on the floor next to the female victim. Did you ask him to move?"

Deputy O'Grady: "Yes, we did. But he refused."

Mr. Sherman: "Did he tell you why he refused to move?"

Deputy O'Grady: "He said that he knew the girl and that he was administering first aid due to her injury. But we didn't believe him. There is no way that this guy could know this girl or anything about first aid."

Mr. Sherman: "Why do you say that?"

Deputy O'Grady: "This lady was completely out of his league. She looked educated and refined. She is a rich white girl with beautiful clothes and a fancy car. He looked like a ranch hand, and it is unlikely that he knew anything about first aid."

Mr. Sherman: "So based on that, you arrested him for killing two people and injuring another?"

Deputy O'Grady: "It's the only thing that made sense."

Mr. Sherman: "Did you test his hands for GSR."

Deputy O'Grady: "No. That was done at the station."

Mr. Sherman: "Do you know the results?"

Deputy O'Grady: "No. But I heard it was negative."

Mr. Sherman: "Did you check the defendant's hands for cuts. It is quite common that one can cut his hand when throwing a knife."

Deputy O'Grady: "No."

Mr. Sherman: "I have nothing further at this time for this witness."

The prosecution rested.

The Judge: "Mr. Sherman, please call your first witness."

Mr. Sherman motioned for the female witness, Anne Sullivan, to come forward. She was sworn in and took the witness stand. She was asked to state her name and spell it for the court reporter.

Mr. Sherman: "Ms. Sullivan, how are you employed?"

Ms. Sullivan: "I am a food server at Carlos and Pepe's restaurant in Palm Springs."

Mr. Sherman: "Have you ever seen anyone in the courtroom in your restaurant?"

Ms. Sullivan: "Yes, I have seen two people in the courtroom in my restaurant."

Mr. Sherman: "Which two people?"

Ms. Sullivan: "I have seen the defendant and the young lady sitting there." (She pointed to Pamela.) They were there on the night in question."

Mr. Sherman: "And what were these two people doing in your restaurant?"

Ms. Sullivan: "It looked to me like they were on a date. They were both dressed nicely. They ordered drinks together. They ordered food together. After they were finished drinking and eating, he paid the check, and they both left together and headed towards the parking lot."

Mr. Sherman: "Was there anything unusual about them?"

Ms. Sullivan: "Only that they are both very good looking. That guy, the one you call the defendant, is so handsome that all of the girls working were swooning."

Mr. Sherman: "I have nothing else."

The Judge: "Do you have any questions Ms. Ryan?"

Ms. Ryan: "Yes. Was the defendant rough with the girl. Could he have been forcing her to be with him?"

Mr. Sherman: "Objection. Relevance."

Ms. Sullivan: "I'd like to answer that question."

The Judge: "Okay. Go ahead."

Ms. Sullivan: "Absolutely not. He was a perfect gentleman. I want one of those."

Ms. Ryan: "I have nothing further."

The Judge: "Mr. Sherman, please call your next witness."

Mr. Sherman motioned for Dr. Adams to come forward. He was sworn in and asked to take the witness stand. He was asked to state his name and to spell it for the reporter, which he did.

Mr. Sherman: "Dr. Adams, how are you employed."

Dr. Adams: "I am a forensic pathologist at the Hobart Institute?"

Mr. Sherman: "How long have you been so employed?"

Dr. Adams: "Twenty-two years."

Mr. Sherman: "What is the nature of your work?"

Dr. Adams: "We perform medical examinations of bodies, both living and dead, to determine cause of death or cause of injury."

Mr. Sherman: "Have you had occasion to conduct such examinations in this case?"

Dr. Adams, "In regards to the attempted robbery at the Circle W Market in question, we examined the two deceased men and the one injured woman who were described in earlier testimony by the Deputy."

Mr. Sherman, "And what did you find?"

Dr. Adams: "With respect to the Asian male, we found that he was shot with a shotgun from a distance of approximately four feet. With respect to the Caucasian male, we found that he was killed instantly by a single knife blow to the neck. With respect to the woman, we found that she fell backwards and hit her head on a display shelf and then very hard on the concrete slab subfloor of the market."

Mr. Sherman: "Do you know approximately how far away the thrower of the knife was standing at the time of his throw?"

Dr. Adams: "Yes, approximately 30 feet."

Mr. Sherman: "Were you given the ballistics report from the Sheriff's Office regarding GSR? If so, what did it state?"

Dr. Adams: "Yes. It stated that the Caucasian male had significant GSR indicative of firing the weapon with which he was found. It stated that the Asian male had contact GSR indicative of holding a gun. Neither the woman nor the defendant tested positive for GSR."

Mr. Sherman, "Based on your findings, how would you say that the incident occurred?"

Dr. Adams, "I would say that the Caucasian male was there to hold up the store. In his effort to do so, he approached the counter where he wound up standing just a few feet from the female victim.

"When he saw the cashier press the silent burglar alarm, he became enraged. This caused him to shoot and kill the cashier. Since a murder was committed during the commission of a felony, he then felt that he would have to kill the girl to keep her from testifying. As he turned and leveled his shotgun to point it at the girl, the defendant threw his knife striking the man's neck, initially paralyzing him and then killing him.

"Allow me to say that this is a move that can only be accomplished by an expert knife thrower. If he threw the knife and it just hit the man, the man would still have had plenty of time to pull the trigger and kill his victim. By throwing the knife where he did, he was able to paralyze the man so he could not use his hands to complete his shot. This takes years of practice and a vast and very special knowledge of anatomy."

Mr. Sherman: "Did you have an opportunity to read the report from the EMTs?"

Dr. Adams: "Yes."

Mr. Sherman: "And what did you learn from this report?"

Dr. Adams: "We learned that the defendant did an excellent job in applying first aid to Ms. Key. Everything he did was right. Firstly, he did not try to move her. Secondly, he aligned her neck with her spinal cord to prevent nerve damage. Thirdly, he applied gauze to her head which was bleeding through her hair as a result of a cut she sustained during her fall. As the gauze became saturated, he was careful to not remove the saturated gauze but to apply fresh gauze over the saturated gauze."

Mr. Sherman: "And your opinion of to the first aid given?"

Dr. Adams: "Frankly, it was right out of a medical text book."

Mr. Sherman: "Would it have been possible for the defendant to leave his post next to the victim when ordered to do so by the Deputy?"

Dr. Adams: "Absolutely not. Leaving her side or allowing her to be moved, except by a professional, could have caused her to lose mobility in one or more of her legs which very well could have meant that she would be confined to a wheelchair for the rest of her life."

Mr. Sherman: "I have nothing further."

The Judge, "Your witness."

DA Ryan, "You say that the Caucasian suspect shot the cashier, killing him, and then leveled his gun at Ms. Key when he received the knife to his neck?"

Dr. Adams: "Yes."

DA Ryan: "Isn't it just as likely that the Caucasian suspect shot the cashier, and then the defendant stabbed him while standing next to him while assisting him with the robbery?"

Dr. Adams: "No. There is no evidence that the defendant was acquainted with the Caucasian suspect, only that he was acquainted with Ms. Key. Ms. Key will testify that the defendant was not with her in the market but was outside waiting for her. Ms. Key will also testify that the knife came from 30 feet away.

"For what you contend to be true, the defendant would have had to make the split-second decision to kill the Caucasian robber with his knife rather than allow him to kill Ms. Key, which would still qualify as defense of others. The only difference would be that for what you contend to be true, he would have had to have made the split-second decision to be more loyal to Ms. Key than to the Caucasian man, and you contend that he did not know Ms. Key before the holdup. Why would he defend someone he does not know and kill the person with whom he allegedly conspired to hold up a market?

"There is no evidence that the defendant was there to rob the market. And there is no evidence that he knew the Caucasian man who was there to rob the market."

DA Ryan: "I have nothing else."

The next witness called was Pamela. She swore her oath and took the witness stand. She was asked to state her name and spell it for the reporter.

Mr. Sherman: "Do you prefer Pamela or Ms. Key?"

Pamela: "Pamela."

Mr. Sherman: "Are you acquainted with the defendant?"

Pamela: "Yes. We were introduced by a friend of mine at work. She invited me to the Indian Reservation for some horseback riding. I knew of the defendant through her, but I did not meet him until the day we visited the Reservation together."

Mr. Sherman: "And how did it go at the Reservation."

DA Ryan: "Objection. Relevance."

The Judge: "The nature and depth of their relationship is quite important. The prosecution is contending that they did not know one another so I have to allow evidence that they did. Overruled."

Pamela replied: "It went very well. We had a great time. We rode out to a waterfall and pond, had lunch, and really had fun."

Mr. Sherman: "Were you attracted to the defendant?"

Pamela: "Of course. Look at him. He's gorgeous."

Mr. Sherman: "Did you arrange to speak with the defendant after you left the Reservation?"

Pamela: "Yes. He gave me his number which usually means he wants me to call."

Mr. Sherman: "Did you call him?"

Pamela: "Yes. And we arranged for a date."

Mr. Sherman: "And was that date on the night in question?"

Pamela: "Yes."

Mr. Sherman: "What happened on this date?"

Pamela: "We decided to meet at Carlos and Pepe's a bar and restaurant in Palm Springs. We met, had dinner, and talked for quite a while."

Mr. Sherman: "And then what?"

Pamela: "I was not feeling well. A female thing. I told Chuck that I would have to go home. He was a total gentleman and cool about the whole thing. He said that he would not come in but that he would feel better if I would allow him to follow me home to make certain that I got home safely."

Mr. Sherman: "And then what?"

Pamela: "I told him okay but that I would need to stop at a small market on the way. He said that he would follow me there but that he would not come in. He would wait for me in the parking lot."

Mr. Sherman: "And then what?"

Pamela: "I arrived at the market and parked my car in the lot, the BMW. I went inside and found what I needed. I was waiting in line behind the Caucasian gentleman. He had a coat under which he concealed the shotgun he used. He pulled out the shotgun and pointed it at the cashier. The cashier went to press the silent burglar alarm. This made the Caucasian man very mad.

"I think that the Asian man went for his shotgun or at least bent down, and the Caucasian man shot him from very close range. I was completely helpless. I figured that the white guy was going to shoot me. I saw Chuck by the door with a knife. As the white guy was about to shoot me, he was hit by the knife and couldn't move. I was moving backwards to try to keep from getting shot. I fell backwards with the back of my head striking a display shelf and then the hard-concrete floor knocking me out. That's the last thing I remember until I woke up in the hospital."

Mr. Sherman: "I have nothing further."

The Judge: "Your witness."

DA Ryan, "Did you actually see the Caucasian man shoot the cashier?"

Pamela: "Yes. I did. Things were happening very fast, and we were all so close together that it was hard to know who was doing what."

DA Ryan: "So, you asked the defendant out on this date?"

Pamela: "Not exactly, but I made it as easy as I could for the date to take place, the same thing that women have been doing for, may I say, years."

DA Ryan: "Do you plan on seeing him again?"

Pamela: "I hope to when all of this is cleared up."

DA Ryan: "But you didn't like him enough to invite him back to your house?"

Mr. Sherman: "Objection. Relevance."

The Judge: "I'm going to allow it. I believe that their relationship is relevant. Overruled."

Pamela: "Firstly, it was our first date, and we were just getting to know one another. Also, I was having that woman thing that we get every month, which is why I needed to stop at the market. I have to say that this is the first time in my life that I have ever been criticized for not sleeping with someone on the first date."

DA Ryan: "Did this make the defendant angry?"

Pamela: "Gosh no. He was very cool about it. Cooler than all of the guys I know."

DA Ryan: "So he was not mad enough to try to kill someone."

Mr. Sherman: "Objection. Relevance."

The Judge: "Here is where you have stepped over the line Ms. Ryan. I am going to sustain the objection and admonish you to not make assumptions that are not supported by facts."

DA Ryan: "Sorry. I have nothing further for this witness."

The Judge: "Do you have anything else?"

DA Ryan: "Yes. I have a demonstration."

The Judge addressing DA Ryan: "As to the demonstration, the bailiff tells me that you brought in a target. Would that be the target that was placed in the far corner of the courtroom?"

DA Ryan: "Yes, your Honor. The purpose of the target is to allow us to see if the defendant can really throw a knife as he says he can."

Mr. Sherman: "The defendant asked me to ask the court if he can take a look at the target to make certain that it is sufficiently secure for the throw."

The Judge: "Very well. Bailiff, would you escort the defendant back to the target so he may get a better look?"

The Bailiff: "Yes."

The bailiff and Chuck went back to the corner to have a look at the target. The bull's eye was a yellow circle about four inches in diameter. Chuck inspected the target and felt that it was sufficiently secure for the throw. Chuck asked the bailiff if he had a black marker. He went to his desk and found a black marker. With the marker, Chuck made one-inch x in the approximate center of the yellow circle. Chuck was asked to take the seat at the back corner of the jury box. This was presumably the farthest point from the target, about 35 feet.

The bailiff cleared everyone out of the path between the jury box and the target moving everyone, including the Judge, all court personnel, all witnesses, all attorneys, and anyone else who remained in the courtroom to the back of the room behind the bench, far out of the path to the target from the jury box. He locked the door into the hall so that no one could come in accidentally.

The bailiff had the knife which had been admitted into evidence. It was in an evidence bag.

The bailiff took the knife, still in the evidence bag, to a location immediately next to where Chuck was seated. The bailiff announced that he was going to remove the knife from the evidence bag and place it in Chuck's hand so that Chuck could aim and throw it at the target.

The bailiff stood next to Chuck. He took the knife out of the evidence bag. As he handed the knife to Chuck, the second it hit Chuck's hand, without aiming, Chuck threw it over his shoulder at the target in a single motion.

The knife not only hit the yellow bull's eye but hit the exact center of the x that Chuck had made on the target with the marker. Enough said.

The Judge asked everyone to return to his or her seat. He said that there was not sufficient evidence to bind the defendant over for trial. He dismissed the case.

Everyone left the courtroom. Taylor and Rick drove home. Pamela drove to work in her car. Chuck and the Chief drove to the Reservation. Dr. Adams and Ms. Sullivan already left the courtroom and the courthouse property after they testified, missing the demonstration.

Chapter 8
The Road Back

Taylor was lucky that Izzy was still young enough to hang out with her. Izzy was coming up on her pre-teen years after which her relationship with her mother would change. She would become more interested in her friends and boys, and her mother would be left out in the cold.

While Izzy was still young, however, she did continue to enjoy going to the Reservation and improving her riding. This was good because it gave Taylor a chance to talk with Chuck privately without worrying about getting caught at some bar or restaurant.

It was Saturday. The weather was perfect. And Taylor and Izzy decided that it would be a great day for the Reservation. Taylor called to make sure Chuck would be there.

They drove over to the Reservation. Taylor went to saddle a horse for Izzy and a horse for herself. Chuck arranged for Michael to take Izzy. This would allow him to ride with Taylor alone. Izzy and Michael took off for the mountains.

Chuck and Taylor rode to the pond with the waterfall in the nearby mountains. They tied up their horses and sat on the rocks.

Chuck said, "I really wanted to thank you for not only helping me but also for believing in me with this whole market holdup disaster. It's very frustrating when you know you are in the right but can't do anything about. That Mr. Sherman was really good too."

Taylor replied, "Yes he was. He's a good friend of Rick's."

Taylor asked, "How have things been going. Have you spoken to Pamela?"

Chuck replied, "It's been really hard to figure out what to do about her. It's been a few weeks, and I have been afraid to call her. I'm afraid that she will always think of me as just an Indian who will forever be blamed if anything goes wrong. That's more pressure than I want to put on another person."

Taylor said, "I get that. Frankly, I don't know her that well so I can't say how she would react if you wanted to re-kindle things. She was out for three weeks with the hospital and rest at home. I don't know if the office has decided what to do with her. I don't know if they want to put her in Indian relations, environmental law, sex trafficking, or transfer her out of the desert altogether.

"Sex trafficking might be good because she could work with me, and the Indians are not really involved. Most of the sex trafficking involves people smuggled in from Mexico.

"Somehow I think that if she stays, she will go into criminal law because that is where there is the most work, and I am sure that the people doing it would be eligible to transfer to a more upscale department."

Chuck asked, "Do you have any plans to speak with her any time soon about her personal life?"

Taylor replied, "I really think that you should do that yourself."

Chuck said, "But she trusts you."

Taylor replied, "As to business yes, but as to personal matters, I am not so sure. I never told you any of this because I felt that you had enough on your plate. Even before you and Pamela met, we talked about you. She thought that you and I were together."

Chuck replied, "Didn't she know that you were married?"

Taylor said, "She did, but she didn't think it mattered. She lives in the white world where things like marriage are fluid. Half of the white people who get married get divorced."

Chuck said, "I guess I would be a liar if I said that I wasn't attracted to you from the first time I saw you. But I knew that you were not only married but also had a child. No matter how attracted to you I was, I would never want to interfere with your family. I only wish that I had two parents who loved me the way you and Rick love Izzy. I would never want to deny that to anyone, especially Izzy who I love like she's my own.

"If Rick was an asshole who beat you and treated you and Izzy badly, maybe I would do something. But he is none of those things. In fact, he is probably the most genuine and supportive white guy I have ever met. He's one of the few white people who doesn't look down on me and the rest of the tribe, but he supports us.

"If you must know, all of the women around the Reservation are in love with him. They dream of landing a kind, rich white guy to get them off of the Reservation and into the kind of life that you guys have. But they hide it well as Indian women learn, for the most part, to only work in the shadows.

"I think you're beautiful, but I could never do anything to hurt your relationship. I initially got together with Pamela because I was hoping that she would be you, or at least like you. I don't know her that well, but I think she might be as close as I will ever get. She seems to be a little looser than you are which might be fun in the short run but might not wear as well. You really have it all."

Taylor was baffled by what she heard, but he was not far off.

Taylor said, "I am flattered, but I am happy to say that I believe that our friendship has developed to a point where it might be our best path. Pamela is young, beautiful, single, and available, the four things you need to start something serious. I really think you should give it a shot. I cannot make any guarantees, but from the little I have seen, I think she might be pretty solid."

Chuck went on, "The single largest problem that any white female person and I will encounter are young jealous white guys. Because she has chosen an Indian, they will berate her. Because she is not attracted to them, to protect their ego, they will have to maintain that there is something wrong with her. This will place me in a position in which I will have to defend her honor all of the time.

"The one night I saw her, I could easily have gotten into a fight in the bar, and to top it off, I was arrested because I was an Indian who could never be with a girl like Pamela.

"White guys will be forever jealous of an Indian with a hot white woman. It's just the nature of the beast. I just hope that I am not in a fight every time she and I leave the Reservation."

Taylor said, "I could placate you and say that such things do not happen anymore in this day and age, but I would be lying. I have to confess that what you say is sad, but it is probably true. I'm hoping that Pamela surprises both of us."

Taylor concluded, "So here is what I say. In the final analysis, you will have to decide whether it is better for you to be with someone you really like who happens to be white or whether to protect yourself from white privilege you should forget about her altogether. I say give it a shot. If risks such as this were never taken, we might never advance as a society."

Chuck replied, "I guess you're right. I will give it a shot."

Chapter 9
Chuck and Pamela

C huck called Pamela to see how she was doing and to feel her out for a meeting. She said that she was pretty banged up, but after some rest, she was feeling better. She was back at work, but they said that they were not certain in what department she would be placed.

They arranged to meet at a coffee bar near her work the following day. When Pamela arrived, Chuck was waiting.

Pamela said, "Hi. It's so nice to see you. I'm so sorry about what you went through."

Chuck said, "It really wasn't that bad, and it just appears to be something I am going to have to learn to deal with. I really hope that this whole episode does not interfere with your relationship with Taylor. I believe that your relationship with her is a good thing."

Chuck asked Pamela if he could call her up for a real date. She said yes and that she was pleased that he still wanted to get together.

He was going to call her.

Chapter 10
Girlfriends

Taylor was of the opinion that maintaining her relationship with Pamela was important. She did not have many female friends, and she sincerely hoped that Pamela and Chuck could have something together.

Taylor asked Pamela to meet her at the bar in the restaurant across the street from their office after work. They met. They were shown to a table. Each ordered a screw-driver.

Taylor told Pamela that she met Chuck at the Reservation and that they had a long talk. She said that they concluded that what may have been between them was just a misunderstanding and that Chuck was looking for an available person to try to start something completely new. She said that Chuck felt that Pamela was the perfect candidate for such a relationship. She said that he felt that Pamela was beautiful, smart, interesting, and capable of being a long-term partner.

In other words, what she was doing here was not lying but just bending the truth a little. In reality, he felt that it was she who had all of the qualities of which they spoke but that since she was taken, Pamela was the next closest person. Taylor was careful to not let on that Chuck felt this way. She kept the conversation focused on Pamela.

Pamela appeared to not only believe what Taylor was telling her but seemed uplifted by it. She indicated that she would pursue a relationship with Chuck.

Pamela and Taylor were finished and were leaving the bar. They were both parked in the underground parking garage under their building across the street. They walked down the car ramp as they were both parked on the first floor.

Three white guys followed them down the ramp. Once out of sight from the street, the lead white guy spoke to Taylor. He said, "Are you the two white girls that like Indian guys? What's the matter, can't get a white guy?"

Taylor said, "We like who we like, and it really does not concern you. We would just like to leave and go home now."

The lead guy said, "No way that's going to happen."

The other two guys grabbed Pamela, restrained her, and took her to one side of the garage. The lead guy pushed Taylor out into the open area as if he wanted to assault her where the others could watch.

Taylor now was separated from the lead guy. They were facing one another as if they were going to fight. The lead guy was 6 foot, 3 inches tall and weighed around 210 pounds. He took out a chromed chain and started to play with it.

He started to come at Taylor with the chain. When he got four feet away, Taylor pulled out one of her knives and threw it at the guy's thigh. It was a direct hit and stuck into his flesh. He fell to the floor seething in pain. He never felt pain such as this before.

The other two guys got scared. They let Pamela go and ran out of the garage to the street. Taylor called 911 and reported the need for an ambulance. She and Pamela went to their respective cars and left the garage. They both went home.

When she got home, she told Rick what had happened. He said that she should report it, which she did. They went to bed, woke up the next morning, and went to work.

At around 11 o'clock, Taylor's intercom rang. She answered and was told that the District Attorney's Office was on the phone. She answered. She was being summoned to the District Attorney's Office for a two o'clock meeting.

She appeared at two o'clock in the DA's Office. She was directed to the conference room. In the conference room, there were two assistant DA's, an older man who appeared to be the lead guys father, dressed in a suit, and the lead guy. There was also a court reporter.

They all introduced themselves.

The lead DA started, "We are here today to investigate the filing of a criminal complaint against Taylor Shaw for a knife injury to Randolph Scott, Jr., yesterday. We have been advised that Ms. Shaw threw a knife at Mr. Scott, and that he sustained serious injuries. Do you have anything to say for yourself Ms. Shaw?"

Taylor answered, "Yes. I do. My friend and I met for a drink at Harry's bar across the street from my office; I am an Assistant United States Attorney. After finishing, we walked back across the street and entered the parking garage below my office. We were followed by three gentlemen, one of whom is here now.

"The three gentlemen made some crude comments about my taste in men. I told him that who I like does not concern him. I told him that I just wished to go home. They separated us with his two friends grabbing my friend and taking her to one side of the garage. The person who is here at the table then squared off against me as if he wanted to fight. He had a chromed chain.

"He started coming at me. As he is nearly a foot taller and outweighs me by nearly 100 pounds, I defended myself by throwing a three-inch knife at his leg.

"The knife stuck into his leg, and he went down. My girlfriend and his two friends left the scene quickly. I called for an ambulance, giving the dispatcher the exact address and location. I then left, went home, and reported his crime to the police.

"I was summoned to this meeting this morning."

The father was livid. He began yelling and screaming, "That story is preposterous. You're just a silly girl. There is no way you can fight my son."

Taylor said, "Perhaps it is your attitude about women that has enabled your son to be what he is, a bully."

The father was now so mad that he stood up and moved towards Taylor. Taylor got up from her chair and began to backpedal towards the wall. The DA stood up and asked the father to return to his seat.

He and Taylor returned to their respective seats, and the DA continued his examination. He asked, "Where did you learn to fight?"

Taylor replied, "That is really none of your business, but I will tell you anyway. I was taught how to fight by the Indians. Initially, it was part of my job at the U S Attorney's Office. Now I go to the Reservation for pleasure."

The father jumped in, "Those Indians are savages."

Taylor replied, "You really do not understand them or how they operate. They have a different attitude about life than white people."

Taylor went on, "In my mind the more important question from this episode is how to protect white women from predators like you and your son.

"A generation ago, white women were protected by white men. No one messed with someone's wife, daughter, or mother without the entire community coming down on him. Now, little girls are kidnapped off of the street outside of their elementary school, college girls are raped and expelled from school if they report it, women walking down the street or leaving bars or restaurants are assaulted, and no one does a thing. I choose to not live that way. I choose to fight for myself or die trying.

"Every woman lives under the constant threat that a man will harm or kill her just because he is bigger and stronger, and there is nothing she can do about it. She can't report it as a crime, because no crime has been committed. The police cannot do anything prospectively.

"She is called paranoid or crazy, right up until the time she is killed. Then, everyone is sorry for the great loss."

Addressing the lead DA, Taylor says, "All of you guys should be embarrassed at the way you have acted. You haul a 5-foot, 6-inch woman who weighs 115 pounds into your office and charge her with what, getting the better of a bigger, stronger man.

"If I had gotten my ass kicked by this guy and pressed charges, you would use your influence to either pressure me to drop the charges or say that no charges should be brought because it didn't happen.

"Sick. The whole thing is sick."

The lead DA asked, "Couldn't you have run away?"

Taylor responded, "No. For a number of reasons. Firstly, if I left, I would be leaving my friend in the grasp of three large men who could beat her or rape her, as she is quite beautiful. Secondly, you're the criminal law expert, and you should know that California is a stand your ground State; I have no duty to run away. In fact, I have the right to stand my ground. Thirdly, I doubt that I could outrun this guy as he is a man, and men are faster than women, generally.

"This has cost me a half day of work, and I am going to leave now unless you have anything else for me."

The father said, "A girl supported by a bunch of Indians. Where were the Indians when you needed them?"

Taylor said, "Sir, you should count your lucky stars that none of my Indian friends were there. That would really have been a mess. But I am sure that they would welcome the opportunity to take on your son and his friends at some Reservation games, such a riding, roping, knife throwing, arrow shooting, fighting, and the like."

The lead DA said, "That will be enough. If we need anything more, I know how to contact you. Thank you for coming in."

Taylor left the office and returned to her office.

Chapter 11
Time Passes

Taylor and Pamela both continued their work in the U S Attorney's Office. They were finally placed in different departments, which seemed to be best.

Pamela started up a legitimate relationship with Chuck. Taylor marveled at just how adept Pamela was at dealing with men.

Pamela decided that if she was serious about Chuck, she would have to learn a little more about him and his culture. She did this by making regular trips to the Reservation and talking with Chuck about his heritage and his hopes for the future. She reasoned that people in general like it if you show concern for them.

Taylor was surprised that Pamela was still interested in pursuing a relationship with an Indian after the near incident in the bar and the actual incident in the market. But Pamela would not bend. She knew what she wanted and was willing to go after it, regardless of the consequences.

Taylor was thinking to herself that maybe Pamela was more solid and more courageous than she thought. Her feelings were not only legitimate, but they were downright honest.

Pamela talked Taylor into teaching in the elementary school at the Reservation one day a week. She loved teaching and even considered becoming a teacher when she was in college. With their educational backgrounds, the ladies were able to teach history, English, and even basic science. Taylor was raised on a farm, so she could teach basic farming skills.

The kids, especially the little girls, loved them. They gave the little girls hope that they could become accomplished and do something with their lives the way that Taylor and Pamela had.

As Pamela and Chuck got to know one another a little better, Pamela decided that she would become a little more open about herself. She reasoned that Taylor was not afraid to show her best attributes to Rick, and rather than making him insecure, it seemed to make him love her more.

Pamela figured that she would start small. She decided to start with her equestrian riding. During their first meeting at the Reservation, Pamela pretended to not know how to ride. This was done so that Chuck would spend a little more time with her and to allow him to show her his skills in this department.

She called her mother and had her send out her English saddle. She had Chuck, Michael, and Roger set up an equestrian course outside of the barn. They set up poles for jumping and other obstacles for maneuvering the horse.

She had her mother send over some of her equestrian clothing. She decked herself out in tan riding pants, high black riding boots, a navy riding jacked, a white zipper shirt, and a navy hat with a chin strap.

Taylor was kind enough to help Pamela saddle the horse. She had never seen an English saddle, but Pamela assured her that it was what was used.

Pamela had the Chief summon all of the children and any of the adults who were interested in watching. In addition to the obstacles, Pamela and Taylor draped red, white, and blue paper runners around the perimeter fence and set out a table similarly decorated for refreshments.

Pamela led her horse out onto the course. She mounted. She then ran the horse through the course, making the several jumps and forward and side steps called for in the program.

The people were thrilled. Chuck was baffled. He said, "Why didn't you tell me that you could ride like that?"

Pamela answered, "Would you have given me as much attention when you were trying to teach me to ride if I had."

Chuck replied, "I see your point."

Even the Chief was beginning to warm up to Pamela. She is a white girl from a rich family. She has a superlative education. But she is a genuine person, and seems truly interested in Chuck. And she seems to be willing to show it rather than just talk about it.

As to Pamela and the Chief, I was not surprised that it would take a significant effort on her part to win him over. Young guys are easy. With her equipment, she can just flash that million-dollar smile and her other assets, and any man would melt. (It was that easy, or even easier, with Chuck.) But the Chief was another story. He was a mature man who knew which qualities were important in a woman, and to win him over would be a job and a half.

Now, as to me and the Chief, that is a different story. I understand why the Chief loves me. Firstly, I was raised on a farm. I was a grower of food. I raised animals and tended to their needs. I had chickens for eggs and goats for milk. My friends were essentially fruit pickers. I was not impressed by money, and went out of my way to help those in need. I raised a beautiful and thoughtful daughter. I was raised much the same as an Indian. These were the attributes of a woman that a man such as the Chief could understand.

In addition, when I dressed as an Indian squaw when we were retrieving Izzy from her kidnappers, Chuck and Roger told me that I looked almost exactly like the Chief's late wife who they had seen before she died.

Pamela, by coming to the Reservation, being interested in Chuck's life, teaching the Reservation children, and participating in Reservation customs, showed that she was serious about having a real relationship with him.

Pamela asked our boss if she could be assigned to the Indian Department and work with the law as it affected the Indian population. Her request was granted, and she began working for the Indian Division at the U S Attorney's Office. Chris Lightfoot, one of the other three attorneys who came up with me, was now head of that department.

This made perfect sense since his parents lived on a reservation. He understood the situation in which the Indians found themselves, and he was willing to fight to make things better.

Over the months, all and all, Pamela won over the Chief, and with his blessing, she and Chuck were married at the Reservation with the Chief presiding. They had a wonderful party which included everyone at the Reservation plus some of our friends from the office, who seemed to be having a good time.

I was her maid of honor, and Rick was a groom. Michael was best man. It was wonderful.

The Chief promoted Chuck to manager of the golf courses. He was now an executive. Between what the two of them made, they were able to buy a house in West Palm Springs, not far from us.

Pamela went to work on Indian affairs with a vengeance. She had quite a quagmire of legal difficulties to work through.

With the law, the Indians experienced many of the same problems that they did with life. They were originally considered a separate, sovereign nation but, as time progressed, even the meager rights they thought that they had were taken from them.

White people cannot live without being right all of the time. They are really full of themselves. And when they are wrong, they simply change the rules and maintain that this is what they meant all the time.

The Indians, even on their own reservations which are supposed to be tantamount to separate countries, are subject to three sets of laws: federal, tribal, and State.

Examine the progression.

The Federal Enclaves Act was enacted in 1817. It provided that federal law applies to crimes in Indian country.

In 1825, Congress enacted the Assimilated Crimes Act which provided that if there was no specific federal law applicable, State law would be used.

In 1885, Congress enacted the Major Crimes Act which gave the federal government jurisdiction over serious crimes in Indian country.

In 1953, Congress passed Public Law 280 which for certain States, including California, transferred criminal jurisdiction in Indian country from the federal government to the State government.

In 2010, Congress passed the Tribal Law and Order Act of 2010 with the purpose of allowing tribal criminal justice in Indian country.

Both the State governments and the federal government have been much criticized for failing to accept cases from the reservations and for generally not pursuing adequate protections for families living there.

Pamela, after being involved with an Indian man and with the Indian people on the Reservation, dove head first into her mission. Fortunately, she had met her new section boss, Chris, at the Reservation and liked him. She felt that he was not afraid to represent the Indians aggressively, which was all that she asked. Regardless of what Chris did personally, he appeared to have the sense to stay out of her way. Taylor had been a good influence.

She went over pending cases. Where things were bogged down, she used TLOA to request the Attorney General to approve concurrent jurisdiction among the federal government, the State governments, and the tribe.

In this way, she could bypass the PL 280 States and persuade the tribes to seek federal intervention which would show an expanded recognition of tribal sovereignty.

She used TLOA to encourage cooperative law enforcement agreements to combat crime near tribal areas.

She worked with TLOA to increase the age for tribal officers from 37 to 47 which would allow experienced officers to continue working and expanding the size of the force.

She used TLOA to permit warrantless arrests based only on probable cause. She used TLOA to obtain training for law enforcement to ferret out illegal drugs and substance abuse.

Pamela went after the nuts and bolts. She went for cooperation, increasing the age of law enforcement, changing arrest criteria, and securing training. She and Chuck spent hours talking about the fate of the Indians.

One of the more perplexing issues was the fear factor. As Black and Mexican gangs became more feared through bolder and more aggressive criminal behavior, their punishment by the courts became more severe.

The Indians, without actually being bolder or more aggressive, were drawn into the same severe punishments.

With the Indians, a lack of understanding of their culture made people fear them. Though this fear was unwarranted, at some point, they will have to be re-educated so that the impression that they project is not quite so misunderstood.

Indian people, even including a person such as Chuck, is known for his special skills in fighting and weaponry. Does this make it so white people want to test them? It seems as if white people may be jealous of Indians and American Blacks for that matter, and the only way they have to combat them is with making them act out in ways that are expected so they can be punished accordingly.

I know that Pamela, Chuck, and the Chief will have to come together to improve the image of the Indian as perceived by white people. Especially because Pamela is pregnant and will be bringing a new child into a rather messed up world. I was thrilled with the news of Pamela's pregnancy.

Rick and I spent many hours with Pamela and Chuck over the past several years since Izzy's kidnapping. Though unlikely, they made a great couple. We all had fun together riding, going to dinner, catching a movie, and just talking at home.

It's odd and almost a little sad that when Chuck did finally succeed in the world, he needed to do it within the framework of the white culture.

Don't get me wrong, I love the Chief, Chuck, Michael, Roger, and everyone else at the Reservation, but, as Chuck told me years ago, success is not measured in the world today by being able to kill, skin, and cook an animal but by making enough money to pick up a cellophane covered Styrofoam plate at the supermarket containing a small portion of an animal slaughtered by others.

The whites who came up with such things as Indian Boarding Schools and mechanical training programs for Indians seem to be horrible people who wanted the Indians to be separated from their culture, their language, their customs, their names, their religion, and even their hair styles.

I hate it, but maybe the Indians would have done better if they had been more willing to adapt. The white man was never going to give the Indian the land they needed to maintain their old culture; the white man simply could not afford to do so.

I remained in the U S Attorney's Office where I was moved from Indian relations to sex trafficking. (I hope they never find any sex trafficking on John's Reservation. I'm certain that the justice would be not only swift, but also final.)

During the five or so years that I worked in sex trafficking since Izzy's return, I was nothing short of a human dynamo. I guess that now I had something else about which to be competitive with Pamela, conviction rate.

I was all over these sleaze bags. I would set up stings. I would lean so hard on the underlings that they would give up their mother if it meant getting rid of me. I had informants deep inside of every criminal enterprise in the tri-counties. I chased them down to Mexico and up to Northern California.

But it got so many girls released from the grip of these creeps that I know that I was doing something right.

Rick remained, as always, my most loyal supporter. However, even he was growing a little concerned, not about the amount of work or the number of hours I needed to spend away from our family, but about how dangerous the work was becoming.

I was no longer in the business of busting some husband with an underage girl in a motel room or setting up a sting of a business man calling in to arrange to see what he thought was one of his regulars. No, that work was increasingly left to local law enforcement.

As time progressed, I became tasked with having my people work their way into giant criminal enterprises. These were businesses so big that they almost came out the other end, particularly considering the number of political campaigns to which they contributed. They not only had their prostitution and forced labor divisions, but also owned many legitimate businesses, through which they could launder their money.

After five years of being over the top, I was contacted by National Woman Magazine and was told that they were giving me the Woman of the Year Award.

With this came interviews of me and Rick for an article in the magazine. I was told that I would be giving a speech at the awards ceremony, which would be held outside and across the street from my office in Riverside.

At some point, I must have said something about it to Rick in passing.

Now, I braced myself for the onslaught.

Chapter 12
It Must Be Awards Season

It was Saturday morning. Taylor, Rick, and Izzy were all home. The land line rang.

Rick announced, "I've got it."

Speaking into the mouthpiece Rick answered, "Hello."

The person on the other end of the line asked, "Is Rick Miller there?"

Rick responded, "This is he. How may I help you?"

"This is Marlene Seifert from National Women Magazine. I don't know whether you know but your wife is going to be receiving our Woman of the Year award for her outstanding contributions to women's rights in the field of law, more precisely law as it relates to sex crimes."

Rick replied, "I think I heard something about that. My wife is not a person who goes around telling everyone, not even me, that she is winning awards."

Ms. Seifert replied, "Well the magazine wants to recognize her for her great work, and as part of our practice, in addition to the award, we would like to do a feature article about her, including a cover."

Rick replied, "And what does that have to do with me?"

Ms. Seifert replied, "We need background material about your wife both for the article and for the awards speech. When Ms. Hawthorne, our Chairperson, gives your wife her award at our annual awards ceremony, she will give a little speech about your wife's life and her accomplishments. Your wife will also give an acceptance speech. We often interview people who know the recipient for background information. And who better to interview than her husband?"

She continued, "On my end, I would like to know firstly whether you would be willing to meet with me at all, and if you are willing, when and where we could meet."

Rick replied, "I would be happy to meet with you. I work all day during the week and have only a little bit of time on the weekends usually around mid-day when I could meet. Taylor usually takes our daughter out at this time, so we could have the house to ourselves.

Ms. Seifert stated, "That would be fine. Either day would work. How about Saturday at 11?"

Rick responded, "That's fine, but I don't know what I can add to what you already know."

Ms. Seifert replied, "Some of her life is public knowledge. Rescuing the kidnapped little girl when she herself was only a teenager, being saved when she was thrown from the roof of a 15-story building, and partnering with the Native Americans to retrieve her kidnapped daughter are widely known, but my editor feels that you might have additional insight, as you were part of much of the action yourself."

Rick replied, "While it is true that I was part of some the action, my part was very small. These are things that Taylor did. Also, after getting Izzy back, things have become pretty quiet. Taylor was promoted from the Indian Task Force to sex trafficking, where she has been for the past few years. Her work there is so confidential that even I know absolutely nothing about it. It might be a pretty boring interview."

Ms. Seifert replied, "I guess I will have to take my chances. I believe that your information about the first part of her now public life will be interesting even if I can't get any information about her sex trafficking duties."

Rick replied, "I will give you as much as I can. As to the confidential stuff, you are on your own with her, which is not a great place to be."

Ms. Seifert concluded, "11 o'clock tomorrow then. Since you think that she will be going out with your daughter, perhaps we can just meet at your house, as you suggested. I have the address. West Palm Springs, I believe."

Rick replied, "Yes, West Palm Springs. I will see you here at 11 tomorrow."

They hung up the phone.

It was after work on Friday, but it was still light outside. Taylor and Izzy dressed and were ready for their evening adventure. They passed by Rick in the living room on their way to the front door.

Taylor asked, "Who was that?"

Rick replied, "She said that her name is Marlene Seifert and that she is with National Woman Magazine. She said that you are receiving the Woman of the Year award from the Magazine and that she wants to interview me to gather information for a feature article which will be included in the Magazine and also in the speech which will be given by the Board Chairperson at the awards ceremony."

"What did you say?"

"I said that I would be available for an interview tomorrow at 11."

"Good. She won't need me then."

"Not tomorrow, but I think that she plans on interviewing you on another day."

Taylor replied, "She's not going to get much information that she doesn't already know. I can't get into any of the details about what I've been doing, and you don't know any of that stuff anyway."

I replied, "I guess that's true."

As she and Izzy made it to the front door, Taylor looked back at Rick and said, "Okay. We're off now. See you here for dinner."

Taylor and Izzy left out the front door, leaving Rick standing by the phone.

Rick went on about his household chores. He cleaned the kitchen, made the beds, and did a load of wash while the girls were out and about.

Taylor and Izzy made it home for dinner, which Rick prepared. After dinner, they all went to bed.

Chapter 13
Taylor, Rick, Izzy, the Reservation, and the Motorcycle Club

Dave Roberts, a food grower/drug dealer, kidnapped Izzy to slow Taylor down in her criminal pursuit of him. Rather than using conventional law enforcement methods, Taylor solicited the help of the Native Americans at the nearby Reservation, including the Chief, his nephew, and others. They were ultimately instrumental in recovering Izzy.

After Izzy's return, Taylor continued to spend time at the Reservation, sometimes taking along Izzy, Rick, or both.

Originally, the Reservation included over 30,000 acres of land extending from what is now Palm Springs, over the desert, and into the mountains. The Indians, the original inhabitants, lived in the foothills. During the Presidential administrations of Ulysses S. Grant and Rutherford B. Hayes, the Reservation was enlarged. It was divided into a checkerboard pattern, with the even numbered squares going to the Indians and the odd numbered squares going first to the railroad and then to white settlers.

After over 30 years of fighting, the Indians were able to make an agreement with the City of Palm Springs and ultimately maintained around 6,700 acres in Palm Springs for the tribe.

The Reservation is located in a larger area known as the Coachella Valley. The Coachella Valley extends roughly from the 10 Freeway to the Salton Sea.

On the south side of the Highway 111, the Reservation runs past Palm Springs into the south mountains. Presently, the area around the foothills south of Highway 111 is maintained similar to a dude ranch. The dude ranch is run by the Chief and his nephew Chuck. Chuck works as a guide.

At the dude ranch, there is a main building which houses a gift shop and the Chief's office. There is a mess hall and a bunk house for guests. The guests are primarily interested in the hot springs a short distance away as well as horseback riding and hiking in the immediate area.

Under the Coachella Valley there is an aquafer which is a vast area of underground water. The Indians used this water for over 3,000 years. When the white settlers began using it, it nearly ran out of water in around 75 years requiring an aqueduct to be built from the Colorado River to replenish it.

Control of the water was given to two white-owned water companies. There were legal fights between the two white-owned water companies and the Indians who sought a voice in the water's management. The Indians were not successful.

The Chief, his nephew, and the others at the Reservation were so kind and supportive that Taylor maintained their friendship and hoped that Izzy would understand their ways and see the world through, perhaps, a slightly different prism than her white friends, many of whom were semi-rich and spoiled.

(Taylor refused to refer to the Chief as "The Chief." She felt that such a nick name was too demeaning for a man so gifted. She called him "John," the English version of his Indian name.)

After leaving the house, Taylor and Izzy arrived at the Reservation and met John. Taylor saddled up a couple of horses, and she and Izzy went for a ride. Izzy was becoming a pretty good little rider. Taylor was an excellent horse person, though not when compared to the Indians who literally became one with the animal.

Izzy was now able to make the horse gallop, cut back and forth, start, and stop. She could mount and dismount by herself. When they were done riding, they returned the horses to the barn, and each gave her horse a rub down. One of the first and many lessons Izzy would learn about horses and life at the Reservation.

They then took a short hike. Taylor and John exchanged pleasantries, and she and Izzy headed home.

In addition to the Indians, Taylor remained in contact with Moose and his motorcycle club known as the Motorcycle Enthusiasts of America or the MEA.

Moose was still located near Haven, which is further down in the desert, where Taylor and Rick were living before moving to West Palm Springs.

When Taylor was just a teenager, she babysat for a 12-year old girl by the name of Tammy Fitzgerald, the daughter of Don Fitzgerald.

The girl was kidnapped from the Fitzgerald home in Haven Lakes located on the new interstate highway running from Haven to Newton.

When the child could not be found by traditional law enforcement, she mounted her own investigation. After her investigation failed, she enrolled in a Constitutional Law class at the nearby junior college. This is where she met Rick, her professor, who was also a practicing attorney in Haven.

Judging from his lectures (and his youthful appearance), she felt that he might help her in her search for Tammy.

She and Rick met, found Tammy, and with the help of Moose and his friends extricated her from the compound of Antony Carbone, a notorious gangster.

Taylor finished college and law school and worked for the State Attorney General first in elder abuse and then in white collar crime.

Rick met several nice ladies after the Tammy Fitzgerald ordeal, but he was so in love with Taylor that he never started a relationship with any of them.

Now that Taylor was working, Rick gathered the courage to call. They began dating. Eventually, they became lovers. Rick invited Taylor to a fancy dinner. The hostess showed her to Rick's table where he took out a diamond ring and asked her to marry him. She said yes, and their life together began.

After they married, Taylor continued on with the State Attorney General. While working there, in response to a tip, she witnessed the death of a worker at a large chemical company during an illegal dumping operation. She was kidnapped and imprisoned at the corporate headquarters building. The CEO ordered that she be thrown from the roof of the 15 story building to keep her from reporting his activities to the authorities. When she was thrown from the building, she was saved by Rick who scaled the outside of the building, ran across the roof, and jumped off the roof tied only to a bungie cord.

She then went to work for the United States Attorney, initially on the Indian Task Force. This is where she met John and the other Native Americans. While on the Indian Task Force, Dave Roberts, a drug smuggler, had her daughter kidnapped in an effort to slow down her pursuit of him. Taylor and her Native American friends extricated Izzy from Roberts, and Roberts was sent to jail, for a very long time.

Chapter 14
The Interview of Rick

The next day arrived. It was Saturday, and neither Rick nor Taylor had to work. They went into the kitchen and made breakfast. Ms. Seifert would not be arriving until 11. As the time approached, Taylor dressed Izzy, and they took off for the day. They were planning on doing some shopping, eating lunch, and catching a movie. Rick was left alone in the house.

The doorbell rang. Rick answered the door. Rick opened the door and let in a tall, attractive lady about 30 years old.

Rick started, "Hello, you must be Ms. Seifert."

She replied, "Yes. And please call me Marlene. Ms. Seifert seems so formal."

Rick responded, "I will. Thank you."

Rick continued, "Please have a seat on the couch."

Marlene sat on one of two couches in the living room that faced one another. Rick sat opposite her on the other couch. They spoke over a coffee table positioned between the two couches.

Rick asked, "How may I help you?"

Marlene replied, "As I mentioned on the telephone, we are doing an article on your wife for our annual Woman of the Year award. I was hoping to ask you a few questions about her."

Rick replied, "I will do my best."

Marlene started, "Let's start with how you and your wife met. Believe it or not, the women who read our magazine are interested in such things. Kind of a modified romance novel."

Rick replies, "My wife and I met when she was a student in a class I was teaching at Newton Junior College, a Constitutional law class. She seemed bright and interested, more interested than most of the other students. She was actually about a year older than most of the students.

"She was bold. She stayed after class and asked if I would meet with her about a private matter. At first, I declined as I thought that it would be inappropriate to get involved with a student away from class, even though she was 19. But she kept after me. She told me that it was about the kidnapping of a person for whom she babysat and that the local authorities could not solve the crime. That night, I checked on line and found a few articles written about the incident. I told her that I would need to know more to get involved."

Marlene interjected, "Well, you're now married to her so something must have happened."

Rick replied, "Yes. We are married now, but many things transpired between our first meeting and our eventual marriage."

Marlene said, "Sorry. I didn't mean to interrupt."

Rick continued, "The case was so intriguing that I decided to get involved."

Marlene asked, "Just the case. She's a very beautiful woman now. At 19, she must have really been something."

Rick went on, "On that score, I would have to either plead guilty or take the 5th. She was far more than just beautiful. She was enchanting. I guess I would be a liar if I said that her looks had nothing to do with my decision to help her."

Marlene continued, "I have to commend you for your honesty. Most men would continue on in denial."

Rick went on, "She arranged for us to meet at a bar outside of town, which turned out to be a biker bar."

Marlene asked, "Why there?"

Rick replied, "Because it was far from town, no one from school went there, and it was dark inside.

Marlene asked, "What did she say?"

Rick responded, "She told me the story about how Tammy was kidnapped, and how the local police could not find her. There was no ransom demand. In time, the case went cold and was closed. There was a funeral for the little girl. Her poor mother was a mess."

Marlene asked, "And then what happened."

Rick responded, "Taylor drafted her old friend Frank Diaz who was a rookie on the police force in Haven. Taylor went to Bryan and met a nice fellow who referred to himself as a court watcher. From him, she learned that the little girl's father and a gangster, Antony Carbone, were in business together. The father was able to get the interstate through from Haven to Newton and to build the fancy subdivision called Haven Lakes along the new route.

"The court watcher told her that he thought that Carbone was the money guy behind Tammy's father and that maybe Carbone kidnapped the little girl to encourage her father to make better progress with Carbone's real project, the building of a hotel and casino at the south entrance to Rock Ridge National Park.

"We flew a drone over Carbone's hilltop compound and saw what looked like a private play yard for a child. We hiked up to get a closer look. Taylor was able to get past the electric fence. I was sent to get Moose from the motorcycle club for help. Unknown to me, Taylor was captured, held, and tortured by Carbone and his men.

Marlene asked, "What happened then?"

Rick continued, "Moose and his men rescued Taylor and Tammy, and I took them to Tammy's mother. No one knew at that time that Tammy's father was involved with Carbone."

Marlene inquired, "Did it seem a little strange that you were involved with one of your students. Some might call that inappropriate."

Rick replied, "In all honesty, it probably was inappropriate. I rationalized it by taking the position that since she could not get help from the authorities, I was her only hope. Besides, I was careful to keep the relationship from becoming romantic. After Tammy was returned, we went through a long period of litigation (criminal, civil, and administrative), during which we did not see much of one another, except in a courtroom or a lawyer's office.

Rick continued, "Various crimes were committed against Tammy and Taylor while they were being held at the compound including kidnapping and, in Taylor's case, torture. Tammy had an obvious civil against Carbone for false imprisonment, assault, battery, etc. Taylor had a similar civil case and a case for torture. On an administrative level, the law enforcement officials were fired and lost their pensions. The civil cases caused Carbone and Tammy's father to lose everything. Taylor used the money she received in the settlement of her case against Carbone to finish college and go on to law school. After graduation, she went to work for the State Attorney General in elder abuse."

Marlene inquired, "So, let me get this straight. Taylor was a student in a junior college class you were teaching. She asked for help with a kidnapping case involving a young girl for whom she babysat. After some minor convincing, you dropped everything to help her, as did Frank Diaz, someone she said was a friend and was now working in the same police department which could not find the child in the first place.

"You flew a drone and gathered DNA evidence. You and Taylor hiked up to Carbone's complex where Taylor was captured. You were able to get Moose and his friends to extricate Taylor and the little girl against great odds. You returned the little girl to her mother. You and Taylor pursued various remedies against Carbone and the girl's father. Taylor went off to college and law school and landed her first job in the State Attorney General's office during which time you had almost no communication with her. How am I doing so far?"

Rick replied, "That's about it."

Marlene continued, "So, you let Taylor go off to college and law school barely speaking to her for several years. You're a good-looking guy with a good job; you must have had other opportunities with women."

Rick said, "I did. But I had such deep feelings for Taylor that I knew that I could not do justice to a relationship with anyone else. I just resolved to wait. Generally, people meet their entire circle of friends in college. I didn't want to be an outsider. Besides, I didn't think that she was that into me."

Marlene weighed in, "You must have thought that she was really special to do all of that waiting."

Rick replied, "Yes, I did."

Marlene asked, "And then what?"

Rick replied, "Honestly, I broke down and called her."

Marlene asked, "And."

Rick replied, "And she was so great. She agreed to meet. We talked for hours and agreed to meet again. We began dating, and eventually, what was a great friendship turned into an even greater love affair. Finally, I arranged for her to meet me at a fancy restaurant for dinner. After she was seated, I got down on one knee and asked her to marry me. Much to my surprise, she said yes."

Marlene concluded, "I guess she never met anyone either in college or law school. Must have been one of those things that was meant to be."

Rick ended, "Yes. I think that her personal relationships may have been adversely affected by her less than perfect home life, her father's abandonment, and her treatment by her mother and her mother's friends. I always gave her a great deal of room to make her own decisions. I never pressured her to be with me romantically. Maybe it worked. Knowing her as I do, I can see that trying to pressure her to do something is going to backfire every time."

Marlene went on, "Now that we have examined the Tammy Fitzgerald case, what happened next? You said something about the State Attorney General's Office."

Rick replied, "Yes. After law school, because she was such an exceptional student and was active civically, she had many offers from top law firms. She chose, however, the State Attorney General's Office."

Marlene asked, "Why?"

Rick replied, "I think that she saw her place in the world as someone destined to help others. She started in elder abuse but was soon moved to white collar crimes."

Marlene asked, "How did that go?"

Rick replied, "It went okay except for the fact that white collar criminals not only have complex cases but also present an element of danger, particularly if you want to make the punishment really fit the crime."

Marlene asked, "What do you mean by that?"

Rick said, "For example, some large companies engage in illegal toxic waste dumping. If they get caught, they might receive a fine, or they might sacrifice a low-level employee. Upper management feels that it is more cost effective to illegally dump and pay a fine than it is to dump legally. In one recent case, however, during a routine toxic waste dump, one of the employees died when exposed to the substance that he was dumping. A small fine and conviction of involuntary manslaughter were levied. This drove Taylor out of her mind. She vowed to seek murder convictions against the highest-level employees in the company for deaths occurring during illegal activities, particularly when ordered by upper management."

Marlene asked, "Was Taylor ever threatened with retribution for being so aggressive with her proposed punishments?"

Rick replied, "Yes. And that was part of the problem. Her intention to increase the penalties became well known around corporate board rooms and high-power law firms. She was not well liked by either, as you can imagine."

Marlene asked, "Didn't I hear that she was the target of corporate backlash?"

Rick replied, "Oh, was she. She received a tip from a whistleblower about an illegal dumping scheduled for that night. She could not reach any of the enforcement divisions at that late hour, so she resolved to go herself. Her investigator volunteered to go with her. It turned out that he was a bad guy planted in her office to keep tabs on her. They went to the dump site in his car. They witnessed not only the illegal dumping but also the death of an employee who died from exposure to the chemical that he was illegally dumping. After he died, his body was sealed in a container."

Marlene asked, "And then what?"

Rick replied, "The investigator knocked her out and took her to the corporate headquarters building of the illegal actor in Riverside. She was told that she would be taken to the roof of the 15-story corporate headquarters building and thrown to her death. As a cover story, she was told that the media would report that she was having an affair with her investigator and that she accidently fell off of the roof during a lover's quarrel."

Marlene interjected, "Sounds serious. Then what happened."

Rick replied, "I gathered up Moose, two of his crew, a computer guy, and Taylor's girlfriend. As it was night, we were able to take over the first floor of the building without revealing our presence to the action on the roof. I cut a hole in a 14th floor window, scaled the outside glass wall of the building, and reached the roof. I pulled Moose and one of his guys onto the roof. I ran towards Taylor just as she was pushed off of the building. I hooked a bungie cord to the railing, jumped off, caught Taylor, and the cord expanded to a location about 10 feet above the ground. I was able to hand Taylor off to one of Moose's guys on the ground."

Marlene asked, "What was the result?"

Rick replied, "Fortunately, Taylor recorded the CEO's speech about how he was going to throw her from the roof. So, the police arrested him and his men."

Marlene said, "That was quite a story. Was Taylor able to go back to work after that?"

Rick replied, "Of course she was. She was back at work practically the next day. She is not a person who sits around feeling sorry for herself."

Marlene asked, "What's next?"

Rick replied, "Taylor and I were married, and around this time, we found out that she was pregnant with our daughter. We were both happy and excited. Never has the birth of a child been so hopefully anticipated and so full of love. We pitched in together, and everything went perfectly. Taylor gave birth to the most beautiful child imaginable, a child loved from conception. I have said many times that I thought that I could never love Taylor any more than I did when we first met. I was so very, very wrong. When I saw how she was with our daughter, I got to see first-hand what love really is."

Marlene asked, "And then what?"

Rick replied, "Believe it or not, Taylor was promoted. She left her job with the State Attorney General and was given her new job, this time with the United States Attorney. The new work would be with the Native American task force. Complaints had come in that the Native Americans felt that they were not getting fair representation from the government. The U S Attorney's Office was asked to seek candidates from outside of the Office. Taylor was selected. We were planning on moving anyway, so the timing was good."

Marlene asked, "How was the work with the U S Attorney?"

Rick replied, "It was great for her and was a much-deserved promotion."

Marlene asked, "How about the work with the Native Americans?"

Rick replied, "That is what made the opportunity really great. Taylor's involvement with the Native Americans turned out to be the best thing that happened to her, to me, and to Izzy on many levels. She was always an outsider coming from a different background than her colleagues. Her involvement with the Indians showed her that she was not the only person in the world who was treated badly for no apparent reason.

"Also, I always admired the Native American culture and read and studied it for years. I could see the injustices. Maybe the transition would have been more difficult if she had been married to someone who disliked or could not accept Native Americans. I know that if I had felt that way, our marriage could not have survived the next several years during which Native Americans would become a large part of our lives. Also, the experience proved to us that race, gender, economic circumstances, disability, and religion had no meaning to either of us. I think that we understood this about each other, and I pray that we are able to instill these values in our daughter."

Marlene asked, "How did things go at the U S Attorney's Office?"

Rick replied, "I don't know how the U S Attorney's Office operates in general; however, with Indian relations, it did an interesting thing. Every person going to work for the U S Attorney in Indian relations is required to spend at least one full day at an actual Indian reservation to see what the conditions are really like. If one wished, a candidate could spend as much as a week at a reservation. Since only one day was required, no one had ever stayed longer than that first day, as everyone was generally anxious to return to civilization as soon as possible. Taylor, of course, was the first person to ever ask to stay longer. She returned the next day and stayed the rest of the week, until Saturday. Her objective was to learn more about the Indian culture. Izzy and I went there on Saturday to bring her home."

Marlene asked, "What happened at the Reservation?"

Rick replied, "According to Taylor, on that first day, she and the other three candidates had lunch and took a hike with the Chief, the Indian gentleman in charge of the dude ranch operation. Throughout lunch and the hike, the Chief explained the reservation system and how this Reservation came to exist in this location."

Marlene continued, "What happened after the first day at the Reservation?"

Rick replied, "As suspected, the other three candidates chose to not return. Taylor, however, did return and stayed until Saturday when Izzy and I came to pick her up. I was told that she did some riding, which she already did well having grown up on a farm, and learned to throw knives, shoot, and fish. When Izzy and I came up, she introduced Izzy to various animals. She is very good with animals as she spent more time with animals than with people when she was young. She showed Izzy how to approach and pet them so that they would not become scared and defensive."

Marlene went on, "And what happened the next week when she finally returned to the office?"

Rick replied, "When she returned to work, her boss told her about the Indian water rights case, the case to which the Chief alluded when he and Taylor spoke at the Reservation. Her boss implied that he intended to involve her with the case. He really didn't want too, but he needed an environmental lawyer from the task force, and she was the only one he had, the other three were criminal law specialist.

"Actually, Taylor's boss hoped that after explaining the complexities of the case to her, she would find it to be so overwhelming that she would decline to become involved. Not much chance of that. He clearly did not know her at all."

Marlene asked, "And then what happened?"

Rick replied, "Taylor's boss explained the case to her. He told her that under the Coachella Valley, there is an aquafer (a pool of water) which runs from roughly the 10 Freeway to the Salton Sea. The Indians used the water from the aquafer for thousands of years. When the white settlers began taking over the valley, after 75 or so years, the water in the aquafer alone could not keep up with the demand. To remedy this, an aqueduct was built which brought water from the Colorado River. This water was added to the aquafer by running it onto the ground and allowing it to seep through the earth and join the water already in the aquafer. The passing of the water through the ground was the only filtration to which the water was subjected.

"The Indians brought a lawsuit for declaratory relief. From what I was told, the case was divided into three Phases. By the time of Taylor's involvement, Phases I and II had already been decided."

Marlene inquired, "What did Taylor's bosses do?"

Rick replied, "Because they had to, Taylor's bosses did ask her to become involved with the case, but that is not what they really wanted. Her bosses had an arrangement with the water companies to allow their large grower client more water than he was entitled to in exchange for money. If Taylor became involved, they knew that she would work for the Indians and that the Indians would not allow the large grower to have the additional water."

Marlene then asked, "And who is this 'client' you mentioned?"

Rick replied, "The client is a person by the name of Dave Roberts, a food grower with the largest crop output of any growing concern in the valley. As it turned out, he was the one calling the shots with Taylor's bosses. Roberts was not only a grower but was also a drug supplier who maintained an elaborate compound in the hills south of the highway opposite Palm Desert.

Even though growing was not his main business, he needed to make enough money from his growing business to convince everyone that it was his main business and would afford him the lavish lifestyle that he displayed. The last thing he wanted was a bunch of Indians and a girl attorney standing in his way."

Marlene asked, "What was going on with the case?"

Rick replied, "By the time Taylor became involved, the District Court had decided that the Indians did have a reserved water right which included ground water. However, it also decided that the Tribe failed to show an injury and, therefore, lacked standing. The Court held that the Tribe could not support its quantification claim as it could not show that it lacked enough water for reservation purposes and that it could not support is quality claim even though dangerous total dissolved solids were present in the water."

Marlene asked, "So, what did Taylor do?"

Rick replied, "She proposed a settlement which would allow the Tribe to maintain a 50 percent ownership of the water in the aquafer and would require the districts to treat the water coming from the Colorado River and keep that water separate from the aquafer. The aquafer would consist only of its original water. The treated water could be sold by the districts and used elsewhere so long as it was (a) properly treated, (b) used for agricultural and irrigation purposes, and (c) insured, that is, the districts would maintain an insurance policy covering loss from the river water naming the Tribe as an additional insured."

Marlene inquired, "How was that offer received?"

Rick replied, "Not well, particularly by Dave Roberts, who was the only person who mattered anyway. When Roberts heard of the offer, which I thought was quite fair, he went ballistic. He reasoned that trying to harm Taylor directly would be of no benefit to him as she had demonstrated that she could take care of herself. So, instead, he decided to do the unthinkable, which was to kidnap Izzy to make Taylor back off of the water use case. Oh, how badly he miscalculated."

Marlene asked, "Taylor must have blown her stack when she found out that her daughter was kidnapped. What did she do."

Rick replied, "She rounded up her Indian friends, and they broke into the Roberts' compound. Taylor rescued Izzy and escaped from the compound on the back of a horse so huge, so fast, and so scary that even horseback riding experts run away from him. (Only the Chief, and now Taylor, have ever ridden him.)"

Marlene asked, "How did you guys get justice for all of this?"

Rick replied, "I organized my law enforcement friends. We obtained a wire-tap warrant and were able to overhear Roberts not only when he admitted to the kidnapping of Izzy but also when he admitted to arranging the murder of the two actual kidnappers. Roberts' life sentence was somewhat mitigated by his giving up Taylor's bosses and the two water district guys. The civil settlement went into a trust account for Izzy's college."

Marlene said, "That is quite a story. After all of this did you guys go back to work?"

Rick replied, "Yes."

Marlene asked, "From the end of the Roberts case until now what has been going on in your lives?"

Rick replied, "Taylor stayed with the U S Attorney and went into the sex trafficking division where she is now."

Marlene asked, "Is there anything you can tell me about her work now?"

Rick replied, "Frankly, no. Firstly, I was personally involved in the Tammy case, the 15-story building case, and the Roberts case. As a result, I can speak to those cases from my own personal experience without relying on what I was told by my wife. I have not really been personally involved with her sex trafficking cases, and even if I was, the information is strictly confidential. I believe the better part of discretion would be for you to ask her about the time since the Roberts case. The information will be much more accurate, and I won't run the risk of violating any confidences.

"And as you can see, I go to great lengths to be fair and honest with my wife, and that is why we have such a great marriage."

Marlene concluded, "Fair enough. I will take up the past few years with Taylor herself. I have arranged to meet with her in the next couple of days at her office."

Rick concluded, "Good. I will show you out."

Rick escorted Marlene to the front door and bid her farewell. He watched as Marlene drove away.

Chapter 15
Prelude to Taylor's Interview

After Marlene completed her interview of Rick and left to return to her office, Rick decided that rather than go to work himself, he would stay at home and wait for Izzy and Taylor. Izzy's school bus dropped her off about three blocks away, and she walked home. She came into the house and saw that her dad was home, which was unusual. They chatted and played some word games in Izzy's room. About an hour later, Taylor came home. It was now close to dinner time.

The three of them had dinner. Having dinner as a family was important, particularly to Rick. He had dinner with his parents nearly every night and found it to be a good time to keep in touch with issues of health and politics.

Izzy went off to do her homework and, after that was complete, watch an hour of television. Izzy then got ready for bed. Each of her parents went into her room separately to say good night.

Rick and Taylor joined each other on the couch.

Taylor asked, "How was your interview with Marlene?"

Rick replied, "Good. Gave me an opportunity to brag about my great wife."

Taylor asked, "What did you think of her?"

Rick replied, "In what way, as an interviewer, as a person?"

Taylor said, "You know what I mean."

Rick replied, "As an interviewer, she was very thorough. Also, she was very well versed in her subject. In other words, she studied up on our lives, at least those parts which would be of interest to her readers, which allowed her to dig a bit."

Taylor asked, "Did you find her attractive?"

Rick replied, "She's not un-attractive. Why do you ask?"

Taylor replied, "Just curious. Everyone around the office who has met her goes on and on about how good looking she is. I just wanted to know what you thought."

Rick replied, "Well, you will be seeing her for yourself in a day or two. I'd be curious what you think."

Rick and Taylor went off to bed. The next day was business as usual. The following day was the day of Taylor's interview with Marlene. They decided to meet at the office after work.

As to the meeting time, as a U S Attorney, Taylor was often required to meet witnesses and other civilians after hours, as she was busy all day either in court or drafting papers during her support staff's working hours.

On many occasions, these meetings would go on past 10 p.m., with some going as late as 12. Taylor's office maintained a safe house in the Riverside area for staff that worked late in the office or had an interview with a witness that ran late. Additionally, Taylor had a good girlfriend living in Riverside, and if the meeting went late, she could spend the night at her girlfriend's apartment if the safe house was occupied. The next day, they would have a leisurely breakfast, and Taylor would work her way back to the office and then home.

The next day, Taylor checked in at her office and worked a full day. After work, around 6, she ordered Chinese food and set it up on the buffet in the conference room.

At 6:30, she met Marlene in the reception area inside of the front door of the office suite. She took Marlene to the conference room for their meeting.

Chapter 16
Interview of Taylor

Taylor moved the large chairs at the end of the conference table around so that she and Marlene could sit facing one another along the end of the table. This would allow them to be separated by less than the full width of the table.

They both sat. Marlene placed some papers from her brief case on the table in front of her. Taylor brought no paperwork, as she was being questioned.

Marlene set up a small tape recorder on the table between her and Taylor. She turned in on and then began. Some of her statements were necessary for the recording.

Marlene started, "Hello, my name is Marlene Seifert. I am a senior staff writer for National Woman Magazine. We specialize in women's issues. Our content is primarily political and academic rather than fashion and cooking. This year, you have been chosen to receive the award for Woman of the Year for your contribution to law and law enforcement. The purpose of this meeting is to gain information about what you have been doing over the past nearly 20 years so that a comprehensive article about you may be written for the Magazine and for our Board Chairperson's speech at our annual dinner, where the physical award will be given to you. You will also be giving a speech at that time."

(Taylor was already familiar with this background information. Apparently, Marlene verbalized it to make a record for the tape recorder.)

Marlene asked, "What have you been doing the past years?"

Taylor responded, "As everyone knows, I grew up on an orange farm. I actually worked the farm, that is, I ran the operation including the bookkeeping and working in the field with the men harvesting oranges and getting them to market. You could say that I worked from the ground up. When I was a teenager, I took a job as a babysitter. The little girl for whom I babysat, Tammy Fitzgerald, was kidnapped. Not being satisfied with the services of traditional law enforcement, I undertook my own investigation. When my investigation reached its end, I enrolled in a junior college. During a class on the Constitution, I met my professor, Rick Miller. I eventually enlisted him and another friend of mine to help me with the kidnapping case. We found the victim, extricated her from the compound of a very bad man, and returned her to her mother."

Marlene asked, "Did this involve a romantic relationship with your professor. Some might argue that the position of teacher makes a relationship no longer consensual. He might be criticized for having a relationship with a student."

(Taylor could see that the interview was drifting towards the adversarial. Was Marlene threatened by her?)

Taylor continued, "Firstly, I was 19 when I met Rick, clearly above the age of consent. Secondly, your premise might hold some water if it was accurate. Yes, Rick and I worked together, but we did not have a romantic relationship at that time. We did not have a romantic relationship for over 5 years when I was 25, shortly after which we got married."

Marlene went on, "Let's not get bogged down on the details. So, after the Tammy Fitzgerald kidnapping, what happened?"

Taylor replied, "There were several Court cases to wade through including the criminal case involving the gangster and Tammy's father, civil cases for both Tammy and me, and administrative cases involving the gangster, Tammy's father, and a couple of police higher-ups."

Marlene asked, "What were you doing during this time?"

Taylor answered, "I was finishing college and law school, taking the bar, and getting my first law job in the State Attorney General's Office."

Marlene asked, "And then what?"

Taylor answered, "I started with the State AG in elder abuse and was then promoted to white collar crimes, primarily investigating illegal toxic waste dumping."

Marlene asked, "And how did that go?"

Taylor answered, "It was going fine for a while. We were prosecuting large corporations for a variety of activities, primarily toxic waste dumping. Then we got a tip late one night. As it was too late to call the enforcement division, I decided to take the call myself. Our investigator decided he wanted to come with me. We went to where we could see the toxic waste dumping site. The trucks rolled in and began dumping barrels of toxic waste in what appeared to be a dry lake-bed. Unfortunately, one of the participants became over-exposed to the waste and died. His body was placed into a barrel and back onto a truck. I wanted to call the authorities, but was knocked out by the investigator who turned out to be working for the bad guy."

Marlene asked, "What did he do with you after knocking you out?"

Taylor replied, "He took me to the underground parking garage at a corporate office building where I was locked in a cage."

Marlene asked, "And then what?"

Taylor replied, "I came to find out that the CEO planned to take me up onto the roof of this 15-story building and throw me and the investigator off claiming that we fell accidentally during a lover's quarrel."

Marlene said, "Wow, that must have been scary. What happened next?"

Taylor replied, "Well, we were taken onto the roof. The CEO made a little speech about his intent to throw us off of the roof which I tape recorded. I was taken to the edge of the building and thrown off. Unknown to me, my husband Rick cut a hole in the glass wall of the building, scaled the outside of the building with suction cups, ran from one side of the building to the other, hooked a bungie cord onto the roof railing, jumped, grabbed me, and the cord expanded almost to the ground below where I was let off. It was really something."

Marlene asked, "What happened after being saved?"

Taylor replied, "Rick and I returned to work as normal. We had a baby. We moved to west Palm Springs. I was promoted to the U S Attorney's Office to be part of the Indian Task Force."

Marlene asked, "And how did that go?"

Taylor answered, "It went great for a while. As part of our Task Force training, we were required to visit an Indian Reservation for at least one day. I stayed the day but asked to stay the rest of the week, as I felt that I was learning so much. I was told that I was the only white person to ever ask to stay the week. I met a wonderful man known as the Chief. He was in charge of the dude ranch operation. I also met has nephew Chuck. I had several long chats with the Chief and Chuck about the Indians. They also showed me how to throw knives, shoot a bow and arrow, shoot guns, and ride horses, though I already knew how to ride."

Marlene asked, "So far, it sounds great."

Taylor replied, "As I said, at first it was great. I then got involved with a water rights case between the Indians and the water companies. My bosses and the water companies were in league with the largest grower in the valley and did not want the Indians involved in the management of the water for fear that they might prevent the water companies from selling extra water to the grower illegally. The grower decided to kidnap my daughter to get me to back off of the water case. Needless to say, I went ballistic."

Marlene asked, "What did you do?"

Taylor replied, "I worked with the Indians, and we rescued my daughter. Rick then was able to get a legal wiretap in which the grower admitted not only to the water scheme but also to murdering the two men who did the actual kidnapping of my daughter."

Marlene said, "I guess that this takes us through the kidnapping of Tammy Fitzgerald, your being thrown from the building, and the kidnapping of your daughter."

Taylor replied, "Yes, this was most of my life between 19 and the time my daughter reached four and one-half."

Marlene asked, "Is it safe to say that these events involved both you and Rick but that the next events were more exclusively about you."

Taylor replied, "Yes, that is true. After I returned to work after my daughter's kidnapping, I was promoted within the U S Attorney's Office to the sex trafficking division. The cases in this division are strictly confidential, even as to one's spouse. I cannot say that it has been easy. Rick and I have been together practically my entire adult life, and keeping things from him is not perfect. Fortunately, he is a lawyer and understands, besides just being great anyway."

Marlene said, "From what I know about the law, the U S Attorney typically prosecutes federal crimes and not State crimes. Aren't sex crimes State crimes?"

Taylor replied, "That is a good point. Let's get into some of the differences. Sometimes a little history helps. The Office of the Attorney General and the offices of the United States Attorney were created by the Judiciary Act of 1789. 1789 is the same year that the Constitution was ratified.

"As to the Attorney General, he is nominated by the President, and his nomination must be confirmed by the Senate.

"As to the U S Attorneys, the country was divided into several federal judicial districts. A U S Attorney is nominated by the President to head each judicial district, and his nomination must be confirmed by the Senate.

"Each U S Attorney serves as the chief federal criminal prosecutor in each district. Also, he represents the federal government in civil litigation in federal and State courts within the federal judicial district over which he presides. Presently, there are 94 districts and 93 U S Attorneys, as Guam and the Mariana Islands share one U S Attorney. U S Attorney Offices are staffed mainly by assistant U S Attorneys, such as I.

"Initially, the U S Attorneys were independent of the Attorney General and were not under his authority. This changed in 1870.

"In 1870 Congress created the Department of Justice (an executive department) with the Attorney General as its head. With the advent of the Department of Justice, the U S Attorneys came under the authority and supervision of the Attorney General and became tasked with handling criminal and civil cases in which the United States had an interest.

"The FBI is the principal investigative agency of the federal government. As part of the DOJ, the FBI reports to the Attorney General and to the U S Attorneys. The FBI is not a national police force. Policing is primarily the responsibility of State and local governments with their local police departments. The FBI does work with such agencies as the ATF and DEA.

"This brings us back to your original question as to whether sex crimes are typically handled by the State.

"As a general rule, most criminal cases involving violations of State law are heard in State courts. However, cases involving violations of federal law may be diverted to federal court. There are some instances where both federal and State courts have concurrent jurisdiction.

"Title 18 of the United States Code sets forth some of the sex crimes which may be elevated to federal offenses and tried in federal court rather than State court. These include aggravated sexual abuse, sexual abuse, sexual abuse of a minor, sexual abuse resulting in death, repeat offenders, human trafficking, child pornography, solicitation of a minor, transportation across State lines, and others.

"In most cases, the accusation almost always begins on the local level when the victim calls the local police department. The local police will interview the accuser and other witnesses. If the local police decide that a crime has been committed, the accused person will be arrested and held in jail.

"Sex crime cases can be tried in both federal and State courts at the same time. The U S Supreme Court has determined that this does not constitute double jeopardy.

"Federal courts can decide which cases it wishes to try. Federal courts are more likely to take on cases where the crime involved includes an activity that crosses State lines, that uses the internet, that involves a minor child, that involves child pornography, that includes aggravated assault or rape, or has been elevated to a federal offense.

"Whether the case is tried in federal court or State court is very important, particularly in terms of penalties. For example, penalties such as prison terms and other consequences are much more severe in federal courts than in State courts. If a child is involved, prison terms and fines may be twice as much in federal court than in State court.

"Sentences are often harsher and longer in federal court due to federal sentencing guidelines which may require mandatory minimums.

"In a federal case, incarceration will be in federal prison rather than a local jail which may further isolate an inmate.

"The stigma associated with a federal conviction may be more damaging than a conviction from a local court.

"Even if there is no conviction, a federal indictment may lead to job loss, loss of a professional license, or injury to one's reputation more-so than with a State charge.

"Under both federal and State law persons convicted of sex crimes must register with the national sex crimes registry.

"So, the short answer to your question is yes, sex crimes are often State crimes, and State crimes are generally tried in State court. However, there is a whole list of sex crimes that have been elevated to federal offenses by federal legislation which allows sex crimes to be prosecuted as federal crimes which have the advantages of much more severe penalties, as we've seen.

"Because the more serious sex crimes, including trafficking, are generally taken up by the U S Attorney's Office, the more serious crimes would fall to me."

Marlene said, "Now I understand why you have been involved with sex crimes. The serious one will go federal and, hopefully, harsher penalties will deter future criminal behavior."

Taylor replied, "Yes. And you are a quick study I must say."

(Taylor had her way of diffusing whatever friction Marlene may have tried to generate.)

Marlene asked, "So, how does your office find out about sex crimes?"

Taylor replied, "The lesser sex crimes, if there can be such a thing, are easier to round up. A mother might find out that her underage daughter is communicating with a predator on line and let the local police know. The local police might have the daughter arrange to meet with the subject, and an undercover officer will intercept him and wrangle a confession. An undercover officer might run an ad in a local throw-away newspaper or on line, arrange to meet with the subject, meet with the subject at a local motel, accept the money, and make an arrest. A subject might pick up a girl on the street posing as a working girl but who is actually an undercover officer. After he tenders his money, he is arrested. A subject might respond to an ad on line, meet, offer money, and get arrested. These are the types of things happening every day.

"Presently, I rarely work with these types of minor sting operations. However, I have handled several such cases in the past. Presently, I typically become involved when the crime turns federal, such as when there is physical violence, when children are involved, and when the parties move their victims across State lines. This type of conduct generally elevates the offense into the federal system."

Marlene said, "Before we get head long into the specifics of your cases over the past several years, I think the readers and audience would like to know a little more about how your relationship with Rick and Izzy progressed from the time that Izzy was returned to you until now. There is a human-interest element involved."

Marlene continued, "I covered with Rick the time beginning with the kidnapping of Tammy Fitzgerald, your kidnapping and being thrown from the 15-story building, and the kidnapping of Isabel.

"Rick pretty much kept to the facts. He did not add much to the romantic part of the relationship."

Taylor replied, "That's just the way he is. In fairness to him, I think he felt that he was walking a kind of tightrope in our relationship. My feeling has always been that he felt that he wanted to try to keep our relationship all business. He wanted me to feel that he was helping me not as a way to start a romance but as a way to solve a problem. I think that he did not want to pressure me, as I was so much younger than he. He wanted me to feel that I did not have to offer romance to keep him working on the case.

"It was really quite sweet when you think about it. Here I was a person with a modest education and no family background whose only experience with men was with men who were trying to hurt me, being treated like a person of substance by a grown, successful, and handsome man, and neither one of us knew how to really deal with it.

"After finally having sex with Rick, I remember thinking to myself that the only sex I knew was from men who were abusive and wanted sex only for themselves. Sex with them was a combination of rough, fast, painful, and generally unrewarding.

"Rick, on the other hand, came to me for sex that was slow and gentle and designed to satisfy both of us and to ultimately foster real feelings. I decided that Rick's way was the way I wanted all of my encounters to be, and so it has been.

"When we were finally both grown-ups, things went much better. We found that we had much to talk about, which is important in any relationship expected to last. The physical part just fell into place, as Rick's way was the only way that I would accept sex as an adult."

Marlene asked, "Was there anything particularly romantic you can share?"

Taylor replied, "Yes. His proposal. We had been dating for a while, and I was beginning to wonder if he would ever ask me to marry him. My deep seeded lack of self-worth was beginning to creep in. There were many times in my life during which I felt that I was not good enough for anyone, and I was beginning to feel that way with Rick. What would a guy with everything want with someone as damaged as I was?

"So, Rick called me up and asked me to meet him at our favorite restaurant, a kind of a fancy place not far from my office. I took off a little early and went home to get ready. I put on everything I had that I thought looked expensive. I fixed my hair and makeup. I was giving it both barrels.

"I knew that whenever I arrived, Rick would already be there. This was just his way. He felt that being late was disrespectful, so he was always early.

"I made my way to the hostess stand to see if someone was waiting. She said that a man was waiting at a table across the room, but she did not know if he was waiting for me. I knew that she was lying. She gave me that look that almost every woman in world gives when she finds out that a hot guy is waiting for someone who is not you.

"I crossed the room to make my way to his table. Later, Rick told me that every eye in the room was on me because I looked so breathtakingly beautiful. I reached the table and asked if I could sit. He said yes. I sat. A few seconds later he got up from the table. I was afraid that he was going to leave the restaurant because I was not what he hoped for.

"Just as fear was coming into my body, he got down on one knee and opened a small box to display a beautiful diamond ring. He said, 'Taylor Shaw, you are the love of my life, and I know that I will never find anyone who I love as much as I love you. Will you marry me?'

"I was stunned. Just seconds ago, I thought that he was leaving the restaurant because he didn't want to be with me, and now he was asking me to marry him basically saying that he wanted to be with me forever. My shock delayed my reply. Ultimately, however, I did say: 'Yes.'

"And with that our most beautiful life together began."

Marlene said, "That is a truly beautiful story. As you know, I interviewed Rick at your home last weekend. I must confess that he is quite a hottie, and I can see why you were attracted to him, even when you were young and generally not really ready for an adult man. But, as I am sure that you know now, he is a nice and supportive person who happens to also be hot. Pretty rare.

"But as you talk with him, as good looking as he is, you find that he disarms you by staying on the topic and being really interesting. Also, he made it so obvious that he is crazy about you, he lets you know gently that there is no room in there for anyone else.

"The fact that at one time you questioned your self-worth is interesting. I think many of us, both men and women, go through a phase when we wonder about self-worth. But it is really hard to imagine someone with your accomplishments ever feeling that way.

"Your life on the farm, your relationship with your mother, and your father leaving are certainly outside factors which could lead to self-worth problems. But the fact that you have overcome all of this and forged ahead with a real relationship is really impressive.

"I probably won't dwell on your modest upbringing and initial feelings of low self-esteem for the article. But I believe that a mention would be good to supply background. How do you feel about that?"

Taylor replied, "I am okay with whatever you think is best. Like anyone, I hope that my achievements are more interesting than my failures, so, in that respect, covering what I have done seems more important to me than my childhood, which was a disaster. Perhaps it could be presented as a way for people to overcome adversity and leave it at that."

Marlene said, "That is a good idea. It allows a truthful rendition of your life without dwelling on a bad childhood, except to the extent that a bad childhood can be turned around."

Taylor replied, "I think that's the approach I would take."

Marlene replied, "I agree."

Marlene returned to the interview and asked, "Before we get too much further, let me hear about Rick. What was it that attracted him to you?"

Taylor replied, "I met him when he was teaching a class on the United States Constitution that I was taking. He took a different approach to the subject than most of the teachers I had in high school. He gave a more realistic assessment of the Founding Fathers than was typical in a survey class. He explained that the Constitution had economic implications. For example, several of the Founding Fathers loaned money to the government which they wanted to get back. Under the Articles of Confederation, each State was autonomous, and the central government had no power to order the States to act together to do things like paying off debts. Under the new Constitution, however, the new federal government would pay off debts existing before the Constitution. Unlike under the Articles, under the new Constitution, all duties would flow only to the federal government which, along with excise taxes, would fund the new federal government allowing it to repay loans to the Founders.

"He pointed out that the new Constitution freed no slaves and gave no women the right to vote. In other words, he was a little more honest about what the Founders were doing than one generally sees.

"His honesty and understanding of the downtrodden, such as slaves and women, was refreshing, at least to me, and I have always tried to lead my life following that sort of example, and so does he."

Marlene asked, "So, getting back to the reality that we are dealing

92

with a women's magazine, was there no romantic interest at first?"

Taylor replied, "All of the girls at school thought Rick was cute, and they probably all wanted to go out with him. I, however, was so wrapped up in Tammy's kidnapping, I could contend that I did not have the time or the interest in offering anything romantic. But that is not exactly true. I probably did hold out a romantic possibility to get Rick interested enough to help me. My bad."

Marlene said, "That's interesting as it dovetails into an age-old woman's issue which is: Do men do things for women exclusively to try to get to know them romantically or can a man really do things for a woman in pursuit of friendship alone?"

Taylor replied, "I'm not a man, but I can't help but believing that the romantic is never far from their thinking. But more importantly, if men were not allowed to do things for women for their romantic interest, nothing might ever get done.

"My situation with Rick was really complicated. I was in a position where I absolutely needed his expertise, but I didn't have the money to hire him. So, how was I going to be able to persuade him to help me in this world based on money?

"I guess I would be a liar if I said that I didn't think that he was helping me at least partly because he liked me in a romantic way, and I didn't try to stop him.

"When we were returning Tammy to her mother, I mentioned to her how much Rick had helped me with Tammy's case. She immediately turned to Rick and thanked him. Rick replied that he was helping partly because he was attracted to me. I guess whether I liked him or not I had to recognize that he had the courage to be honest about his motivation. I have to say that his honesty is one of the many things that finally drew me to him.

"I was such a mess and was put down my entire life by my mother that I felt that I would never love myself enough to allow someone to love me. With some maturity and successes of my own, I hope that I have finally grown out of all that, thank goodness."

Marlene replied, "Well, I think that we might put this part behind us and concentrate on what you were doing and why those things led you here.

"Aside from the obvious things in your professional life, how was your life away from work?"

Taylor replied, "The Tammy kidnapping, my kidnapping, and my daughter's kidnapping took up the greater part of the first five years of our marriage. During this time, I was able to have outside friendships with Moose and his people and with John and the Native Americans. Those relationships started as business, Moose and his bookkeeping and John and his water rights, but developed into worthwhile friendships.

"From Moose, I learned how to fight and stand up for myself. At my urging, Rick also developed a friendship with Moose and did learn important things. It's a good thing that Rick opted to attend the urban training part of his work with Moose. Otherwise, he might never have learned how to scale the outside of a glass building and jump from a roof to save me tied to nothing but a bungie cord.

"Before Izzy's kidnapping, my relationship with the Native Americans was fairly brief, and Rick did not really participate. It is interesting to note that after Izzy came home, I spent a great deal of time with John and his tribe and learned many things of great value. Rick could see the value in all of this, and over the past several years, he and I have spent a considerable amount of time at the Reservation and learned many things together. Rick is a closet egalitarian. He believes in the Native American culture and has worked hard to understand it and to benefit from its teachings.

"Now, Rick and even Izzy can ride, shoot, throw knives, fish, and live outside. Another of the things that has made our relationship so great is that we both understand how badly the Native Americans have been treated and work to treat them as our friends. Neither of us really has too many friends in our own circle. We both seem to prefer exposure to other cultures."

Marlene said, "That is very interesting. From what I have heard, you don't really publicize your work with the Indians."

Taylor replied, "True, but it is not really work. They are our friends."

Marlene went on, "I know, but none of the various things that have been written about you get into any depth about your relationship with the Indians."

Taylor replied, "No one has ever taken an interest in that part of my life, or even asked about it."

Marlene continued, "I can see that, and it makes sense. Magazines are in business to make money so they emphasize the things that will interest their readers."

Taylor went on, "Also, when a woman is married, it is hard for her to maintain friendships with other male people. Whenever a woman is seen with a man, it is presumed that they are having an affair, even when 90 percent of the time this is not the case. Friends of a woman's husband seem to take some kind of perverse pleasure in pointing out to him that his spouse has been seen with a man, even if they were at a bait store buying worms. It's sad.

"Rick supports my outside relationships with men and women, but I am sure that he dislikes being reminded that I have them."

Marlene continued, "I guess I don't have to tell you that you and Rick have a special relationship, a relationship based on mutual respect and trust. That is not always the case."

Taylor replied, "I know, and believe me, I feel blessed."

Marlene asked, "Do your jobs require you guys to be apart from one another for long periods of time?"

Taylor replied, "Not for long periods of time, but our jobs, particularly mine, require me to be away from home for several days at a time."

Marlene asked, "Why?"

Taylor replied, "As you know, I am in sex crimes. The typical case often involves taking out an ad in a throw-away newspaper or on the internet and luring someone to a motel room. Other basic cases involve picking up an undercover cop on the street. With these types of cases, there is not much travel involved. The location of the crime can be confined to the local jurisdiction.

"However, as the cases become more complicated, the main perpetrator will be removed from the immediate action. For example, a main perpetrator might be running an illegal gambling operation along with providing ladies. He would have underlings actually operating either or both of the businesses, and his identity would be kept far from the public.

"As it does us little good to arrest one or more of the underlings, we need to be more creative with determining and capturing the actual perpetrator."

Marlene interjected, "How is this done?"

Taylor replied, "The only way that the actual perpetrator can be ferreted out is through the use of witnesses. For example, let us assume that a lady has been provided to a john. She obviously knows the underling but often also knows the perpetrator. She might even have been the actual perpetrator's girlfriend when she was young and beautiful and just starting out. As she aged, she might be re-purposed to working for the perpetrator in another capacity.

"If she is caught, she might be willing to testify against the actual perpetrator. Remember, he turned her out to do his dirty work after dumping her.

"If we are going to take these cases to trial, we will need a witness. And part of my job is interviewing these witnesses. These interviews can take place away from the venue, even in other cities. They often require being away from home for a few days. We have safe houses in which I can stay if I am away from home."

Marlene asked, "Is Rick ok with this?"

Taylor replied, "It's just part of the job. And it is made more difficult by the fact that I cannot tell him everything that I am doing or where I am going to be due to the danger of being located myself. Keeping all of these secrets has always been a problem, and I would say that it is one of the few things about our relationship which is unrewarding. So far, he has been better than a good sport, but eventually things could become strained."

Marlene said, "Well, he's a better man than I. I don't know if I could live with my spouse going out to meet strange people at all hours and maybe not coming directly home."

Taylor replied, "But this is what I do, and it is the only way that it can be done."

Marlene asked, "Can you tell us about some of the witnesses you have interviewed? How they acted. How they dealt with the pressure of becoming a target protected only by the federal government?"

Taylor replied, "Frankly, no. All of this is strictly confidential. Everyone knows that we need and get witnesses, so we cannot keep that a secret. But the identity of the people themselves cannot be revealed."

Marlene said, "So we have your fake ads, car pickups, and more complicated cases involving witnesses; are there any other newer types of cases you can tell us about?"

Taylor replied, "I guess if pressed, I could say that there have been a couple of fairly recent developments in sex and sex trafficking laws, the use of RICO and cases where a victim of a sex crime seeks revenge against her perpetrator. I can talk about these types of cases because they have been covered in the newspapers and are already fairly well known, but I cannot get into specific suspects.

"On my end of things, which is criminal, RICO allows us to go after the top leadership in addition to the perpetrators of the criminal activity.

"Something that might be of interest to you and your readership is the situation where the victim is rescued, the perpetrator is punished, and, later, the victim seeks out the perpetrator and causes him great bodily harm or even death. This is more of a frontier justice approach.

"Many victims of sex trafficking come from dysfunctional families who do not provide them with the basic necessities. They fall prey to men and women who promise to give them food, shelter, and clothing. After they begin receiving these items, the perpetrator forces them to have sex with the perpetrator's clients for money.

"Even after being rescued, many victims suffer severe psychological consequences as a result of being trafficked causing them to cope in self-destructive ways such as drug use or violence. This behavior often brings them back into the criminal justice system where they are penalized for their reaction to their own trauma.

"There are several cases where victims of sex trafficking have been legally penalized for killing their trafficker.

"In Wisconsin, a victim was facing a life sentence for killing her trafficker. The State Supreme Court ruled that she will be allowed to argue in Court that her actions were the direct result of being trafficked which could allow an acquittal.

"In Tennessee, a victim was sentenced to life in prison for killing a man who raped her. She has been granted clemency after spending many years in jail.

"In California, a victim was sentenced to life without the possibility of parole for killing a man who trafficked her. She was granted clemency.

"Marcela Howell, the CEO of the non-profit group In Our Own Voice states the case succinctly: 'The decision to prosecute Lewis and the subsequent sentence sends a clear message to Black women, girls and gender expansive individuals – the law will not protect you – and if you defend yourself, you will pay a high price.'

"Anglo-American law is based on legal principles that are centuries old. At the time of their formulation, the relationship between men and women was much different. Men wrote the laws, and, in many ways, our laws reflect the interaction between one man and another man.

"In these cases where the victim of sex trafficking comes back and kills her trafficker, the most sought-after defense for homicide, the defense of self-defense, cannot be used by its own terms.

"A quick look at the jury instructions for self-defense will illustrate my point. With self-defense, the defendant must reasonably believe that he is in imminent danger of being killed or suffering great bodily harm. The defendant must reasonably believe that the immediate use of deadly force was necessary to defend against that danger.

"In other words, self-defense only works during the transaction in which the defendant believes that his use of force is necessary.

"After the imminent danger passes, such as after the trafficker is no longer in the victim's presence, self-defense is no longer available.

"The jury instruction drives this point home and further informs that self-defense will not be available when it says, 'Belief in future harm is not sufficient, no matter how great or how likely the harm is believed to be.'

"We, as women, are, therefore, rendered helpless. When a man perpetrates a crime against us, after he is released, he can come back after us at any time. Our chances of surviving against him in a one-on-one confrontation in which we might be able to claim self-defense is non-existent. He is too big and too strong.

"And we are unable to apply our cunning by going after him for that which we are certain that he will do in the future. It's a man's world out there.

"I have heard that in some jurisdictions Judges are allowing victims to argue that their actions are the 'direct result' of being trafficked and allowing victims to assert being trafficked as a defense, but I would maintain that this might be a long shot at trial."

Marlene said, "I have never heard it summed up that way before. It does bring into focus how difficult it is for the law, as it is, to protect us as women. I think that these are great points for our CEO to address during the awards ceremony, perhaps a little tempered."

Taylor replied, "I'm sorry, but some things really make me mad, such as these. I myself have spent hours and hours training with my Native American friends. It is so unfortunate that our culture has created a situation where women, under some circumstances, have to fear men, as they do. And they call the Indians savages."

Marlene said, "Oh my, look at the hour. I think that we covered a great deal. However, I will take what I have to my boss and see if we need more. When can we meet again?"

Taylor replied, "Tomorrow night I have a meeting with a witness in a very big case. The meeting will be in Riverside, not far from my office, but may go so late that I need to stay either in a motel or our safe house, depending upon whether it will be in use."

Marlene replied, "I will call you to about meeting a couple of days from now, if it is necessary."

Taylor replied, "Good. I will wait to hear from you."

The first part of Taylor's interview came to an end.

Chapter 17
Taylor's Witness

With all of the interviews and such going on, Taylor nearly forgot that she still had work to do.

After finishing with Marlene for the evening, she drove home to Rick and Izzy.

She parked her car and entered through the front door. It was late. Her interview went until midnight. She went into the master bedroom, changed into sleeping attire, and got into bed with Rick.

Rick asked, "What have you been up too? It's pretty late."

Taylor replied, "The interview went longer than either of us thought. I didn't feel right about taking time from work so I waited until my work day was over before we started. As a result, it got pretty late."

Rick said, "No worries. I'm not going any place, but Izzy does like to see her mom before she goes to sleep."

"I know. I'll make up for it in the morning. Tomorrow is going to be a late night too. I have a witness to interview in that sex trafficking case on which the office has been working. The interview will be in Riverside, I think at the office or someplace close to the office."

They turned out the lights and went to sleep. The next sound was the alarm clock at 6 a.m., the time for which it is always set.

Rick said, "Morning honey. I'll make us breakfast." He got out of bed and headed for the kitchen. After a couple of minutes, Taylor joined him. A few minutes after that, Izzy wandered in.

Izzy said, "There you are mommy. I missed you at bedtime."

Taylor replied, "Sorry sweetie. I hope to be home in time to tuck you in tonight."

Izzy finished her breakfast and left for her room where she would get dressed and ready for school.

Now in the kitchen without Izzy, Rick asked Taylor about her plans for the day. Taylor replied, "I have a full day of office work scheduled, and after office hours, I have that witness to prep for her upcoming trial I told you about."

Rick asked, "Can you tell me which witness?"

Taylor replied, "No honey. It's a very big case, and everything is confidential. I'll tell you all about it then the trial is over, and the perp is behind bars, where he belongs."

Rick said, "Okay."

Taylor went to the master bedroom and dressed for work. She came back into the kitchen where she said goodbye to Rick and left the house. Rick would take Izzy to school on his way to work.

Chapter 18
Taylor at the Office

Taylor had been with the U S Attorney for several years now. She moved from Native American relations to sex crimes. Her new boss is Daryl Drake, a career bureaucrat. It is said that he passed up several opportunities to go to work for one of the mega-firms he was fighting on a daily basis, which were always looking for lawyers with inside experience to benefit their very good paying clients.

One of the assistants is Rob Fulton. Rob is not quite as robust as Daryl in his work efforts. He treats his work more as a job than a calling. He is a little jealous of Taylor who, due to her heroic efforts on all fronts, is well admired for her work even though she does not have many friends.

There were other accomplished young people in the office. She made friends with Pamela Key, a privileged Stanford Law graduate. In her effort to help some of the young attorneys become familiar with the work, she went out of her way with Pamela. Even before Pamela visited the Reservation and met Chuck, she knew of Chuck and of Taylor's interest in him.

As a new hire, Pamela did not want to intrude into the social life of any of the established attorneys so she intimated to Taylor that she would leave Chuck to her, if that is what she wished. Taylor protested claiming that since she was married, there was no need for Pamela to be concerned. Pamela took Taylor at her word, but the implication is that Chuck's involvement with Pamela or any other woman was not particularly favored by Taylor.

Taylor took Pamela to the Reservation where she met Chuck and found that she was even more attracted to him than she thought she might be. She also learned that she was not particularly attracted to Chris, one of the other lawyers, who was a very nice man.

Taylor and Chuck, after a long chat, finally came to grips with their mutual feelings. Taylor decided to maintain her relationship with her husband and daughter, and Chuck was encouraged to pursue Pamela, which he did, as they ultimately married.

After Chuck and Pamela married, Pamela became pregnant. She left the office and tended to her pregnancy, the child's birth, and child rearing. In the Indian culture, she could devote herself to child rearing without being demeaned for not getting back to work immediately.

With Pamela gone, Taylor lost her office girlfriend.

Taylor went about developing new friendships. Her new friend was Sharon Robbins. Sharon Robbins was a young woman who worked very hard and played it straight down the line with everything that she did. She came from a solid family background and the finest schools. She was only 26.

Though she and Taylor were friends, she was also trying to learn from Taylor, whose outstanding work was well known.

Sharon was a person who was smart enough to not try to compete with Taylor. She wanted to learn, and Taylor loved teaching. Taylor welcomed a woman to woman relationship built on trust and not on under-cutting, which was often prevalent in their workplace.

Taylor's secretary was Margaret Heller, also known as "Margo." She was smart, organized, and worked hard to make Taylor's life a little easier. Taylor was so appreciative of Margo's work that she built her up whenever she could. She actually refused to refer to her as her secretary and asked that everyone with whom they came in contact also not refer to her as her secretary. She preferred "assistant."

With Sharon and Margo, Taylor had herself quite a team, and a team was needed with the tough cases that would be coming up.

Rob tried his best to ingratiate himself with their boss Daryl. He felt that this was his path to moving up in the ranks. Rob was in Daryl's office often during the day to talk about upcoming cases and various strategies.

During one such meeting Rob asked, "So, who are you going to put on the Franco case?"

Daryl replied, "Taylor."

Rob asked, "Why Taylor?"

Daryl answered, "Because she is the best attorney in the office, no offense. But if you are asking because you wanted me to assign the case to you, I gave it to her because she has a lighter case load right now, and I think that she will do a better job with the female witness than you would, and this female witness is crucial to the case."

Rob said, "You're making a mistake. She is not ready for this case. I would do a much better job."

Daryl replied, "You might, but yet you probably would not. Besides, it is my decision, and I have made it."

Rob said, "The trial is starting pretty soon, and she has not even interviewed the important chief witness, what's-her-name, yet."

Daryl replied, "Her name is Elizabeth Ann Forrester. Her stage name is 'Crystal Covington.'"

Rob replied, "I think they call that her 'stripper name.'"

Daryl said, "The trial is not for a while, and she will meet Ms. Forrester in plenty of time. Until then, Ms. Forrester is with the Marshals in protective custody. As we know, Ms. Shaw will have plenty to do here in the office that is unrelated to the Franco case, one of which is to give the orientation to the new hires about sex trafficking and the RICO Act."

Rob replied, "She is going to do that. Is she your favorite assistant now? I would probably feel better about it if I thought you were having sex with her. But she is such a straight arrow and so boring in that department that I doubt it."

Daryl replied, "She doesn't need to have sex to get ahead. She does it by being a better lawyer. You should try it some time."

Rob said, "Very funny."

Rob continued, "When will she meet the witness?"

Daryl responded, "I don't know. It all has to be coordinated with the Marshal."

Rob seemed to be angling for the time and location of Taylor's meeting with the witness. Fortunately for Daryl, he really did not know.

Rob and Daryl left for the evening. Everyone else had already gone home.

Chapter 19
Sharon Robbins

T he next day at the office was business as usual. As is generally the case at a prosecutor's office, the staff has several cases in various stages of completion. The Bobbie Franco case was just one of them.

Though Sharon had only recently joined the office, she and Taylor were becoming friends. As with many of Taylor's relationships, people were drawn to her because of her superior knowledge. Talking to her was an education.

They decided to meet after work for a drink. There was a bar across the street. They agreed to meet there at 5:30.

They left work together, rode down in the elevator, and walked across the street. They entered the bar. It was pretty typical. It was dark inside with dark walls and booths. As they had been there before, they showed themselves to a booth along the side wall. The place was not too bad. It was relatively clean, and the staff was presentable.

They were both attired in business-wear. Taylor was in a dark blue suit with a knee length skirt and a matching jacket. She wore a white shirt and low heals. Sharon was dressed similarly, but her suit was grey.

Sharon started, "So glad that you had time to see me. I thought that you might be too busy with the Franco case and all."

Taylor replied, "I'm a little busy, but most of the work with the Franco case has already been done. The only thing I have left is interviewing the witness relative to the sex trafficking and prostitution. Another lawyer is handling the related case of tax evasion. We need two predicate crimes for the RICO part of the case. We'll be covering that in the orientation lecture.

Sharon asked, "And when will that be?"

"Tomorrow," Taylor replied.

"And who will be giving it?"

Taylor replied, "I will."

"Good, then it will not be boring. If I had to sit through a lecture from Mr. Drake or Rob, I might go out of my mind."

Taylor asked, "What would you like to drink?"

Sharon replied, "White wine is good for me."

A cocktail waitress came to the table and asked for their order.

Sharon replied, "White wine."

Taylor replied, "White wine is good for me too."

Sharon asked, "Are you sure you have time for this. I know you're married. Do you have to get home to your husband?"

Taylor replied, "Rick is guest lecturing at Desert Junior College this evening. He won't be home until after 9."

Sharon asked, "Is Rick the guy in the photo on your desk?"

Taylor replied, "Yes."

Sharon asked, "Don't you worry about him being around all of those college girls. Judging from his photograph, he is a good-looking guy, and those college girls can be aggressive."

Taylor replied, "Funny you say that because that's how I met him. I was enrolled in a class he was teaching. I guess I was one of those college girls once."

Sharon asked, "What happened?"

Taylor replied, "He helped me, and after the victim was rescued and all of the legal stuff was dealt with, things just sort of developed, and we ultimately got married."

Sharon replied, "I would call marriage quite a development."

Taylor replied, "Perhaps it was, but it was just one of those once-in-a-lifetime things."

Sharon asked, "What do you think of Rob? He has been flirting with me, and I am wondering if you think that it would be okay to date someone who works in the office."

Taylor replied, "As to the second part of your question, to tell you the truth, I don't know what the rules are for office hook-ups. I presume that it is alright. As to the first part, the part about what I think about Rob, I really don't think about him at all. But I will say this, he is just the kind of guy from whom I generally try to stay away."

"Why's that," Sharon asked.

Taylor replied, "I really don't like cocky men. They tend to try to accomplish things with bluster rather than with reasoning, and I don't have time for that."

"Don't you think that he is good looking?" Sharon asked.

Taylor replied, "He may be, but his looks have no meaning to me. Good looking guys tend to get by on their looks and are unreliable in a pinch. I already have a good-looking guy at home, and talk about reliable, he would walk over hot coals for me."

"But Rob is so cute."

"If you really have strong feelings about him, you might give him a try. The last good-looking co-worker I had got me thrown off of a 15-story office building."

"What happened?"

"Rick and our friends saved me. Rick actually dove off of the building tied to a bungie cord to rescue me. Like I said, he would walk over hot coals for me."

Sharon replied, "I guess I'll give Rob a little more thought before taking him up on his several offers to go out."

Sharon continued, "How did you meet Rick anyway? I need details."

Taylor replied, "You probably would not believe it."

Sharon replied, "Try me."

Taylor said, "As I said before, I was a student in one of his classes at Newton Junior College. I was dirt poor, and I took on babysitting jobs for friends of my mother. A little girl by the name of Tammy Fitzgerald was kidnapped. The police did such a poor job on the case that I decided that I would mount my own investigation. When that failed, I enrolled at Newton Junior College. When one of my professors announced that he worked for the DA and had experience with criminal investigations, I cornered him into helping me."

Sharon asked, "How old were you?"

Taylor replied, "I was 19."

Sharon said, "19! I doubt that you needed to do much cornering. As beautiful as you are now, you must have really been gorgeous at 19. The poor guy had no chance."

Taylor went on, "But I was really messed up. My father left me and my mom when I was 10. My mother was an alcoholic and entertained some real winners. I worked all day on an orange farm and looked like hell. But Rick was so great. No one ever treated me the way he did. It took a lot of nurturing and patience on his part over five years. I finished college and law school, improved the farm for my mother, and started with the AGs office before I was even able to see him."

Sharon asked, "And what did Rick do?"

Taylor replied, "He did what he always does. He made it easy for me to do the things that I needed to do without worrying about himself. I am one lucky girl."

Sharon said, "Working on an orange farm. Dirt poor. Knowing you now, I never would have thought that was possible. I just figured you were an upper middle-class white girl who went to one of the finest schools and landed a job with the government before going to the other side and making big money. Wow, you have really come a long-ways from those days. I heard from rumors around the office that you are going to be Woman of the Year. Some leap."

Taylor said, "I don't advertise my background. I am telling you this because I like you and trust you, and I hope that I can help you achieve what you seek."

Sharon replied, "Your secret is safe with me. I actually admire you even more than I did. Not to change the subject, but I was hoping that I could ask you for some advice about our retirement plan here at work. Do you think that I should invest in it?"

Taylor replied, "We have what is called a 401K. With it, money is taken out of your paycheck and invested in your retirement account. You cannot get this money out of the plan until you are 59 and a half without significant penalties. At some places, an employer will also make contributions to your account. This is known as matching.

"That said, if the employer matches or also puts money into your account, the general rule is that you might as well do it, as you are getting free money in addition to the amount taken out of your check. If you are only utilizing the money coming out of your own check and there is no matching by your employer, you might wish to consider other methods of retirement savings.

"A 401K plan is what is known as a qualified plan. With a qualified plan, the money you put in the plan is tax deductible. With a non-qualified plan, the money you put in the plan is not tax deductible. With either plan, the money in the account grows tax deferred. In other words, you do not pay money on the growth until you take it out.

"Qualified plans generally consist of 401K, IRA, and Defined Benefit. As the money put into the plan is tax deductible, the amount is limited by statute.

"There is also something called a Roth Plan. A 401K or IRA may be a Roth Plan. With a Roth Plan, the amount that you may contribute is limited and the amount contributed cannot be deducted from your income tax. However, at the end, when you take you contributions and the growth out, both come out tax free. With a non-Roth plan, your contributions come out tax exempt but not your growth.

"An annuity works similar in some ways. A fixed annuity allows either fixed interest or an amount tied to an index such as the S & P 500 to enter the account. A variable annuity allows the insurance company to invest in funds which mirror generally available funds. These can go below zero whereas a fixed annuity's value cannot. Money in either a fixed or variable annuity grows without tax until it is taken out. Annuities have features such as allowing the value to be converted into payments which are guaranteed to last the rest of your life.

"As to life insurance, there is term and permanent. With term insurance you buy coverage for a certain period of time. With permanent, it lasts until you die. Permanent insurance may also have a cash value. You can recoup your contribution tax free, and you can borrow out your growth, also tax free. This cannot be done with an annuity.

"If you don't want to contribute to your employer's plan or have your money with a life insurance company for either an annuity or life insurance policy, you can have your own professional manager."

Sharon asked, "What do really rich people do?"

Taylor responded, "Really rich people invest in stock in their own companies. Rich people receive stock in their own companies through many means. As the stock appreciates in value, their net work increases commensurately. They have what is known as an unrealized capital gain on which they pay no tax until they sell the stock."

Sharon replied, "That sounds a little unfair."

Taylor replied, "That is because it is completely unfair."

Sharon said, "So you said that you will be giving your lecture tomorrow. Who will be included?"

Taylor replied, "I think Mr. Drake said that there would be four, you, Ben Adams, Lisa Williams, and Howard Moss. I believe that it will be at 10 a.m. in the conference room."

Sharon replied, "Okay. I'll see you then."

Taylor and Sharon finished up at the bar and went home. Taylor arrived home at about 8. She relieved the babysitter. She checked on Izzy who was in her room. Izzy was going to watch a little TV and turn in. Taylor went into the living room to wait for Rick. Around 8:30, Rick came home, and they went to bed to get ready for the next day.

Chapter 20
Taylor's Lecture

Taylor arrived at the office at 8:30. The receptionist told her that Mr. Drake wanted to see her in his office. She went to Mr. Drake's office and knocked gently on the door.

"Come in."

Taylor entered the room.

Mr. Drake said, "Please, take a seat."

Taylor sat.

Once seated, Mr. Drake started, "I want to thank you for taking on the lecture this morning. I have been so slammed with the Franco case that I don't think that I could endure giving another one.

"I believe that I gave you the names of the four people who will be attending, Sharon, Ben, Lisa, and Howard, I think. They are the new hires, and have been, as you know, tapped to be part of the sex trafficking team."

Taylor replied, "I'm fine with that, and giving the lecture is no problem."

Mr. Drake replied, "Thank you. I'll let you go and get ready."

Taylor got up and left the office. She returned to her office to review her notes for her lecture. Taylor collected her notes and headed for the conference room. The room had a large rectangular table in the center. On one end, there was a lectern which Taylor would use to address her small audience.

There were two water pictures on placemats in the center of the table along with some empty glasses. Along the side wall, there was a long narrow table. On the table, there were soft drinks and light snacks. This table would be used to stage lunch, if it became necessary.

Taylor was the first to arrive. She placed her written material either on the lectern or immediately adjacent to it. There was a stool with a high seat for her to sit if it became necessary. The table had four chairs, two on either side, for the attendees.

The four would-be team members entered the room. Each took a seat at the table. When things settled down, Taylor addressed the group.

"As you probably know, you have been chosen to supplement the sex trafficking department here at the firm. The purpose of today's lecture is to acquaint you with the development of the law in this area.

"Before I start, I would like us to go around the room and introduce ourselves. Let's start here to my left."

Immediately to her left was a gentleman. He introduced himself as Ben Adams. As the others, he is a new attorney from what Taylor would consider to be a second-tier law school, similar to her own. Ben communicated that he was opposed to sex trafficking on several levels and expressed how anxious he was to get started prosecuting criminals who engaged in it.

The next person told the group that her name was Lisa Williams. She was also from a second-tier law school. She had some familiarity with sex trafficking as one of her childhood friends was kidnapped and impressed into service in the sex industry. She was hoping to channel her anger towards prosecuting criminals who would prey on people as her friend was preyed upon.

Coming to the other side of the table, the next person introduced himself as Howard Moss. He was also from a second-tier law school and a modest family who worked hard to get him into law school.

The last person sitting immediately to Taylor's right was Sharon Robbins. She introduced herself and spoke about how anxious she was to be of help to victims of sex trafficking. She was from a top law school, and her poise and deportment relative to the other hires could be seen. She was the only candidate from an upper-class home.

Taylor thought to herself that she was pleased with the group and its makeup. She felt that coming from less might make their contributions more robust, similar to her own background. She felt that the three of them, the candidates other than Sharon, might really throw themselves into their work, as the work they were undertaking was very important to not only the U S Attorney's Office but to society in general.

Taylor started, "Thank you all for letting us know about your backgrounds and that you envision yourselves as contributors willing to work hard to obtain our objectives. Let me start now."

Taylor began her lecture, "For the past many years, the United States has considered human trafficking to be a fundamental human rights violation. To that end, in the year 2000, the Trafficking Victims Protection Act (the 'TVPA') was enacted and began to make great strides in fighting the war against modern slavery.

"However, as time went on, human trafficking became more complex and began to resemble other forms of organized criminal enterprises often involving multiple planners and perpetrators and complex webs of illegal activities. In addition to human trafficking, human traffickers also became involved in such crimes as drug distribution, robbery, extortion, kidnapping, and human smuggling. Initially, Congress addressed this issue by repeatedly amending the TVPA.

"As parallels between human trafficking and other forms of organized crime became more apparent, prosecutors began using the Racketeer Influenced and Corrupt Organizations Act ('RICO'), in conjunction with TVPA to fight traditional crime and human trafficking.

"Though prosecutors have been able to use RICO in human trafficking cases since 2003, the first RICO human trafficking indictment was not filed until 2009.

"From a historical standpoint, human trafficking has always been lucrative in the United States. For one, people from all over the world want to come to the United States anyway, it is low risk because it operates in the netherworld of illegal aliens, and human beings are a resource which may be re-used.

"Prior to TVPA, human traffickers were prosecuted under involuntary servitude and slavery statutes. As these prosecutions were difficult, the TVPA was created to address trafficking

"The loudest critics of the TVPA felt that it gives preference to victims who are willing to act as witnesses and tends to favor victims of serious trafficking.

"Due to the limitations of the TVPA, prosecutors came up with the idea of using RICO for human trafficking cases working on the theory that human trafficking has become a form of organized crime involving more people and more types of related crimes than it ever did before."

Taylor asked the group, "Is everybody following all of this so far?"

All four nodded in unison.

Taylor said, "Okay. I'll go on with the more specific provisions of RICO and then how RICO applies to human trafficking.

"In 1970, Congress enacted RICO as part of the Organized Crime Control Act of 1969. The bulk of the RICO provisions are set forth in 18 U.S.C., Sections 1961 to 1968. By 1972, thirty-three States adopted State RICO laws."

Taylor continued, "Under RICO, it is a crime for a person to belong to an enterprise that is involved in a pattern of racketeering, even if the racketeering is committed by other members of the enterprise. To be convicted of racketeering, there must be proof of at least two specified criminal offenses within a 10-year period.

"These specified criminal offenses are known as 'predicate' offenses and may include offenses which do not ordinarily violate federal statutes, such as murder, kidnapping, gambling, arson, robbery, bribery, extortion, or dealing in drugs as well as numerous federal offenses such as loan sharking, mail fraud, wire fraud, obstruction of justice, prostitution, trafficking, and obscenity. The Supreme Court has added that the two predicate offenses must be related and that the perpetrators must pose a threat of continued criminal activity."

Ben asked a question, "Ms. Shaw, if a mob boss has already committed two crimes, why not just charge him with those crimes. Why use RICO?"

Taylor replied, "That is a very good question Ben. Under your scenario, the mob boss would be charged with the under-lying crimes and could be sentenced for one or both of them, if found guilty. However, RICO creates offenses and penalties over and above the predicate crimes, including a $25,000 fine and imprisonment for 20 years for each count. These penalties are imposed on top of the criminal penalties resulting from the predicate offenses.

"In short, the RICO penalty may be greater than the penalty for the under-lying crime or crimes. If the penalty for the under-lying crime is greater than the RICO penalty, the underlying crime's penalty may still be used. The prosecutor has no down side. He or she will get the greater penalty either way.

"In addition, the RICO violator must forfeit all profits and interest in any business gained through racketeering, even those gained through a legitimate business or through a legitimate part of a business.

"Further, a U S Attorney who decides to indict someone under RICO has the option of seeking a pre-trial restraining order or an injunction to temporarily seize a defendant's assets to prevent him from transferring assets which he might need to satisfy a judgment.

"In many cases the threat of a RICO indictment may force a defendant to plead guilty to a lesser charge in part because the seizure of his assets would make it difficult for him to pay a defense attorney.

"As you may see, RICO gives the prosecution the ability to seek greater penalties than the under-lying crimes as well as the option to seize a defendant's assets before trial. I would call these pretty strong weapons for one to have in his or her arsenal.

"Does this answer your question?"

Ben replied, "Yes. I see now why RICO is such a great tool."

Taylor continued her lecture, "An enterprise includes any individual, partnership, corporation, or other legal entity, but may also include any association of individuals even if they do not form a legally recognized entity. This type of combination is known as an association in fact. The association in fact is the most common type of association for a criminal enterprise.

"Though perhaps not as important to us, RICO permits a private individual damaged in his business or property by a racketeer to file a civil suit.

"Both civil and criminal components allow recovery of treble damages.

"While Congress amended RICO to include human trafficking as a predicate offense in 2003, it took six years before it was used.

"Because RICO prohibits racketeering activity that is continuous, a prosecutor might be able to bring a RICO charge even if the Statute of Limitations has run on the under-lying crime.

"As we discussed above, an additional incentive for prosecutors is Section 1963 which requires asset forfeiture of any interest or property gained as a result of a RICO violation, including property gained legitimately. This was included by Congress to break the economic power of organized crime as well as to punish offenders.

"RICO also has a more flexible conspiracy provision. Unlike general conspiracy statutes which require an overt act to affect the object of the conspiracy, under RICO all that is necessary is an agreement for a common purpose even if the conspirator did not agree to the commission of the act. Once the conspiracy is shown, the defendant's connection to the conspiracy need only be slight, and it is not necessary the he be part of the overall conspiratorial agreement.

"From our point of view, RICO allows a great deal of prosecutorial discretion. For example, an indictment does not have to specify the type of enterprise that forms the basis of the racketeering charge.

"RICO allows the joining of multiple crimes that might otherwise not be permitted. With RICO one is only trying to prove the existence of an enterprise and not the commission of a particular crime.

"Further, because the forfeiture provisions of RICO are mandatory, RICO gives prosecutors a substantial amount of sentencing control normally reserved to a judge or jury. Fear of financial repercussions brought about by the forfeiture provisions of RICO may produce more cooperative defendants when it comes time to make a plea bargain.

"As we may see, RICO offers us a number of ways to combat human trafficking in our war against modern day slavery.

"With RICO, the prosecution may reach the members of the enterprise who are not the perpetrators, may gather ill-gotten assets, and may enjoin the transfer of assets needed to satisfy a judgment pre-trial.

"Before we break, it might be a good idea to go over some of the basics of the indictment process. Does anyone wish to weigh in?"

Howard raised his hand and said, "I'll take a crack at it."

Taylor replied, "Okay. Good."

Howard started, "A grand jury is different than a trial jury. A grand jury is convened to determine whether there is enough evidence to charge a person with a crime and not to determine guilt beyond a reasonable doubt. There are 16 to 23 grand jurors. Only the prosecutors and witnesses are allowed to present their case at the hearing. 12 jurors must agree to proceed with the case."

Taylor replied, "Those are the basics. We will have much more about grand juries as we go along. This is all I have for now. Are there any questions?

Howard asked, "Will we be seeing RICO cases in this office?"

Taylor replied, "Most certainly. We have a couple now. Anything else?"

There were no further questions. Taylor was not certain whether all of the material was understood, but she and the rest of the senior staff would always be available to answer questions. They did not intend to throw the new hires into the RICO fire without offering a great deal of help.

Taylor concluded, "That's it for now then. You may all return to your respective offices where I am certain there will be a full day's worth of work waiting for you. Thanks for your attention. I hope that we all learned something."

The group broke up and left the conference room. It was now time for a late lunch, which is where Taylor was headed.

Chapter 21
United States Attorney – Riverside Branch Office

T he Office of the United States Attorney and the office of the Attorney General were created by the Judiciary Act of 1789, the same year that the Constitution was ratified. The Act also created the United States Federal Judiciary including the District Court system.

The Act provides for the appointment of a person learned in the law to act as the attorney for the United States in each judicial district and to prosecute criminals and handle all civil actions in which the United States shall be concerned.

Initially, the U S Attorneys were independent of the Attorney General. However, in 1870 the Department of Justice was created after which time the U S Attorneys came under the supervision of the Attorney General.

The U S Attorneys are appointed by the President for a term of four years subject to confirmation by the Senate. A U S Attorney may continue in office after the expiration of his term until a successor is appointed.

Each U S Attorney handles criminal prosecutions and civil actions in each of the federal judicial districts. There are 94 federal judicial districts headed by 93 U S Attorneys as Guam and Northern Mariana Islands share one U S Attorney. The day to day work of the U S Attorney's Office is carried out by Assistant U S Attorneys. Taylor is an Assistant U S Attorney.

The United States Attorney's Office, Central District of California, has a branch office in Riverside. Taylor works in the Riverside Branch Office. The Riverside Branch Office prosecutes federal crimes that occur in San Bernardino and Riverside Counties.

Riverside Branch Office Assistant U S Attorneys work closely with virtually every federal law enforcement agency as well as with State and local law enforcement, including the District Attorney's Offices in Riverside and San Bernardino. Taylor's husband, Rick, works for the District Attorney.

Chapter 22
Daryl Drake

It's 2 o'clock, and Taylor finished lunch and returned to her office to work. Her intercom buzzed. She picked up the phone and immediately recognized Margo's voice. "Hi, Mr. Drake would like to see you in his office as soon as it's convenient."

Taylor replied, "Thanks Margot. I'll go over there right now."

Taylor got up from her desk and walked down the hall to Mr. Drake's office. She knocked gently on the door. Mr. Drake, expecting her, asked her to come in. She entered the room.

Mr. Drake said, "Please sit."

She sat down in a large chair that was facing his desk.

Mr. Drake started, "I see that you finished the lecture on RICO and that everyone is back at his or her desk."

Taylor replied, "Yes."

Mr. Drake asked, "How did it go?"

Taylor answered, "I thought it went well. It's pretty complicated stuff for new hires, but I think they have enough to know that they need to ask before doing anything stupid."

Mr. Drake went on, "All good. Speaking of RICO, how is your RICO case coming along"

Taylor replied, "It is coming along pretty well. You might find the charging and some of the theories interesting. Eventually, though, I will need to interview the witness."

Mr. Drake replied, "I'm working on that. It seems that the threats to the witness have been taken so seriously that she has been placed in deep protective custody with 24 hour a day guard service from the Federal Marshal. No one knows where she is. Not even me."

Taylor responded, "That is unfortunate because it may take a while to get an indictment with another 70 days to get to trial."

Mr. Drake is a good-looking man around 50. He has grey hair. He keeps himself fit with regular trips to the gym and tennis on the weekends. He wears well-fitting suits, usually dark blue or grey. He is about 6 feet tall. At 175 pounds, he looks trim.

One would have thought that after a couple of years with the U S Attorney he would have taken a job in a private law firm. Even in the upper levels of a government law office, one would think that he would want more with his credentials and experience.

From his wall, it appears as if he went to UCLA, which should be sufficient for a large firm. Hard to say why he went the government route.

Our relationship has been cordial. I've caught him looking a couple of times, but he is careful to not cross any lines. He respects my work, but mostly because my success reflects on him. Whether he supports me for his benefit or mine is unknown. Everyone in the office, including me, knows that he has been married for 20 years and that he has three children in high school and middle school. All of them are boys. He's a nice-looking guy for his age with greying hair and a nice tan.

I understand that his wife works and has a pretty good job with the county. The two salaries allow Mr. Drake to be a little less concerned about raising a family of five on what he alone would make working for the U S Attorney.

Mr. Drake asked, "So, what is your plan for Bobbie and his friends?"

Taylor replied, "I am thinking RICO. His activities definitely amount to an enterprise. Under RICO, we don't need to specify what the enterprise is, and we can join other crimes with some of their conduct, even crimes that could not be joined under the Federal Rules.

"In addition to requiring two acts of racketeering within a 10-year period as required by Section 1961, the Supreme Court has held that for RICO, it must also be shown that the predicate crimes are related and that they amount to a threat of continued criminal activity.

"Section 1962 makes it unlawful to invest in an enterprise using income derived from racketeering, to acquire or maintain an interest in an in an enterprise through racketeering, or to operate or manage an enterprise that conducts its affairs, either directly or indirectly, through a pattern of racketeering. It is also unlawful to conspire to violate any of the above.

"We have at least three people in the upper echelon of the enterprise, in addition to Bobbie himself, this includes Luis Foley, and

Sergio Marks. Though they will argue strenuously that they are not a partnership, corporation, or other legal entity, they are definitely an association in fact.

"We will be able to show that the three men met regularly to discuss their crimes and that each defendant had a different role within the enterprise.

"1962(c) also requires that a defendant participate directly or indirectly in the conduct of the affairs of the enterprise with some level of control. This allows prosecutors to charge low and middle level employees under RICO."

Mr. Drake asked, "I know that we will be arranging an opportunity for you to prep the witness before the indictment. She will not be able to have an attorney during her hearing before the grand jury, so this preparation will be very important. She will have to be well coached as to what to say, within, of course, those things about which she has personal knowledge. I know that you have not been given time for an in-depth interview, but have you had a chance to learn at least some of the things that she knows?"

Taylor replied, "The information about which she knows is sketchy at this point. I have heard that she will be able to testify that Mr. Franco, Mr. Foley, and Mr. Marks or their underlings would go to Tijuana and solicit young women to come to the United States to work. They would assisted them in illegally entering the country. After learning their fate, that is, to work as prostitutes, they would become slaves and be forced to work. Any fees that they generate would be embezzled by their bosses. They would additionally be required to act as drug mules trafficking drugs into the United States. Money would be laundered through several legitimate business run by the enterprise.

"We have a variety of predicate crimes including assisting people to illegally enter the country, slavery, embezzlement, drug trafficking, and money laundering, all occurring with the 10-year time period. The crimes are obviously related and pose a threat of continued criminal activity.

"From a standpoint of plea-deal tactics, RICO should work well for us. Section 1963 (a) requires that all of the assets gained as a result of a RICO violation must be forfeited. This has been interpreted to mean all of the businesses run by an enterprise shall be forfeited even when some of them are legitimate. As a result, all of the assets, even the ones obtained legitimately, would be forfeited, including buildings, vehicles, and other legitimately obtained items. Further, the proceeds gained from a RICO violation as determined by the Court would be forfeited, even if the defendant no longer has them.

"Another great feature is that pre-trial we can get a temporary restraining order and/or injunction to keep the defendants from transferring assets so that there will be assets available if we win at trial."

Mr. Drake said, "That is a pretty far reaching law. If we can get at the legitimate assets, we might be able to force a plea deal."

Taylor replied, "That would be my hope. When you consider the expense and inconvenience of protecting a witness, a plea-deal begins to sound pretty good."

Mr. Drake said, "If that is all that you have, let's call it a day and get back to our regular work."

Taylor replied, "Okay."

Taylor returned to her office to finish up for the day. Rick was not teaching tonight, so she thought that she could prepare a nice meal for the three of them and turn in early.

Chapter 23
Bobbie, Luis, and Sergio

Bobbie Franco was a low level, want-to-be, hoodlum from New Jersey. His rise up the criminal ladder has been similar to the rise of a corporate intern. People above him move to other jobs, get fired (or killed), die (under suspicious circumstances), or move out of the area (often into witness protection).

In New Jersey, Bobbie did well with sports betting and gambling. He then found his true calling – prostitution. He was a natural. He hated women, particularly his mother; he was rough and uncouth; he would do anything for money; and his gall was unmitigated. He was the perfect pimp, except he did not dress as well as pimps generally dress, and his car was also a little more understated.

He treated his girls so badly that they eventually turned on him. He lacked the people skills to reign them in.

While on a trip to California, he met his eventual partners, Luis Foley and Sergio Marks. They too took a perverse interest in prostitutes. But they had all of the swagger, the fancy clothes, expensive cars, and jewelry. Unfortunately for Luis and Sergio they loved the game but lacked the money. Bobbie, on the other hand, had money but lacked the "pimp hand" necessary to run a prostitution business.

Luis and Sergio convinced Bobbie that they would do the heavy lifting with the girls if Bobbie would supply the funds.

By this time, Bobbie had worn out his welcome in New Jersey. The three of them decided that a move to California would be in order.

As Los Angeles was already saturated with players, and competent players at that, they decided that the desert might be their move. People came from all over the country to stay in the desert for a short time. Short timers were really the bread and butter of the industry. They did not spend the time or effort to actually strike up a human relationship with anyone. They could sneak away from the wife and kids for an afternoon saying that they were playing golf, and meet up with a working girl.

Also, the desert was a pretty direct shot to Mexico. What better business plan for a pimp than the ability to grab a few girls from the streets of Tijuana and convince them to come up to the States to work and be taken care of. A pimp's dream.

Between the three of them, they put together quite a business smuggling girls, turning them out as prostitutes, and creating a pool of forced labor. True gentlemen.

Chapter 24
Attorney for the Defense

With Bobbie's reputation, one can only imagine how sleazy his attorney would be. But though Bobbie is many things, he is not stupid. When Bobbie felt the Feds closing in around him, he immediately booked a consultation with his lawyer, which is something even legitimate and honest business people occasionally fail to do.

Bobbie's attorney's name is Leonard "Red" Shultz. He was given this nickname for being painfully aggressive and completely unafraid to present far-fetched theories on behalf of his clients, as if he had taken a shot of Red Bull, and because of his red hair. His lies have been so huge that people often think that he must be telling the truth. No one could make something like that up, so it must be true.

Bobbie's office, if you can call it that, is in a ghost town called Eagle Mountain located outside of Joshua Tree National park. Allowing the town to remain unknown and in an apparent state of disrepair, Bobbie remodeled the insides of buildings leaving the outsides in their broken-down state. He built an office for himself with a kitchen, quarters for his guards, quarters for his girls, and a storage building for his drugs. From the outside, it continued to look like a ghost town.

With the girls, most of their service would be out-call. That is, the girls would be chauffeured to the customer's hotel room. Additionally, they would provide some in-call service at the Desert Spring Inn in Indio. The Desert Spring Inn is not lavish, but it appeared clean, and one could access the rooms without passing through a lobby.

One reaches Eagle Mountain by taking the 10 Freeway from Palm Springs east through Cathedral City, Palm Desert, and Indio to Desert Center. On this part of the journey, the 10 Freeway passes the Indian Reservation and Joshua Tree National Park. The 10 ultimately reaches

Desert Center. At Desert Center, one turns north and takes Kaiser Road to Eagle Mountain. Taking this route, the trip from Eagle Mountain to Palm Springs is approximately 85 miles. The long distance is partially due to the fact that one needs to travel around the outside of the National Park when taking the 10 Freeway. Taylor Shaw's home is in west Palm Springs.

The town was originally founded by Henry J. Kaiser of Kaiser Steel in 1948 at the entrance to the Eagle Mountain iron mine. Kaiser had a steel mill in Fontana. The increased iron shipments in 1948 led to the utilization of the iron mine at Eagle Mountain, and a town grew up around it. Environmental concerns and foreign competition led to a reduction in iron output, and the population in Eagle Mountain diminished. In 1981, Kaiser phased out the Eagle Mountain operation rendering the town a virtual ghost town, which is its present state.

No one knew where Bobbie's compound was located. If you wished to visit Bobbie at his compound, you would be taken in one of his cars and would be required to wear a hood over your head.

Bobbie had his attorney Leonard picked up and taken to the compound. Luis and Sergio were also picked up and taken there.

After the long trek, the they finally arrived and assembled in the dining area. Bobbie had a secretary set up a table and chairs and put out drinks, water, and snacks.

The four of them sat around the make-shift table. Bobbie called the meeting to order.

Bobbie started, "Well gentlemen, I imagine that you are wondering why I called for this meeting. Believe me, I would not have requested it unless I thought it was absolutely necessary.

"My sources at the U S Attorney's Office tell me that they are planning an assault on our business. I have heard that in addition to charging us with various crimes directly, they are also considering a RICO indictment.

"I, for one, am no lawyer, and I have little reliable information about RICO and its ramifications. I don't know whether it is something that we should fear or whether it is just so much smoke?

"So, I asked my attorney to meet with us and explain to us how all of this works so that we may plan our next move.

"Luis and Sergio let me introduce you to Leonard Shultz, my long-time attorney. He is also known as Red. It has been my experience that Red is well versed in all things criminal law, and he has given me terrific counsel in the past which has kept me out of jail so far.

"So, allow me, on behalf of all of us, to ask Red, the important question: Is this RICO thing something about which we should be worried or not?"

Red answered, "As with all things in the law, the answer is that it depends. If one did not do anything that would give rise to a RICO indictment, he would have no worries. If, on the other hand, a RICO case could be made against him, he needs to move quickly because the penalties can be significant.

"At this point, I do not know exactly what you are doing. Remember, the attorney-client privilege might not come into play if a defendant admits to his attorney that he committed a crime or is planning to commit one."

Bobbie replied, "Perhaps I could give you a hypothetical situation?"

Red answered, "Better to ask about penalties."

Bobbie replied, "That's fine. What would the penalty be if someone trafficked young women for prostitution and made use of them to transport drugs for illegal drug sales?"

Red replied, "Obviously, that person would be liable for the trafficking and for the illegal drug sale, and would probably be liable for money laundering in connection with the profits. He could be charged separately for each offense and be sentenced to the penalty prescribed for each, which could be a fine and imprisonment for a period of a few years, which could be reduced.

"Perhaps the more serious problem would be that he might face a RICO indictment. Under RICO, if a defendant commits two acts of racketeering, known as 'predicate' crimes, within 10 years, he might be liable for a RICO violation. The penalty for a RICO violation could mean a fine of up to $25,000 and a sentence of 20 years per count. In addition, the defendant would be required to forfeit all money as well as all interest in any business gained through his pattern of racketeering, whether the business is legitimate or not.

"Predicate crimes are 35 crimes, 27 of which are federal crimes and 8 of which are State crimes. They include all of the usual suspects such as murder, kidnapping, extortion, arson, bribery, theft, embezzlement, fraud, slavery, money laundering, and drug trafficking.

"As you can see, the 20 year per count jail sentence is quite stiff.

"However, if the sentence for the under-lying crime is more severe, the prosecution could seek it instead. For example, if the underlying

126

crime is murder, the prosecution may use the sentence for murder, the underlying crime, which could be 25 years to life or worse, instead of the 20-year RICO sentence.

"One of the really draconian parts of the RICO law is the forfeiture provision. Under RICO, all ill-gotten gains and interests in any business, whether legitimate or not, must be forfeited.

"And if that is not enough, under RICO, the prosecutor has the option to seek a pre-trial restraining order or injunction to seize a defendant's assets and prevent their transfer before the trial.

"Does any of this make sense?"

Luis and Sergio were dumbfounded. They were unable to speak after hearing about RICO.

Bobbie said, "Can this all be true? Can they really choose the greater sentence, confiscate your money, and get a restraining order against transferring your property?"

Red replied, "They most certainly can and probably will."

Luis asked, "Is there anything we can do?"

Red said, "I'm going to stay out of planning. That is not my job. My job is to explain the law."

Bobbie was uncharacteristically logical. Using some judgment, he said, "I think that we have learned all we need from Red, and all of the information was useful. Unless either of you object, I think I will let Red go home now. We can stay and talk about the case."

Though Red did not show it, he was more than thrilled about that outcome. Bobbie had one of the cars take Red back to Palm Springs where he was staying. Bobbie returned to his meeting with Luis and Sergio.

Luis asked, "Should we have let him go without getting more help?"

Bobbie replied, "It's only his job to explain the law and penalties. It is not his job to plan crimes. I believe that what we have to do is so painfully obvious that we do not need a lawyer to tell us.

"It's pretty clear that RICO would be the end for us. We have had successful businesses, both legal and Illegal. We might have been able to get out with a short sentence and minor fine, but with RICO, sentences are 20 years per count, and they can take away all of our businesses, even the legal ones. This is too much. Our only option is to beat the RICO charge.

"From my sources, the only evidence they have is the testimony of that bitch Crystal. She knows enough to bury us. She did all of the work with the importing of the girls, collecting and skimming all of the money, laundering the money through our legitimate businesses, selling all of the drugs that the girls brought in, and basically running the entire enterprise.

"I am sure that she made a plea deal where she will get immunity or, at very worst, pay a small fine and do no jail time at all. She has been and will remain in protective custody until the trial."

Luis asked, "So, what can we do?"

Bobbie replied, "Pretty obvious. We have to get rid of her. We have no choice. It's that or spend the next 40 years in prison."

Luis replied, "I see your point. But the witness is in protective custody and is being watched 24 hours a day. It is going to be nearly impossible to get close to her."

Bobbie replied, "And we need to reach her before her grand jury testimony. Remember what Red said. He said that before the trial, they can get a temporary restraining order or injunction to seize our assets. This alone would devastate our operation. If we can't get to her before she testifies and they get a restraining order, we're finished anyway. On the other hand, if we can keep her from testifying before the grand jury and make the indictment go away, we will be fine."

Bobbie continued, "Here's the thing. Yes, she is in protective custody. While in protective custody, during the days and nights, she will be in some motel room or safe house where she will be nearly impossible to reach. However, at some point, she has to be moved to meet with her attorney. Though she is not allowed an attorney in the grand jury room, they are certainly going to have an attorney speak with her before her testimony."

Luis replied, "I see your point. We will get her when she meets with her lawyer."

Luis continued, "There is not much chance that they would do that at the safe house, as safe houses are very lived in, if you know what I mean. They will have to do it at the lawyer's office or some other neutral place. Can we find out?"

Bobbie replied, "I'll take care of that. I have someone on the inside. Okay, let's break for now. We need to get moving on this project right away. We should be ready to roll immediately, depending on when she meets her lawyer."

The meeting broke up, and the three men left Eagle Mountain for their respective homes.

Chapter 25
Rob

Rob Fulton is a good looking, 6 foot, two inches tall, white guy weighing in at 185 pounds. He comes from a modest family. His father is a wheeler-dealer accustomed to living above his means. Rob appears to be following in his father's foot-steps. Though from modest circumstances, with his good looks, he has been able to present himself as several classes above his actual station in life.

He talked his way into one of the better law schools by making a fairly reasoned plea during the oral portion of the admissions process. Rob was able to convince the admissions board that the school needed white men from less than wealthy families to balance out the school's efforts to award admission to minorities.

It worked, and Rob got through school with some plagiarism and assorted cheating from his classmates, particularly the intelligent and reasonably attractive women upon whom he prayed, not unlike a jackal praying on the remains of a dead animal.

The bar exam was more difficult to fool. He did manage to get through on the third try after tutoring from a young female lawyer with whom he struck up an intense but brief relationship until the results were made public, at which time he dumped her unceremoniously.

Rob talked his way into the U S Attorney's Office. It appears as if he is somehow related to Daryl Drake, his immediate boss; apparently Mr. Drake is his mother's second cousin.

Rob decided that he would get ahead by kissing up to his boss, a strategy that worked for him from time immemorial.

Rob has been with the U S Attorney for four years. He is now around 30. Taylor is approaching 38, and Sharon is just 25, and a brand-new hire. At her young age, Sharon is open season for an experienced user such as Rob.

Rob is a good-looking guy, and all of the women in the office ogle him daily. This just feeds into his already overly large ego. In addition to his looks, he somehow presents an aura of financial success. He wears flashy clothes; has expensive-looking jewelry; has an expensive car; and has an expensive apartment. He somehow does this all on his salary, which is on the meager side.

How does he do it? If you ask him, he says that he receives some money from family. Most people drop the inquiry there.

Sharon already asked Taylor her opinion of Rob, which she gave. She then proceeded to ignore it, not unlike many young women.

Chapter 26
Sharon and Rob

Sharon was in her office working late. It was around 6:30. She heard a gentle knock on the door. She got up from her desk and went to the door, as it was her custom to keep her door locked after 6.

Sharon asked, "Who is it?"

An answer came from the other side of the door, "Rob."

Sharon opened the door. She saw that it was Rob and let him in. She directed him to one of the two chairs which were placed across the desk from her.

Sharon said, "Please have a seat. And what may I do for you?"

Rob replied, "Nothing really. I just stopped by to say hello and see how you are doing with your new job."

Sharon replied, "Thank you. Everything is going fine. So far, I love it here. It's very challenging, and the people are great."

Rob replied, "That's all good. You get along okay with your boss?"

Sharon said, "You mean Daryl. Yes. He's great."

Rob continued, "And the other senior staff, like Taylor?"

Sharon said, "Oh, yes. She's a dream. She has been so helpful and such a good friend. I consider myself lucky to know someone like her."

Rob went on, "I didn't know. I don't have much to do with her. We work different cases."

Sharon said, "That's okay."

Rob asked, "I was wondering if you would be interested in getting a drink or having dinner with me."

Sharon replied, "I guess that would be okay. I am not certain about dating a co-worker. It can be a problem."

Rob said, "I was thinking about something very casual. Not a real date. Like we could meet at the bar across the street after work."

Sharon replied, "I guess that that would be okay."

Rob continued, "How about tonight?"

Here the rubber and the road would meet. If she really didn't like him and really didn't want to start anything with him, she would just decline, saying that she was uncomfortable being with a co-worker away from the office.

If, on the other hand, she did like him and did want to explore being with him away from the office, she was stuck. If she turned him down because it was too soon to say yes, he might not ask again. If she accepted, she might appear desperate, and he might get the impression that she was easy.

She apparently did like him and did want to explore being with him so she said yes.

Rob excused himself to return to his office to grab his jacket and brief case. She collected her things and went to the reception area where they were going to meet. They met and rode down in the elevator to the first floor. They walked across the street, entered the bar, and sat at a table in the bar.

Sharon was not really Rob's type. Her looks were serviceable, but she was not a knock-out. Rob thought of himself as God's gift to women and felt that any woman that he was with would have to be beautiful beyond comprehension. Sharon was not that. She dressed well, but conservatively. She wore functional clothing, which was not revealing.

But Rob romanced women for other reasons; reasons which will become clear. So, the fact that she might not measure up to his usual standards was not important. She gave the impression that she felt that she was inadequate. But because he made the first move, she was beginning to allow herself to feel as if she might have a chance. Poor thing.

They arrived at the bar. Rob gallantly held the door for her. He addressed the hostess and arranged a table in the bar area for the two of them. Once seated, Rob asked her what she wanted to drink. She opted for white wine. Being ever the gentleman, he ordered a white wine for her and a greyhound for himself. The drinks came and were placed on the table in front of them. Their conversation ensued.

Rob started, "You said that you like your job and co-workers. That's a good thing."

Sharon answered, "Yes. Much better than the alternative. How about you. Do you like your work here?"

Rob actually did not like his work at the U S Attorney's Office at all. It was too slow and pedestrian. He knew that at his level, he was just the hired help with little chance of advancement.

However, he was afraid to say so. He was afraid that if Sharon thought that he did not like his work, he might not appear to be a person as serious as she might like. And it was essential for Rob's purposes that Sharon think of him as a possible future love interest, even if he did not have those feelings and didn't think that those feelings would develop.

So out of fear, Rob responded to Sharon's question by saying, "The job is a good one. It gives us a chance to fight the good fight for the Indians and for the little guy against the big corporations. Who knows, this job might change me into a crusader."

Sharon said, "That's good. I too think we can really do good here."

Rob was beginning to see that if he wanted to get anywhere with Sharon he would have to temper his rhetoric a little and appear to be more of a do-gooder. He was coming to believe that his typical non-caring thing, which generally worked so well with women, would not work with Sharon. Maybe she was one of those rare girls who was not just looking to tame a bad boy but was actually looking for something meaningful.

Rob said, "That's true. We really can. We have all of the tools and contacts to really make a difference."

Sharon said, "Yes we do."

Apparently, his new plan was working. She was beginning to come around.

Rob asked, "What kind of cases are you working on?"

Sharon replied, "As you know, I am just a beginner. They give me some arraignments and other pre-trial hearings. Mr. Drake was talking about giving me some Indian cases. Apparently, there are many crimes committed on Indian reservations, and some of the assistants do not wish to handle them."

Rob asked, "Wasn't Taylor really involved with the Indians?"

Sharon replied, "I don't really know. I wasn't working here then, but I understand that she was involved. In fact, I think that she mentioned that she still sees some of her Indian friends and goes to the Reservation often to visit, even taking her husband and daughter and some of the attorneys from the office. One of the girls from the office married an Indian man. Taylor says he's really nice."

Rob replied, "That sounds about right. It seems as if now that she has gotten in on the good side of Mr. Drake, she is getting the plumb assignments."

Sharon said, "From my understanding, she has earned whatever assignments she has been given without the necessity of getting in on anyone's good side."

Rob could see that he had unintentionally drifted to the not-so-well-hidden anti-feminist side of his personality. He would have to correct course if he wanted to hang in with Sharon. As with all of the women in the office and most of the men, they liked Taylor and respected her as a person and as a lawyer.

Rob went on, "No. I mean Taylor has progressed to the point where she is getting the best cases. I mean I heard that she has been assigned the Bobbie Franco case, which is probably the biggest case to come to our office in many years. I was hoping for a shot at it, but it was given to her."

Sharon, being supportive, said, "You shouldn't worry about it. She's the senior person, and it stands to reason that she would get that case."

Rob went on, "That's true. And there will be other cases for me."

Here he used self-deprecation to wiggle back into Sharon's good graces, and he did it well. His next step would be to equate himself with her by offering the following:

"You and I will have to wait our turn to get the really big cases, but I am certain that we will. I know that you work hard enough to catch the eye of our bosses."

Sharon replied, "Thank you for being so understanding. I think you're right."

"Understanding" was so far from Rob's vocabulary that he barely knew its meaning. But if appearing to be understanding was what it was going to take to win Sharon over, he would be understanding.

They had each ordered and consumed their second round of drinks, and Sharon was getting a little light headed and was becoming a little more unguarded, as white wine tended to do to her.

Rob was then ready to perform his next trick which is not only one of the oldest tricks in the book, but often netted results.

He said, "I don't think it's safe for you to be driving. I think I better drive you home. I can come back in the morning to bring back your car."

Sharon replied, "I think that's a good idea. The last thing I need is a DUI."

They walked across the street and entered the parking garage. Rob directed Sharon to his beautiful Porsche. He opened the door for her. She asked, "My, this is a beautiful car. How can you afford it?"

Some people might be offended by such a question, but not Rob. He replied, "My family has money." This was not true, but Rob thought that it would sound good to Sharon. He had some side hustles about which he preferred to not tell Sharon, or anyone else for that matter.

They drove to Sharon's apartment. It was in a nice building. She was able to live in such a nice place because in her case, her family actually did have money and paid most of her rent. They made their way up to the top floor. Sharon was sober enough to find her way but drunk enough to barely get into the elevator.

When they reached the door, Rob pulled out all of the stops. He held Sharon close and aggressively kissed her on the mouth. She initially recoiled, but then decided to go with it.

All of the women in the office thought that Rob was so good looking and such a great catch, particularly since he was so close with the boss. She was in the position many find themselves in that she could have sex on the first date and probably have a 50 percent chance of never seeing the guy again or she could reject him and have a 90 percent chance of never seeing him again.

He needed to be careful here. His interest in Sharon was not just for sex. If that were the case, he would give it his best shot and move on. However, his interest was driven by something else. He needed to keep himself in Sharon's good graces because he needed information from her for his side hustle. This was much more important to him than sex.

He would take the sex if it was offered, but if it wasn't, he would have to back away gracefully, because it was more important to keep himself in her orbit than it was to get laid. If things deteriorated to that point, he would have to pivot to his nice-guy routine saying that he wanted to be friends and that sex was not important. He would then use that new strategy to try to get the information he needed.

He said, "May I come in, or should I go?" (He would never offer this as an alternative under normal circumstances. He would just barge in.)

Sharon replied, "Why don't you come in."

Sharon opened the door, and the two of them entered her apartment. Once inside, Rob said, "This is quite a nice place."

Sharon replied, "Thank you. Between you and me, my parents help me with the rent. They say that it's important to them that I live in a safe neighborhood."

Sharon continued, "Would you like a night cap?"

Rob said, "I think I'm fine. But thank you." (He was really on his best behavior.)

Sharon said, "I'd really like to get out of these clothes. Would you excuse me while I put on something a little more comfortable?"

Rob replied, "Certainly."

Rob felt now that rejection was out of the question. He was elated as he would not have to go to his nice-guy routine which was getting a little old, and painful.

Sharon went into her bedroom. She was there for a while. Rob could hear the sounds of her undressing and then dressing. She came back out to the living room in a very cute ensemble consisting of a short night gown and a sheer robe. She came over to the couch and sat next to Rob.

Wasting no time, Rob grabbed her, and they started to kiss passionately. Rob maneuvered her into the bedroom and onto the bed. He removed his clothing and her night gown with one hand. This was not his first rodeo. Rob had been a purveyor of sex for years and had used his prowess to gain an advantage over women on too many occasions to count.

He moved his mouth down her body below her waist. When he contacted her there with his mouth, she became almost uncontrollable with pleasure. He was a real pro.

He then moved up her naked body to a position where his face was next to hers. When seeing her in this light, he thought to himself that she was really quite beautiful. For him, sex was business. It was a way of getting control over a woman to ply her for information he could sell. Whether his mark was beautiful or was really not so beautiful was irrelevant. In fact, the less invested he was, the easier it was for him to obtain what he needed.

When he found her to be beautiful, rather than please him, it scared him. Was he getting soft? She was so sweet and so kind he wondered if he could be falling for her? That would certainly ruin everything.

136

He needed to maintain control for his purposes. If he actually liked her, this might be more difficult to accomplish. He quickly swept all of those thoughts out of his head and readied himself for the main event.

They were now lying face to face. He entered her. She moaned. She felt so good. He, as a seasoned veteran, was able to keep it going inside of her for 30 minutes. This would be 28 minutes longer than any of her previous encounters. Her body raised up with ecstasy. They finally climaxed together. It took him a minute to gain the strength to move.

They finally separated. Rob rolled off to Sharon's right. Sharon nuzzled her head under Rob's left arm. They were both spent, a feeling to which neither was accustomed; Rob because he never cared about his partner, and Sharon because she never had a partner with Rob's skills.

Sharon spoke first, "Rob, that was really something. No one has ever made love to me like that before in my life."

Rob replied, "That makes me feel good to hear, but with your beauty you must have had many lovers." (This was a BS line that Rob brought out to convince her that he cared, which he did not.)

Sharon said, "I hope that we can do this again. I hope that we can be friends."

Rob replied, "Certainly honey."

They fell asleep in each other's arms.

At 5:30 they both awoke. She reached out for him. He moved in and kissed her hard on the mouth. They made passionate love again, even more passionate than the night before.

When they were done, Sharon cuddled into Rob's arm where they stayed for quite some time. It was time for a little pillow-talk.

Rob said, "I heard from Mr. Drake that the Bobbie Franco indictment hearing will be very soon."

Sharon replied, "Yes. I heard the same from Taylor."

Rob said, "I know that the witness cannot have an attorney present, but I presume that she can be interviewed by an attorney. I guess Taylor will do that. If she intends to interview the witness, she does not have much time left.

Sharon replied, "Yes. That is true. I think she will do it tonight after work."

Rob said, "I hope they use our office. I heard that the witness has been in witness protection, and witness protection is typically done in a sleazy motel where everyone has been sitting around all day watching TV and eating pizza. It gets a little rank in there."

Sharon replied, "Yes. She said that they would use the office."

Mission accomplished. Rob got the information he was after. The witness interview would be tonight after work at their office. He could now sell this valuable piece of information to Mr. Franco because the only opportunity he will have to grab her will be when she is moved out of the office after the interview.

When she is being brought in before the interview, it will be early enough to make grabbing her difficult. Everyone will be fresh, the Marshals will be on high alert, and there will still be some unrelated left-over security people in the building.

On the other hand, when the witness interview is over, it will be late, and everyone will be tired and not as vigilant as they might otherwise be.

Rob got out of bed and took his clothes into the bathroom. It was now 6:30 a.m. He came out of the bathroom fully dressed.

Sharon asked, "Are you ready to go now. Can't you stay for a while?"

Rob replied, "I'll stay until you get dressed for work. I forgot you need a ride to the office."

Rob violated several of his own rules. He stayed all night. Usually, he would leave by 3 a.m.

He made love to her twice. Usually, once was his limit. He offered to take her back to the office. Usually, he would call an Uber. He agreed to be friends. Usually, he prohibited discussions relating to the future. But worst of all, actually worse than all of the rest combined, he allowed himself to have feelings for her. He never, ever developed feelings for anyone, even his mother.

Notwithstanding his transgressions, he accomplished his mission. He got the information about where and when the witness interview would be taking place. He would now sell that information to Mr. Franco. And now we know how he makes the money he uses to afford his apartment, his car, his clothes, his jewelry, and his other accoutrements.

Rob took Sharon to the office and dropped her off. He told her that he needed to return home to change clothes.

When he arrived home, a two-way radio had been placed in his locked mail box. It was off. He turned it on and made a call to another two-way radio. He reached Mr. Franco, who was waiting for his call. He told Mr. Franco the time and place of the witness interview. Mr. Franco arranged to wire $100,000 to a private account for him. He turned off the radio and put it back in the mail box. It would be picked up within five minutes. The two-way radio was used because every cellphone signal can be intercepted whereas a two-way radio is nearly impossible to track.

Chapter 27
Witness Interview

Sharon was torn whether to tell Taylor about her tryst with Rob. It was a fairly busy day and both of them would have plenty of work to do. Sharon decided that she would hold off telling her until tomorrow, after the witness interview would be finished.

Late in the afternoon, Taylor would have her last meeting with Mr. Drake to go over some of the details of the interview.

Taylor's intercom buzzed. It was Mr. Drake asking Taylor to come to his office at 4:00.

The day flew by. It was 4:00, and Taylor was collecting her things so she could meet Mr. Drake and then the witness.

She went to Mr. Drake's office and gently knocked on his door. He asked her to enter, which she did. She was directed to a chair in front of Mr. Drake's desk. She sat.

Mr. Drake started, "Thought we could talk about a few things before the witness interview for the indictment hearing.

"I realize that you have attended many indictments in the past, but I am always told by my boss that it is necessary for me to go over our responsibilities with the assistant who will be appearing. We need to play by all of the rules. Here are the rules:

"Grand juries are selected from the same jury pool of ordinary citizens as those who serve on trial juries. Those selected generally serve between 18 and 36 months, usually meeting a few times a month. They have the power to issue subpoenas and to question witnesses.

"As we know, an indictment is a one-sided affair. A grand jury makes the decision to indict an accused. A trial jury decides his guilt or innocence. For this reason, the burden of proof is much lower with a grand jury than with a trial jury. A grand jury need only find probable cause that a crime has been committed and that the defendant committed it. The decision need not be unanimous.

"A grand jury may have between 16 and 23 members, usually 23, and at least 12 must agree before an indictment will issue. On the other hand, a trial jury must establish guilt beyond a reasonable doubt by unanimous verdict.

"More importantly, with a grand jury indictment, only the grand jurors, the prosecutors, and the prosecution witnesses are allowed in the room. A prosecution witness is not allowed to have an attorney. In some rare cases, a potential defendant is allowed to present some evidence, but no defense attorneys are ever allowed in the room. There is no cross-examination of the prosecution's evidence.

"It is recommended that the prosecutors meet with the victim to help determine whether to charge the defendant at all. When meeting with a victim, it is necessary to have law enforcement present. Otherwise, the prosecutor could become a witness.

"It is important for us to remember that a prosecutor's grand jury role as an investigator is different than his role as an advocate in a trial. At the indictment stage, a prosecutor's duty is not to win but to seek justice. The prosecutor's client is the public and not a particular governmental agency.

"The 5th Amendment to the United States Constitution provides that no person shall be charged with a serious or infamous felony except by indictment. This was done to prevent the government from charging people with serious felonies without the participation of the people, that is, the grand jury.

"The prosecutor's role is to ensure that criminal investigations are not based on partisan, political, or personal considerations and do not discriminate based on race, ethnicity, religion, gender, sexual orientation, political beliefs, age, or social or economic status.

"Criminal investigations shall be in the public interest and shall remain secret and confidential.

"I prefer to characterize your meeting tonight with the witness as an interview rather than as a preparation. It is not really our job to coach the witness, as one might do with an expert. The interview tonight is for you to hear what the witness has to say and determine whether it is enough to get an indictment.

"At the indictment hearing, you will be doing your share of talking, but it has always been my experience that grand juries prefer to hear from the witnesses.

"You, of course, have a right to change your mind about the witness and her story. The prosecutor may inform the witness whether he or she is considered to be a witness or a subject, as their status may change during the investigation.

"So, I have done my due diligence. It is much to digest."

Taylor replied, "I'm familiar with all of the rules. I'm really more concerned about the logistics of the meeting."

Mr. Drake replied, "As you know, the witness is in protective custody with the U S Marshal. The Marshals will bring her here to the reception area. They will text you, and you will meet them and escort the witness to your office for the interview."

Taylor asked, "Will the Marshals stay in my office during the interview?"

Mr. Drake replied, "No. They would get too bored. They will leave her with you and wait either outside or in the parking garage until you are finished. When you are finished, you can text them and take her to where they direct."

Taylor responded, "Is that safe? This will all take place after hours when there is almost no security in the building. I'm not armed as I am told that guns are not allowed in the building."

Mr. Drake replied, "No need to worry about that. No one knows when she is supposed to be here. That information has been kept from everyone. I'll be going home for the evening, so you will be on your own."

Taylor replied, "Okay. Guess I will have to make due."

It was now just before 6. Taylor returned to her office and waited for the text. Promptly at 6, she received a text message from the Marshals that they were at the building and were ready to bring her in for the interview. Taylor texted them back and asked them to bring her to the reception area for the suite. With the security desk being closed, the Marshals were able to bring her directly to the U S Attorney's suite.

Taylor went to the reception area to wait. A few minutes later, the door opened, and two Federal Marshals brought the witness into the suite.

Taylor thought to herself that this must be Ms. Forrester. She was in her late 30's. She looked as if she had had a hard life of late nights, partying, drinking, stripping, escorting, and taking drugs. She was not unattractive but was a disheveled mess. Her hair looked dry and appeared to have been colored many times. Her skin was rough and pitted. Her makeup was misapplied. She looked pretty bad, but with her resume, it was to be expected.

As to her attire, she looked like a 40-year old trying to dress like a teenager. Her clothes were dirty, ill-fitting, and very revealing, even though there would be no one left who would be interested looking at whatever might be revealed. It was tragic. Taylor thanked the Marshals for bringing the witness to her.

She then addressed the witness directly, "You must be Ms. Forrester."

She replied, "And you must be Ms. Shaw? I was told that I would be meeting with you here at 6."

I said, "Yes on both counts. Come with me back to my office so we can get started."

She followed me through the door to the hallway for the private offices. We went around the corner and entered my office.

I said, "Have a seat. Would you like anything?"

She replied, "I'd like a double bourbon neat, but I doubt that it is on the menu. I'd settle for a Coke, though."

Just outside of Taylor's office in the secretarial area, there were some soft drinks in a small refrigerator. Taylor excused herself, left her office, retrieved a Coke from the refrigerator, and returned to her office. Once in her office, she poured the contents into a glass and handed it to Ms. Forrester. She thanked Taylor.

Ms. Forrester, Coke in hand, sat in a chair opposite Taylor's desk.

Taylor began her inquiry, "Hi. May I know the name that I should use when addressing you?"

The witness began, "Well, my actual full name is 'Elizabeth Ann Forrester.' My stage name is 'Crystal Covington.'"

Taylor replied, "I don't think that Crystal Covington would be appropriate for what we are doing. Can we go with Elizabeth?"

Elizabeth replied, "That's fine, but I was always called Lizzy when I was growing up."

Taylor replied, "Lizzy is fine with me. Let's use Lizzy."

Lizzy replied, "That's fine."

Taylor began her questions, "Do you know why you are here?"

Lizzy responded, "I believe that it has something to do with Bobbie Franco."

Taylor replied, "Yes, it does. An indictment of Mr. Franco is being considered, and you were referred to us as someone who may have

143

witnessed relevant conduct on his part."

Lizzy responded, "What exactly is an indictment?"

Taylor replied, "An indictment is an old legal concept. In fact, it showed up in the United States Constitution in 1791. The 5th Amendment provides that in order to hold someone to answer for a serious crime, he must first be indicted. At this time, the Americans had just suffered through a long war of independence with England. Before the war, the English could hold people to answer for serious crimes just by charging them. As this did not sit well with the people forming the new government, after the Revolution, they required that to charge someone with a serious crime, he would first have to be indicted.

"With an indictment, a grand jury of ordinary citizens is assembled. If the government is going to charge a person with a serious crime, the prosecutor will first present the facts of the crime to the grand jury. The grand jury will determine whether there is sufficient evidence that the accused committed the crime and vote whether or not to indict him. If the grand jury votes that there was not sufficient evidence, the accused would be set free. If the grand jury votes that there was sufficient evidence, the accused would be indicted, arraigned, and ordered to stand trial.

"What we are going to talk about today is the indictment. We will not be trying Mr. Franco to determine his guilt or innocence. We will only be considering whether there is sufficient evidence to hold him over for a trial.

"In a trial, the prosecuting attorney acts as an advocate for the State. He or she presents evidence to try to convict the accused of the crime charged.

"With an indictment, the prosecutor is only required to present enough evidence to show that the accused committed a crime and, as a result, should stand trial.

"In the indictment setting, it is the prosecutor's duty to seek justice and not to win cases. According to the American Bar Association, with an indictment, it is the duty of the prosecutor to develop sufficient factual information to enable the prosecutor to make a fair and objective determination of what charges should be brought and to make sure that an innocent person is not prosecuted. His duty is to develop legally admissible evidence sufficient to obtain a conviction of those who are guilty and deserve prosecution.

"The prosecutor must ensure that criminal investigations are not based on partisan or improper political considerations and do not discriminate on the basis of race, religion, gender, sexual orientation, or social or economic status.

"It is our mission here this evening to find out what you know, first-hand, about Mr. Franco's activities. It is not my intention to have you twist your story in any way. I just want to hear about what it is that you actually know first-hand."

Lizzy interjected, "I think I see what is going on. You need my testimony here to see if you have enough to indict Bobbie or Mr. Franco?"

Taylor replied, "That is correct."

Lizzy asked, "What's in it for me?"

Taylor replied, "Hopefully we will be able to treat you as a cooperating witness which could include limiting your own criminal liability or provide you with immunity from prosecution altogether. Frankly, I don't see how the case can be successfully prosecuted without your assistance. I don't see where giving you immunity would be detrimental to the public interest. Everyone has been in a tight spot before."

Lizzy replied, "Okay. I understand. How much of my back story should I get into?"

Taylor replied, "I really can't advise you, but the interest here is the criminal activity, if any, carried out by the accused."

Lizzy replied that she understood and started her story:

"I was born into a poor family. Guess that is no surprise when someone finds herself in my present situation. My father left us when I was little, and I never heard from him again. My mother had no way to make a living so she started working as an escort and selling drugs. Again, no surprise.

"As I became a teenager, I guess I became sort of a commodity to the escort seekers. I was desperate and didn't mind sex, so I started escorting. I got to see some okay hotels. I got a few free meals. And I made enough for a small, horrible apartment in a really bad part of town. Some of my clients introduced me to drugs. I guess they thought that drugs would loosen me up and give them more sex.

"You meet all kinds escorting. Most of the men just want to get in and get out as fast as they can. Some found the need to get physically abusive, which just made matters worse for both of us. Every so often, you might even meet a nice guy. Most of these guys were too nice and not terribly attractive so they had no other way to get sex.

"As is the case with many girls in my line of work, along the way I met an older man who offered to take care of me. My older man was Bobbie Franco. When this happens, the girl drops all of her other clients and becomes the exclusive property of her care-taker guy.

"I came to find out that this kind of relationship creates more problems than it solves.

"The type of man who will pay for an exclusive girl is typically insecure and becomes possessive to the point of being dangerous. The relationship tends to break down over time. Then the guy becomes bored with the girl, and the girl does not have the skills to make herself useful to him or to anyone else, and, in most cases, she is no longer beautiful. She can only take whatever he is still willing to give.

"I was luckier than most. Most girls in this spot as they get older and their looks begin to fade are just thrown out. Now they are older, no longer attractive, and have nothing to fall back on. To complicate matters, most of them are strung out on drugs. So, they have no money, no looks, and need drugs for which they need money that they do not have. They wind up living on the streets hustling for any money they can get to support their drug habit.

"In my case, however, though Bobbie was not in love with me and was a complete asshole, he did feel badly enough for me to figure a way to keep me from going into complete free-fall.

"Bobbie started as a really low-level hood in New Jersey. In New Jersey he started with sports betting and gambling, pretty clean when compared to robbing banks and murder for hire. Because it was pretty clean, sports betting and gambling did not bring in as much money as some of the other lines of work.

"Bobbie then hit on prostitution. It was his true calling. He was a natural. He hated women, which is a must for this line of work. He hated his mother, which also helps. He was the perfect pimp except for the clothes and car. He treated his girls so badly that he considered leaving New Jersey. A guy with a bad rep like Bobbie's found it nearly impossible to get girls to work for him.

"Finally, things got so bad for Bobbie in New Jersey that he decided to take a look at California. While on such a trip to California, he met his eventual partners, Luis Foley and Sergio Marks. They had the contacts, but no money. Bobbie had the money, but no contacts.

146

"Having worn out his welcome in New Jersey, Bobbie decided to move to California. As Los Angeles was already saturated, he opted for the desert, which worked out well. It gave him a straight shot down to Mexico where he could pick up girls and bring them to the States with promises of easy work. They also used the girls to smuggle drugs in from Mexico. Luis and Sergio were satisfied with the business plan and joined in happily.

"As for me, Bobbie offered to take me to California with him. He could see that I was at least capable of helping him with his business, and if the business grew, he would need help out in California, where he didn't know or trust anyone. So, I packed my bags, and we headed to California, winding up in a place called Indio. Indio was chosen because it was fairly close to Palm Springs and other places known for tourists and to an abandoned town that Bobbie could get his hands on to lease called Eagle Mountain.

"Once in Indio, Luis and Sergio shared a house that they bought, and Bobbie bought his own house and allowed me to live there so long as I was valuable to his business.

"Eagle Mountain was transformed into a hide away. The outsides of the buildings were left to continue to look like the ghost town that it was. The insides were modified to become an office for Bobbie, a kitchen, a storage building for their drugs, and a dormitory for their girls and whatever help they had. It was less than an hour to Indio by car, just far enough.

"Business began as usual. They would send me to Mexico to meet girls and try to talk them into returning with me, and, unknown to them, bring in a load of drugs. The girls were very nice. In Mexico, they lived in squalor. It was not even as nice as Eagle Mountain.

"I begged Bobbie to let me take the girls on little excursions to resorts or movies. He turned me down flat saying that the only way the girls would see anything outside of Eagle Mountain was with a paying customer. If a customer wanted to pay, he could have a girl for as long as he wanted and he could do whatever he wished. A few customers took him up on this, but most opted for the one-hour special either at a hotel in Indio or at the customer's hotel.

"Large quantities of drugs were taken back with the girls. They were dropped off at Eagle Mountain, along with the girls. The girls were taken to their quarters where they were cleaned up and be fitted for new clothes. The drugs were taken to the storage building and left in the care of Hank and Dan.

"Bobbie, Luis, and Sergio built up the drug business. As they were the only people in the area with significant quantities, they could use runners to deliver and collect for their product."

Taylor said, "I don't want to interrupt your interview, but some detail about the arrangements for the girls and drugs would be good."

Lizzy continued, "Sorry. I would drive a fairly large vehicle from Indio. I was set up as a shuttle service with a three-row van. Bobbie worked his many contacts near the border, and they had their patrol people take only a quick look at what I was doing. In theory, I was there to shuttle women to come to the United States to work in the fashion industry. This was good for Mexico because it usually meant that money made in the U S would be sent back to Mexico to enter the economy.

"Bobbie, Luis, and Sergio had several legitimate businesses. They manufactured ladies' sportswear. This factory was where the ladies were supposed to work. Some did work as seamstresses, but others worked as escorts. They owned several dry-cleaning businesses, some small markets, and several apartment buildings. Money from their illegal businesses would be infused into the legal businesses.

"They would take money out of their legal businesses to pay for their living expenses such as homes, cars, yacht, airplane, etc. This allowed them to launder the profits.

"The bookkeeping for the legitimate businesses was pretty straight forward. Except for the infusion of money from escorting and drug sales, the books appeared almost legitimate.

"On my end, for the purposes of getting in and out of Mexico, everything was legal. I had a passport card that allowed me to proceed through the Ready Lane by the electronic reader. We always had a temporary permit for the vehicle while it was in Mexico complete with a deposit and an insurance rider. We always stayed within 20 kilometers of the border.

"Though the papers for the ladies were fake, they were the correct fakes, that is, instead of using a fake tourist visa which would expire, we used fake work visas. Again, Bobbie's contacts allowed us to cross back with only a cursory look at the ladies' papers.

"In short, Bobbie smuggled the girls into the U S.

"I typically drove the van from Indio, south past the Salton Sea, past Imperial, and to Calexico. I would cross the border at Calexico and enter Mexico in Mexicali. I would stop downtown to pick up the papers. While the girls were in the waiting area of the forger, I would look them over and tell him which ones we wanted. I would go off to pick up the drugs, and he would tell the chosen girls that they didn't need to go home. He put the finishing touches on the papers for the girls who would be leaving with me.

"I went around the corner to pick up the drugs. Bobbie's drug of choice is Fentanyl. It is so deadly that it can be sold in small quantities. This made it easier to move and store. Its small physical size made it easy to conceal and carry. Though it sounds dangerous, the drugs were put into glass containers and sealed before loaded in the van. Though drugs are typically moved in plastic bags, plastic is very porous and may be sniffed by dogs through a plastic container. This is not the case with glass.

"The drugs were loaded within the floor boards of the van where it would take significant equipment to remove them, much more work than a routine inspection at a border crossing.

"I would then pick up the chosen girls and drive the van back to Eagle Mountain where the girls and drugs would be unloaded.

"From this point, my work would include getting the seamstresses situated at their new work and explaining to the escorts what they would be doing. We had a phone secretary who would handle the calls on the several escort lines coming in from various websites and ads. The girls would be booked out either in-call, to our hotel in Indio, or out-call, directly to the customer's hotel room.

"Much of my time would be coaxing the girls to work, fielding their complaints about their customers, going to their location if things got out of hand, arranging medical treatment for those who were beaten or otherwise abused, and providing pep-talks to those in need of encouragement.

"It's a horrible business for a girl. It completely denigrates you as a human.

"Bobbie, of course, could not care less about what happens to the girls. This is why he is the perfect person to be a pimp. The worse it gets, the better he likes it. Poor guy is really sick.

"I was not, thank goodness, as directly involved with the drug trafficking as I was with the escorts.

"I did keep track of the escort business and the drug sales and accounted for all of the cash making it available to Bobbie, as I was the only one he trusted.

"The Fentanyl thing is almost too much. Thousands of dollars are realized from its sale, and many people die from its use."

Taylor asked, "Are there any records?"

Lizzy continued, "No. These guys are way too smart. They have records for their legitimate businesses, but the girls and drugs are separate. Just cash, which is not even put in the bank. These guys are so paranoid that they don't even use cellphones. Everything is done with walkie-talkies.

"I wouldn't want to have anything to do with records, even if they had them. If anyone tried to make records they would be killed. It's really too dangerous. I didn't even count the money. I just picked it up and delivered it to Bobbie."

Taylor said, "You don't have to worry now. They will not be at the hearing. You will not be cross-examined. It will just be me and the grand jury."

Lizzy replied, "That is a good thing, but eventually, if it goes to trial, they will be represented, and I will be cross-examined."

Taylor added, "In all honesty, that is true. But it is getting late now. Presuming that we have everything that you know, which it appears we do, we have all that we need. The grand jury might subpoena evidence if it needs to. Thank you very much for meeting with me. You have been a great help. After tonight, I guess the next time I see you will be at the grand jury meeting.

"I was told that the Marshals would be available to pick you up. I am supposed to text them when we're done. I'll text them now."

Taylor sent a text to the number she was given for the Marshals. She received a return text that read as follows: "Send Ms. Forrester to Parking Level 1. We will pick her up and take her back to the safe house."

Taylor said, "They want me to send you down to Parking Level 1. I don't feel right sending you all by yourself. I'll come with you and stay until your ride comes."

Lizzy replied, "Thank you. That's sweet."

Taylor ended, "Just doing my job."

The two of them left Taylor's office, left the suite, and entered the elevator. Taylor pressed P1, and the cab began a downward descent towards the first level of the underground parking. At P1, the cab stopped, and the doors opened. Lizzy and Taylor exited onto the bare concrete of the parking garage floor.

Chapter 28
The Kidnapping

After Lizzy and Taylor exited the elevator cab and the elevator doors closed, two large men came from the shadows. One grabbed Lizzy and used his taser gun to subdue her. She was docile within seconds. He handcuffed her and placed a black cloth hood over her head.

The other man grabbed Taylor. Taylor put up a pretty good fight, and he was becoming agitated.

However, her work attire and heels coupled with the element of surprise and his taser put her at a disadvantage. After getting in a couple of good licks, the man was able to taser her, which nearly knocked her unconscious. He was able to handcuff her and place a black hood over her head.

Both of the hooded girls were placed in the trunk of the perpetrators' town car. Off they went. Destination unknown.

While riding in the trunk, both ladies slowly gained consciousness. Lizzy began to panic. Taylor tried to calm her down.

Taylor said, "If they were going to kill us, we would already be dead. They must be taking us someplace to meet their boss."

Lizzy finally calmed down and said, "They must be taking us to Eagle Mountain." Among other improvements, Bobbie built a jail with two jail cells to house anyone who became unruly.

Taylor could not tell exactly which direction they were going, but she presumed from the light traffic that they were heading south and east into the desert. If they were heading north, they would be passing through Riverside towards Pasadena or Los Angeles, and the traffic would be much heavier.

The drive felt like an eternity and was made more intolerable by not knowing where they were going and what their fate would be.

The ladies were kidnapped around 9:30, when their meeting ended. They drove for a long time. Before midnight, the car finally stopped.

The ladies were still in the trunk. Not knowing what else to do with them, Hans and his associate Sully took them to the jail and placed them into one of the cells. Hans and his associate went to the bunk house where they would remain until their morning meeting with Bobbie.

The two ladies would remain in the cell until the morning when, it was presumed, they would meet their kidnapper.

The cells had stone walls on three sides with no windows. Floor to ceiling vertical metal bars ran from one wall to the other. The cells were divided by perpendicular metal bars running from the floor to the ceiling. Each cell had a door, and each cell had a toilet and a small basin in its far corner.

Each cell had a bunk bed along its stone wall.

When they were placed in the cell, Lizzy became unglued. She must have known that her fate would be death. For her to escape death, she would have to recant everything she was prepared to say and vow to leave town forever. And these promises would probably not work.

Taylor was upset, but she tended to keep her emotions bottled up not because she was okay with dying but because she knew that a show of emotion was a sign of weakness which would work against her.

At this point nothing would be happening until morning, which was still eight or nine hours away. For the bad guys, with the witness in their custody, there was nothing pressing anymore. At least from a standpoint of time.

The girls both sat on the lower bunk. They were too keyed up to sleep, as these could be their last hours on earth. They started a conversation.

Lizzy said, "I feel so horrible about all of this. Here, I've dragged you into such a mess, and you might not make it out. You have a husband and a daughter, don't you?"

Taylor replied, "Yes, I have a husband and a daughter, but my office really went out and solicited you to testify."

Lizzy continued, "You are such a nice person and you've been kind and respectful of me when no one else ever has. You probably come from a nice home with great parents who loved you and took care of you, and you are now passing that along to the people you meet. I, on the other hand, had a terrible home life. My father left when I was little. My mother only cared about drugs and when she would be getting high again. She was an escort and turned me out when I was 16. She kept all of the money I made and used it to feed her habit.

"When I was 17, I met Bobbie. Like many such relationships, he offered to take care of me. He would give me drugs, and we'd have sex. He was rough with me. He used to beat me if I said anything. He made me do many horrible things both with him and his friends. I never finished high school. I had no interest in learning anything except how to get my next fix. Like my mother, he only criticized me and told me that I wasn't good enough. He kept me from going to school or learning anything. It was all for him.

"The relationship with Bobbie was nothing but destructive for both of us. I don't know why it even went on.

"By the time that I no longer looked like a teenager, I was totally dependent on him, and that just put more pressure on him and more beat downs for me.

"I've often wondered about this beating women thing. Do men really enjoy that? Somebody must because it seems to exist all over the world. Are men really that self-loathing and insecure that they have to beat up on someone who can't fight back?

"He did finally take pity on me, putting me to work. But what was that work? Driving to Mexico to pick up women with forged papers to work for him as escorts and to pick up drugs. Both of these jobs are so dangerous for the driver and so safe and financially rewarding for the boss that they do not amount to opportunity at all. All for him, all of the time, as usual."

It was Taylor's turn, "Believe it or not, the beginning of my life was not much different than yours. Your speculation that because of the way I am now, I must have come from a loving and economically privileged home. That was certainly not the case.

"I was not born into privilege. I was born on an orange farm. My father left us when I was 10. My mother was a raging alcoholic and could not take care of me or herself.

"By a very young age, I was made to run the farm so support my mother and her habit. Similar to Bobbie, she continually told me that I was not good enough, not pretty enough, and not smart enough to ever amount to anything. All I would ever be able to do would be to run the farm and take care of her. A less than modest life.

"By 17, I would make a little money babysitting for an upwardly mobile family. The little girl was kidnapped. The police made a half-hearted effort to find her. I, being stupid, mounted my own investigation. But the rantings of a teenager from very common circumstances were easy to ignore.

"At 19, I decided to go back to school. I enrolled at Newton Junior College, not too far from the farm. There I met a young professor who was also an attorney with the DA's office and who worked with criminal investigations. He was pretty cute, and all of the girls liked him. I have to confess now that I thought that I could bat my eyes at him, and he would do anything I wanted. I've never told this to anyone, and I will deny it if you do.

"Along with another friend, we set out on a journey to find the kidnapped girl. Working together on the case gave us a reason to be together. He was from a loving family, and boy can you see the difference. It's palpable. Our work together was never about him. It was always about our objective. Though our relationship was never about sex, we did ultimately have it when we went out of town to interview a witness. And it was wonderful. It was kind, gentle, and mutually gratifying. I learned then how to separate the good from the bad.

"He never went down that road where he would be my caretaker. He always encouraged me to make my own decisions, to be my own person, and to have my own successes.

"As I think back on it now, he was fearless. He did not fear losing me if I found out that I didn't need him to survive. He encouraged me to finish school and go to law school.

"He reasoned that if it was really meant to be, we would be together. I think deep down he felt that if you have to do something in order to have a relationship with another person, you really have no relationship at all.

"When I finished school and landed my first job with the State Attorney General, he called and asked me out on a date. I guess at this point he felt he had nothing to lose. Since I finished school and had a job, there was nothing else he could do for me to get me to be with him in that way.

"I hid it pretty well as I hemmed and hawed and finally said yes to a date. We went out finally, and it was a flood. I forgot how much I enjoyed being with him. Now, I could truly see how it felt to be with someone just because we like each other.

"I have to confess, I was pretty cute in those days. Also, I was educated and had a good job. I was quite a catch, if I do say so myself. I had many chances to go out. Many guys came after me. But I always felt that they were playing one angle or another. When he came to me finally, I never had that feeling. He knew the real me, and rather than letting that bother him, he embraced it.

"Eventually, he asked me to marry him, and I said yes. On that day, our most beautiful life together began, and I have never looked back. Izzy was born, and when I see the kind of father he is, I know that I made the right choice. He would die before leaving our daughter or letting anything happen to her, and I mean that literally.

"Throughout our marriage, he has always given me a lot of room. He trusts me, and I think that even if he didn't, he knows that if your partner chooses someone else, that's just the way life is going to go.

"I love spending time at the Indian Reservation. John, the Chief, Chuck, his nephew, and everyone there have been so great with me. They accept Rick and love Izzy like their own. Izzy has learned a great deal about animals and people from the Indians. I have spent years perfecting my riding, animal tending, knife throwing, shooting, fishing, cooking, cleaning, and all of the other things necessary for the Reservation.

"When my daughter was kidnapped, the Indians were the ones that helped me get her back, and for that, I am forever in their debt.

"I just pray that I can get us out of this mess as I would hate to leave my daughter without a mother."

Lizzy said, "That is quite a story. When I hear you tell it, I see the many mistakes I made. I hope that I can get out of here and try to undo them and get on about a productive life. You did it with your background which gives me hope that I can do it with mine."

Lizzy continued, "I heard that you are up for Woman of the Year from National Woman Magazine?"

Taylor replied, "That is correct."

Lizzy said, "That's great."

Taylor responded, "It's really not a big deal. I do handle women's issues at work, so I guess I just outlasted everyone else."

Lizzy said, "You're too modest. Anyway, I hope we can get out of this mess so you can get your award.

Taylor said, "I have no plans on giving up yet."

Chapter 29
Bobbie Franco Has Finally Met His Match

Bobbie was in his office at Eagle Mountain waiting for news about the kidnapping of Lizzy, aka Crystal Covington. Finally, Hans and Scully, the two thugs he sent to kidnap her, showed up at Eagle Mountain. The buildings at Eagle Mountain had been left to look like a ghost town, complete with a dirt road in front of Bobbie's private office.

Hans and Scully entered Bobbie's office.

Bobbie asks Hans, "How did it go?"

Hans replied, "Well, it went okay. I was able to disable the security cameras in the parking garage where we were set to grab her, and the only other cameras were outside attached to other buildings and cannot see into the garage.

Bobbie replied, "Why then was it just okay. What went wrong?"

Hans replied, "Well, in order to grab Crystal, we had to grab the other girl too."

Bobbie asked, "What other girl. There was only one girl set to testify."

Hans replied, "That may be true, but when Crystal showed up, she was with another girl, and to grab her, we had to grab the other girl too.

Bobbie, agitated, asked, "Who is this other girl?"

Hans replied, "I am not 100 percent certain, but I think that she might have been the lawyer questioning her. I could be wrong. She looked so young she might have been a secretary or just someone coming down in the elevator at the same time."

Bobbie said, "You idiot. The whole idea was to grab only Crystal. If she doesn't show up, they will have to dismiss the indictment. We can say that she got cold feet and left town. But there would be no reason for the other girl to disappear, whether she is an attorney, a secretary, or just someone who got off the elevator. Crystal has a plausible reason to disappear, the other girl does not. In fact, the other girl would have every reason to stay to return to her normal life.

"I worked very hard and paid a great deal of money to make it so the Marshals would not be in the parking garage at the time set to grab Crystal. You have ruined my plans. Now I will have to get rid of both of them.

"Go get them and bring them here."

After his dressing-down, Hans took Sully to the jail cell where the ladies were being held. They got the ladies out of the cell, handcuffed them, and marched them across the street to Bobbie's office.

As they crossed the street, they could see that they were standing in the middle of a virtual ghost town, right out of a western movie. The outsides of the buildings appeared in their original condition.

There were several store fronts connected by an elevated wooden sidewalk. There were doors into some of the stores. There were a couple of horses tied up in the street. Taylor presumed that they were used to patrol the surrounding desert, as even off-road vehicles cannot go where horses can.

Hans opened the door to Bobbie's office and led the ladies inside. Bobbie looked them over.

Bobbie said, "Please have a seat. We have some things to discuss."

Lizzy became agitated, "What is the deal with kidnapping me? I worked for you for years, and this is how I'm treated."

Bobbie replied, "Shut your trap bitch. I don't want to hear a peep out of you. You were going to rat me out, and when someone threatens to do that, they magically disappear. In fact, Hans get her out of here. I'll deal with her later."

Hans dragged Crystal out of the office and took her back to her cell. He returned to Bobbie's office.

As Hans returned, Taylor could see that he was carrying a hand gun. It looked like a nine-millimeter Beretta from the outline of the gun that she could see through his jacket. This is a serious gun; he is not playing. His associate, Sully, was sent to the kitchen, leaving only Bobbie and Hans with Taylor. The office is at street level behind a western façade. The street itself is dirt in this location. Two horses were tied up outside of the large window in the front of the office.

Bobbie said, "Where are my manners. Hans, can you please take off the handcuffs?"

Hans briskly unlocked the handcuffs and removed them. He set

157

them on a nearby table.

Bobbie continued, "Please sit and make yourself comfortable."

Taylor replied, "I prefer to stand. I've been either locked in the trunk of a car or sitting in a jail cell for the past several hours. Standing feels good."

Bobbie said, "Okay then stand. So, what is your position in all of this? Are you Crystal's attorney?"

Taylor responded, "No."

Bobbie asked, "Well what were you doing in the parking garage?"

Taylor responded, "Getting my car. I work in the building."

Bobbie asked, "Are you an attorney?"

Taylor replied, "Yes, a prosecutor."

Bobbie said, "You're a liar."

Taylor replied, "Believe what you wish. You're a real tough guy when you're beating up women. Why not be a gentleman and let me fight one of you?"

Bobbie motioned for Hans to move closer to Taylor. He then started to order Hans to restrainer her saying, "Hans, please ..."

Before Bobbie could finish his sentence, Taylor picked up a long chrome letter opener from the desk and stabbed Hans in the neck at his carotid artery. He began to bleed. He needed both hands to try to control the bleeding, which was allowing blood to run down his body.

Bobbie went for the desk drawer where he had a hand gun. Taylor, still holding the letter opener, threw it at him striking him in the neck, also at the carotid artery. He too began to bleed profusely.

Taylor dove through the fixed pane window of Bobbie's office landing on the wooden sidewalk. She then mounted one of the two horses, and took off running.

Instinctively, Bobbie's men took off after her. All of the men stationed at Eagle Mountain joined in the pursuit of Taylor. Most were on horseback, but two were on the ATVs.

She was an expert horse person. She guided her horse through some very rough terrain. She entered Joshua Tree National Park, which is immediately adjacent to Eagle Mountain, taking her poor horse to a rocky area. She vowed to the horse that she would take care of her first chance she had.

She maneuvered Bobbie's men into a clearing in a box canyon surrounded by high vertical rock walls. She came around the back of the rock walls winding up high above the clearing from where she could look down and see them.

She used a long branch to dislodge enough rocks to start a small avalanche which allowed rocks to fall down and block the entrance into the clearing trapping Bobbie's men inside. Bobbie's men would now have to clear the rocks just to get back to Eagle Mountain, which would be without Taylor.

Chapter 30
Taylor's Escape

There was a method to Taylor's madness with respect to her attack on Bobbie and Hans. She reasoned that though both of these idiots were probably asleep during physiology class in high school, they had been in the killing business long enough to know that you did not mess with the carotid artery.

Everyone in the killing business knows that if the injury to the carotid is severe, the injured person needs immediate, professional medical attention. Otherwise, he runs the risk of death by bleeding out or brain damage within minutes.

If the injury to the carotid is not severe, even though the injured person might not bleed out immediately, the repair to the artery would require clamping and stiches. These procedures would require a trained medical professional and a hospital setting.

With an injury to the carotid artery, it is necessary for someone to maintain pressure at the bleeding site with his fingers. It would, of course, be better to have a nurse or medic do this. It is essential that an open airway be established and maintained and that the head be packed with ice. These measures are necessary to prevent brain damage pending the repair.

Taylor reasoned that with the prospect of death or brain damage running through Bobbie's mind, he was likely to be distracted from his efforts to re-capture her. She was, however, only partially correct.

Due to his vast experience, Bobbie was pretty savvy. For gunshot and knife wounds and for run-ins with the local wildlife, Bobbie kept a medic on call, and he could have the medic at his office within minutes. Presuming that the damage was not severe, the medic could have the injured party stabilized and ready for transportation, by helicopter, to the closest hospital, where the injured person would probably make a full recovery.

Though their injuries kept Bobbie and Hans personally out of the hunt for Taylor, Bobbie was still able to have his men pursue her.

If she could not be apprehended by his men, he ordered one of the remaining men to locate her address through Don Green, a local PI, and to send two men there and wait for her. In his mind, he figured that she had no place else to go, other than home. If Taylor made it home, they were instructed to bring her, her husband, and her daughter to Eagle Mountain. If she did not make it home, they were instructed to bring her husband and her daughter.

In his mind, he thought that he would have a little fun with them before killing them as payback for his injuries.

If Taylor was not at home when Bobbie's two men got to her house, Bobbie wanted the search for Taylor to continue on horseback and with the two ATVs until she was caught.

After Bobbie and Hans were taken away by helicopter, Bobbie's men worked to move enough rocks to get out of the clearing in which they were trapped.

Taylor took off riding through the National Park towards Palm Springs and the Reservation.

Bobbie's men did extricate themselves. They returned to Eagle Mountain where they learned that Bobbie and Hans had been taken to a hospital.

Taylor had no money. She was afraid to borrow someone's phone for fear that Bobbie would find the person and punish him or her. As she rode west in the direction of the Reservation, she came upon something that she had not seen for quite a long time, a pay phone.

She dismounted, got some water for the horse, and made a collect call to the Reservation. She announced her name to the operator. Thankfully, the call was accepted by John's assistant. She asked to speak with John. John came on the line.

She said, "Hello, is this John?"

The voice on the other end said, "Yes. And this must be Taylor."

Taylor replied, "How did you know?"

He said, "Because I know your voice, and you are the only person who calls me John."

Taylor said, "I am so sorry to call you with this. I have asked for your help so any times, I hate to ask now."

John replied, "Please let me know what you need."

Taylor said, "I just finished interviewing a witness, and I was walking her downstairs to the parking garage. She was in protective custody, and somehow her protection detail disappeared. I was thinking that maybe they went to a bar for a drink because they cannot drink at the safe house. I should have anticipated that something was wrong, but I figured that they would return to the parking garage.

"When we reached the parking garage and exited from the elevator, we were immediately grabbed. Hoods were placed over our heads, and we were put in the trunk of a car.

"My witness was scheduled to testify against a very bad man known as Bobbie Franco. I presumed that she was kidnapped and that I was taken because I happened to be with her.

"This Bobbie Franco is a gangster involved in trafficking prostitutes, cheap labor, and drugs. My witness was going to offer testimony that would land him in jail for a long time with all of his property being confiscated.

"I presumed that we would be taken to Mr. Franco's compound and kept there until the next day, when we would talk to him. As it turned out, we were taken to his compound and were placed into a cell until the next day. The compound, we came to find out, is located in a place called Eagle Mountain, which is a distance from Palm Springs along the 10 Freeway.

"After being put in the cell at Eagle Mountain, the next morning, we were taken to speak with Mr. Franco. I presume that Mr. Franco felt that the testimony of the witness would be so damming that he had no alternative but to get rid of her, and, because I was there doing my job, I guess he felt that he would have to get rid of me too.

"The next morning, we were brought to Mr. Franco's office. The witness became so agitated that Mr. Franco ordered one of his henchmen to take her back to her cell. I was left alone with Mr. Franco and another of his henchmen, Hans.

"Mr. Franco and I had a truly unpleasant verbal exchange. You can imagine that I was very upset with him and what he intended to do us. This angered Mr. Franco who motioned for Hans to discipline me by, I presume, restraining me or slapping me. Before he could complete his move at me, I picked up a sharp letter opener and stabbed him in the neck at the carotid artery. Hans needed both hands to stop the bleeding.

"Seeing this, Mr. Franco went to his drawer to reach for his gun. I took the letter opener with which I had just stabbed Hans and threw it at Mr. Franco, also hitting him in the carotid.

162

"The fact that Hans and Mr. Franco each needed both of hands to stop the bleeding, gave me enough time to jump through a plate glass window, mount a horse tied up outside, and take off. His men chased me on horseback and with two ATVs. I eluded them, and I guess they went back to their compound. I continued riding and saw a pay phone. As I had no money, I called you collect. I'm sorry."

John said, "Well it sounds like you were able to get out of there. I know that white guys will never catch you on a horse. You're too good a rider. What do you need?"

Taylor said, "Mr. Franco has money so I presume that he will get his needed medical care. In the white world, if you have money, you get the best medical care, even if you're a gangster and have just kidnapped two people.

"But here is my fear. I'm afraid that Mr. Franco will find out where I live and send someone there to get Rick and Izzy and take them to the compound where he might have them killed, even if I surrender.

"I hate to ask for a big favor, but here goes. I was hoping that you could send Chuck and someone else to my house to round up Rick and Izzy and take them to the Reservation. The problem is that if the guys get to my house before Chuck, I don't know what they'll do."

John replied, "No problem. I will have Chuck and Michael go to your house and pick up Rick and Izzy immediately. I am sure that they will get there before Mr. Franco's men as they are just minutes away by horseback. If they encounter anyone from Mr. Franco's organization, I will have Chuck take them out into the desert and lock them in a cave. They will be in a place where they will never be found. We'll keep them alive until this blows over. Who knows, they might learn to like it."

Taylor replied, "Thank you so much John. Now for favor number two. Can I come and stay at the Reservation with Rick and Izzy, just until this mess is cleared up?"

John replied, "Of course you can. We would love to have you."

Taylor has been to the Reservation several times over the years. When she is there, she always cooks and cleans, helps with the animals, helps with the farming, tells stories to the children, teaches the children with Pamela, and does anything and everything for the people living there. As a result, she is encouraged to come back any time she wishes. These are the things about which the Women of the Year Award givers know nothing.

Chapter 31
Getting Rick and Lizzy to the Reservation

C huck and his buddy Michael left for the Miller house immediately on horseback. They had the horses at full gallop, as they wanted to beat anyone there who was sent by Mr. Franco.

They reached the Miller house within minutes. They were coming from higher ground behind the houses which gave them a vista of the area. They saw a town car approaching from a couple of miles away. It appears as of Bobbie Franco's plan was already underway.

Chuck made it to the Millers' front door. He knocked. Rick answered the door.

Chuck said, "Hi Mr. Miller, I'm Chuck from the Indian Reservation."

Rick replied, "I know. We met several times when I went to the Reservation with Taylor. How can I help you?"

Chuck replied, "It seems like Taylor may have gotten into a little trouble. She called my uncle, you know, the Chief, and asked him to send someone here to collect you and Isabel and take you both to the Reservation. It seems that she was kidnapped, and she is afraid that the person who kidnapped her might send someone here to pick up you and your daughter."

Rick replied, "Kidnapped? Where is she now."

Chuck said, "It appears as if she escaped, and she is now riding from Joshua Tree National Park to the Reservation. So, she is safe for now. However, as I said, she is afraid that her kidnapper might send guys to kidnap you and your daughter to get leverage against her."

Rick replied, "I see. And I presume that this kidnapper has something to do with the guy against whom she is trying to get an indictment?"

Chuck replied, "I don't know, but we really need to get you out of here now. If they are coming, they should be here soon."

Rick replied, "Okay. I'll tell Izzy."

Michael, who had been watching the street, came over to tell Chuck that a town car with what appeared to be two men was approaching from the highway. They agreed that a town car looked a little out of place.

Chuck decided to have Rick and Isabel stay inside of the house. Chuck reasoned that if these are the guys that the kidnapper sent, they will try to get into the house. Once they do this, they will know that these are the bad guys, and they will deal with them accordingly.

The town car drove slowly down the street which implied that they were checking addresses to find the Miller house.

They parked on the street in front of the Miller house and got out of their car. They proceeded towards the front door. They were dressed in business suits and looked very out of place in the desert.

When they reached the front door, they were in the entry below the overhanging roof. They each drew a gun.

This was all the Chuck and Michael needed to see. As they drew their guns, they were descended upon by two very pissed off young and strong Indian men. And the Indians beat the ever-loving daylights out of them. Using fighting techniques that these guys had never seen, Michael smacked Sully so hard on the side of his head that his head almost came off of his neck. He then threw him to the ground and stomped his stomach, neck, and head, while the guy was crying out in pain.

Chuck reserved some even more brutal tricks for Steven. He pulled his head backwards so hard that his neck almost snapped. If he had been instructed to kill him, he would be dead. He left just enough of his spinal cord to keep his head on and his legs still usable.

They pulled black cloth hoods down over their heads, tied their hands, and threw them into the trunk of the town car. To keep them from yelling, they were gagged.

At this time, Rick and Isabel came out of the house. Each was carrying a small bag with clothing for an overnight trip.

Chuck told Rick to take himself and Isabel in his car to the Reservation and ask for the Chief. Chuck explained that though they fended off the first two bad guys, others would be coming and that it would be better for everyone if he and Isabel were in a safe place surrounded by friends.

Further, a second group of bad guys would be more skilled, greater in number, and more heavily armed than the first group. The first group of bad guys were not well prepared as they expected their mission to be easy.

Chuck told Rick that by keeping the house vacant, it might appear as if no one was home which might discourage a second kidnapping attempt.

Chuck said that it was important for Rick to drive himself to the Reservation. This would give he and Michael time to hide the car and to make ready the cell in which Sully and Steven would be kept while this matter was being resolved. Also, he did not want Isabel to see the condition of the prisoners or any conduct modifications that might be necessary to keep them in line.

Rick and Isabel took off for the Reservation. The two prisoners remained in the trunk with their hands bound and the hoods pulled down around their heads.

Chuck drove the town car out of the subdivision and onto Highway 111. He turned right onto the turn off road for the Reservation. Along the turn off road, a dirt road extended at nearly a right angle. After a few yards, the dirt road turned towards the mountains. Chuck turned onto the turn off road and then onto the dirt road. He followed the dirt road up towards the foothills of the San Jacinto Mountains.

In a very desolate area out of sight of the highway, the turn off road, and the dirt road, there was a shack about the size of a one-car garage. Chuck got out of the car and unlocked the pad lock on the door, pulled the hasp, and swung the doors open. He drove the town car into the shack.

He started to hear a great deal of pounding from the inside of the trunk and trunk lid; he presumed that the prisoners were getting agitated, particularly since the vehicle was now stopped.

Chuck figured that he would wait for Michael to come with the horses before letting the prisoners out. He did not want to contend with the two of them by himself. A few minutes later Michael came. Though he was on horseback, the distance across the desert was shorter than taking the highway.

Chuck and Michael pulled the prisoners out of the trunk. They were hopping mad, but since they were gagged, whatever it was that they were saying could not be deciphered. They were now standing outside of the barn-like structure still hooded and gagged.

In a fit of empathy, Chuck removed the hoods and gags, thinking they he should give them some water. Instead of being appreciative, they became abusive.

Sully said, "You two idiots have really done it to yourselves now. You have signed your own death warrants. My people will kill you two on site. This is inhuman what you have done to us."

Chuck said, "You two are lucky that we don't kill you where you stand. If it wasn't for my boss, you would both be dead. Firstly, where we are taking you, you will never be found. Your associates might guess that you were taken by two men and that the two men roughly match our description, around 6 feet tall with brown hair, but that describes almost everybody under 35 in the entire valley. Their matching that description to us is not likely.

"As to inhumane, you are the last two people on earth who should be talking about inhumane. You are sent to someone's home to kidnap her husband and her 10-year old daughter and then deliver them to your boss who will certainly kill them. Killing another man in a fair fight is one thing, but killing a 10-year old child, particularly a female child, is so far beyond the bounds of decency that you cannot even be referred to as human.

"As I said before, if it was up to me, you would be dead already, and it would have been a long and painful death. For reasons I do not understand, my boss wants you kept alive, and for this reason alone, you are still alive. And rest assured that if you make your confinement difficult for us, I will go against my bosses' orders, and I will kill the both of you.

"You white people are all the same. When you are dishing out pain, everything is fine. But when you are receiving pain, the person inflicting that pain is a monster. So, shut your mouths because if you irritate me, I will kill you. Trust me on that."

Sully and Steven were beginning to grasp Chuck's seriousness.

Chuck and Michael tied ropes around Sully's and Steven's ankles just long enough for a normal stride. They bound their hands behind their backs. They fastened ropes around their necks so that the two would be connected together. They ran a pull rope from the rope between them. They gagged both of them, partially for their own protection, as Chuck was disappointed that he could not just kill them.

Chuck and Michael mounted the two horses. Chuck took hold of the pull rope and pulled Sully and Steven along behind his horse.

Chuck said to Sully and Steven, "The two of you will be walking from here."

Knowing that they would be curious about where they would be walking and knowing that they could not ask in their present gagged state, Chuck said to the two of them, "In case you are curious, we will be walking to your new home, a jail cell in a mountain unknown to everyone in the world except me, Michael, and my boss, oh, and now you."

Their caravan continued up into the mountains. The path was quite steep and difficult to navigate, except for experienced hikers and expert horsemen. The horses led the way, and Sully and Steven were pulled by the rope around their necks along the path.

As they reached the higher level in the mountains, the terrain became too steep and difficult for the horses. They tied up the horses and continued on foot with Chuck and Michael leading the way. They finally reached their destination, an opening into a cave in the mountain.

They directed Sully and Steven into the cave. There were several empty buckets in the back of the cave along with some blankets. While Chuck shackled both prisoners to the back wall of the cave, Michael filled 6 buckets with water from the nearby creek and two buckets with beef jerky, grains, and fruit. Michael placed the buckets inside of the cave.

The front opening of the cave had one inch in diameter steel bars with an entry door. The bars were embedded deeply into the rock of the cave's opening. Chuck and Michael exited from the cave and locked its door behind them.

Chuck announced to Sully and Steven, "Welcome to your new home. We have left you with water, some food, and blankets. You will stay here until the situation with your boss is resolved. Getting out will be impossible. The locks cannot be cut with bolt cutters. If someone should try to pull the bars out of the cave's opening, the entire mountain will fall into the cave, killing anyone in the area. Someone will be back to refill your water and food supply. If an attempt is made to escape, you will both be killed. We will be leaving.

Chuck and Michael hiked down the hill to their horses. They rode across the desert to the Reservation.

Chapter 32
Holding Up at the Reservation

By the time Chuck and Michael returned to the Reservation, Rick and Isabel had already arrived in Rick's car, and Taylor had arrived by horseback after her escape from Franco's compound.

When Taylor arrived, she took her horse to the barn and gave her a good rubdown, something the horse never had before. She then walked over to the main building where Rick, Isabel, and the Chief were meeting.

Rick moved out to greet her. They embraced. Rick said, "Honey, it's so great to see you. Are you alright. How did you get away from those people?"

Taylor replied, "It's kind of a long story, but the short version is that I stabbed Franco's henchman with a letter opener and then threw it at Franco. Those knife throwing lessons here at the Reservation really came in handy. I then commandeered a horse and rode across Joshua Tree National Park to get here.

"I knew that Franco would send guys to go after you and Izzy, so I asked John to send Chuck and a friend to meet them and to ask you to come here."

By this time, Chuck and Michael had arrived and taken their horses to the barn. They exited the barn and came over to join the group in front of the main building.

Taylor asked Chuck, "Did Franco send his men to my house?"

Chuck replied, "He certainly did."

Taylor asked, "What happened to them?"

Chuck replied, "We had a little fun with them and then took them to a cave in the mountains where we left them for now."

Taylor responded, "Good. Neither of you appears to have gotten hurt."

Chuck replied, "No. We're fine."

The Chief stepped in, "That is all well and good. Now we need to figure out where we go from here. Let's adjourn to the mess hall."

Taylor, Rick, Isabel, the Chief, Chuck, and Michael walked to the mess hall, entered, and sat down around one of the tables.

The Chief asked one of the elder women to take Izzy over to the office and give her a couple of things with which to play. He did not want to expose her to the plans he had for Mr. Franco and his men.

Once everyone was seated and Izzy was out of the room, the Chief began:

"I believe that it would be in our best interest to move quickly. From what I understand, Taylor's witness is in Mr. Franco's custody. I believe you said you were both in a jail cell. I presume that she was returned there at the time of your escape. As her testimony is essential, we presume that the indictment proceeding will be postponed until she can be recovered and made ready to participate.

"The fact that she is probably still at Eagle Mountain is good for us. The topography and the dirt roads will work to our advantage with the horses.

"I would propose that we gather a group of braves, ride out to Eagle Mountain, and take out Mr. Franco's men one by one. We will use arrows and knifes dipped in curare to render them unable to fight back once hit.

"After we have taken out all of the men, we will remove the witness from the cell, and place the unconscious men in the two cells. I understand that there are two cells.

"We will then return the witness here to the Reservation where she can stay pending her testimony."

Directing his comments to Taylor, the Chief continued, "As to the indictment, because of your personal involvement, you might not be able to pursue it yourself. So, you will have to search your soul to determine whether there is anyone in your organization that you trust enough to bring this case to the grand jury in a capable manner. I'm afraid that I won't be able to help you with that decision. I'll leave that to you and Rick.

"After the hearing date for the indictment is set, we will have to figure out a way to get the witness to the hearing without getting her killed in the process. I believe that I will enlist my braves as her escort, as I am a little wary of white people, particularly where money is concerned, as money seems to be the thing that most drives them. I tend to trust those who are driven by loyalty rather than money. I cannot depend on white people to be loyal if they are offered the right amount of money."

Taylor jumped in, "I agree with your plan completely. I really see no other way. I don't know what the status is of Franco himself. I know that he and his main henchman needed medical attention, but I presume that by now they are back in action."

Taylor continued, "While we are riding to Franco's compound, I thought Rick's services could be used to see what property Franco owns. With the RICO proceeding pending, we can go after all of his businesses, both illegitimate and legitimate. He might not even own Eagle Mountain.

The Chief put out the call for braves, and 15 showed up. Chuck and Michael could not wait to go. And Taylor herself would make an even 18.

Rick asked Taylor, "Are you going with the braves?"

Taylor replied, "You bet."

Rick asked, "Isn't that a little dangerous?"

Taylor replied, "Everything in life is dangerous. But things are made more dangerous by not shutting down bad guys before they have a chance to do more damage. Besides, I am the only one who knows where everything is located in the town, so I have to go."

Rick conceded, "Okay then."

Rick was not surprised. As well as he knew Taylor after all of these years, he still expects the improbable.

Chapter 33
The Ride to Eagle Mountain

T o prepare for the ride to Eagle Mountain, Taylor asked the Chief if she could borrow some clothes. Even though the Chief's wife had passed away years ago, she somehow knew that he would still have some of her things. She knew when she dressed as an Indian before rescuing Izzy from her kidnappers, the Chief looked at her and said that she reminded him of his late wife. She knew that a man such as he, with his depth of character, would be with someone for life, and that would be that.

The Chief was a little bit in love with Taylor, and why not. She was everything, beautiful, smart, courageous, a great mother, and a great companion. To him, regrettably, she was a cross between the wife he lost entirely too early and the daughter he was never able to have.

He was so kind and patient with Izzy that it took all of her strength to hold back the tears when they were together. He was teaching her how to care for the animals, work at the ranch, and to accept people not for what they have but for what they are. The grandfather she always wished Izzy could have.

The braves assembled. They dipped arrow heads and knives in curare to make them ready for the impending fight.

When Taylor came out, she was so beautiful, but she was also unrecognizable. You could almost feel the pain in the Chief's eyes when he saw her. The pain of great loss and unrealized possibilities. But he masked it well. He knew that he had to go with it to survive.

15 braves, Chuck and Michael, and Taylor rode off in the direction of Eagle Mountain. They crossed the highway and turned northeast towards their destination.

It would be a nearly two-hour ride, but by using the horses, they did not alert the other side that they were coming. This would give them the opportunity to capture 75 percent of the enemy before the others knew that they were in the fight of their lives.

They tied up the horses and set out on foot. Some would circle around to the northeast towards the other side of the ghost town. Some would drop down to the southeast to flank. Some would pursue directly east into the heart of the town, where most of the people would be located.

After Taylor's escape, Franco greatly fortified the town with additional manpower. Instead of the few people he once had, he now had 20. 5 were on guard duty on the northeast. 5 were on guard duty on the southeast. And 10 were left in the town itself.

On the northeast, 5 braves synchronized their arrow shooting to strike all 5 guards at precisely the same time. In this way, none of them could warn the others. The 5 guards were knocked unconscious by the poison arrows. They were tied up and placed in a shed located just outside of the town.

The same tactic was attempted on the southwest. 2 of the guards were struck with arrows and were rendered unconscious. Of the other three guards, one engaged one of the braves in a hand to hand test, which the brave won. The other 2 were struck with thrown knives and became unconscious. These 5 were tied up and placed in the shed.

The remaining 10 men heard the commotion and moved to the center of town to prepare for an attack. This group had the advantage of being able to use the town's buildings as cover. This group included Mr. Franco and Hans.

Hans, who was not having very good luck with knives this week, took a knife blow to his thigh. This was not good but was better than the stab to the carotid that he received from Taylor the day before. He went down and became unconscious.

Chuck and Michael squared off against two of the bad guys. Unfortunately for the bad guys, they were no match for them. They took a savage beating before being tied up and put into an empty room in the building which housed Franco's office. Hans was brought to this room which made a total of three guards, leaving 7 guards, including Franco.

Taylor was just outside of the town. Her hours of practice with a bow and arrow was going to be tested. She kept out of sight, particularly out of the site of Franco, as identifying her might interfere with her ability to pursue the indictment or cause the indictment to be dismissed.

The standard for dismissal of an indictment is extremely high.

Dismissal is appropriate only if it is established that the violation substantially influenced the grand jury's decision to indict. The defendant must prove actual prejudice. The participation of a prosecutor in the recovery of a witness from imprisonment by the defendant would surely be a case of first impression, but Taylor reasoned that because her involvement might affect the government's ability to prosecute Franco, she would back out, using her significant personal involvement as a kidnap victim as a reason.

Taylor was able to work her way around the side of the town where she could not be seen by Franco. She spotted two of his men concealing themselves from the other direction. Using her bow and arrow and the quick release firing she practiced for so many hours from horseback, she got off two shots which struck each of Franco's men in the upper thigh. They both went down and were taken to the storage room.

This left four guards and Franco. They were in his office in the main building.

Taylor found Chuck and Michael on the outskirts of town. She said to Chuck, "I think it's time to get the witness from the jail. Do you think that the braves can handle Franco and his four guards?"

Chuck replied, "Yes."

Taylor said, "The jail is across the street from Franco's office. We can get in around back so we won't be seen."

Chuck replied, "There's no need for you to come with us. It will be dangerous as the braves and Franco will be locked in a cross fire."

Taylor said, "Don't worry about me. Besides, I know where the keys are hidden. Also, if she sees me, she will not get as hysterical as she might if she thinks that she is just being kidnapped again by someone else."

Chuck replied, "I see your point."

Taylor, Chuck, and Michael circled around the back of the jail building and entered through a door that was not visible from Franco's vantage point. When Crystal saw her, she looked relieved.

Crystal said, "I didn't think that anyone would come looking for me. The law enforcement in this town is probably on Franco's payroll, and the attorneys are not much better."

Taylor went into the desk and removed the false bottom to reveal the keys. She opened the cell door, and Crystal followed.

Taylor said, "We need to go out this door and move to the rear of

174

the building. Franco is held up in his office across the street which is the other direction. We want him to think that he still has you locked up and under his control."

They moved outside and then to the rear. They moved to the outskirts of town where they could sit and watch the raging battle. At this point, the braves took Franco's office. Franco and four of his men remained. The braves rendered two of the four remaining men unconscious.

They then captured Franco and his last two men and took them to the jail and placed them in one of the two cells.

The other braves carried all of Franco's remaining unconscious men from the storage room to the jail and placed them in the cells.

This left Franco and all of his men locked up. Some were unconscious and some were not.

Chuck, who was the un-appointed leader of the braves, left Taylor, Michael, and Crystal and went to the jail.

Franco was livid. He screamed at Chuck, "I am going to kill each and every one of you Indians. I demand to know what you intend to do with us."

Chuck replied, "I will let law enforcement know where you are. I presume that they will come and get you out."

Franco yelled, "Where is the girl?"

Chuck replied, "Do you mean the girl that you kidnapped and held here as your prisoner or the little girl you sent your two goons to kill?"

Franco screamed, "Very funny. You know who I am talking about. The girl that was being held here in this cell."

Chuck replied, "Oh her, she is going with us. We will look after her until she testifies against you."

Franco was now out of his mind with anger. All of the work and planning he went through to kidnap the witness against him and to keep her from testifying was up in smoke. If she was merely returned to the Federal Marshals, he could just buy them off and get her back. But she was now going to be under the protection of the Indians. That was a different matter. They were not driven by money. No, they answered to a higher authority, duty and honor, two things about which Franco knew nothing.

Chapter 34
Return to the Reservation

Taylor, Chuck, and Crystal made their way back to the Reservation where the Chief and Rick waited impatiently.

Michael and the other braves left like the wind: You will never know exactly when they will appear, and you will never know exactly when they leave. Taylor barely had a chance to thank them.

Rick was very happy to see that Taylor made it back safely. He asked, "How did it go?"

Taylor answered, "It was difficult, but we were able to get Crystal back, and we will be able to look after her until she testifies."

Crystal, who was close by, referring to Taylor said, "She was really something over there. You should be very proud of her?"

Rick replied, "I'm proud of everything she does not only as an attorney and law enforcement helper but all that she does for me as my wife and for Isabel as her mother. Those are the important things to me."

Crystal said, "Yes. You are a lucky man. And she says that she is lucky to have you. Guess you are both lucky. I hope I have some of that luck one day."

Rick replied, "Maybe all of this will bring you closer to that objective. We all need to remember that choices have consequences. Taylor chose me, sort of a plain vanilla guy, when she could have had anyone she wanted."

Crystal said, "Don't sell yourself short. You're a great guy. But the choices I made in that department were not very good, and I have paid dearly for them, which almost included death."

Rick directing his question to Taylor asked, "And how about your case?"

Taylor replied, "Obviously, I will not be able to handle the RICO case against Franco for several reasons. Firstly, because an indictment is a one-sided affair where, in most circumstances, only the prosecution will be presenting evidence, the prosecution is held to a different standard than in a trial. The prosecutor is held to a standard where he or she is providing justice.

"Further, I will now be a witness to Crystal's kidnapping, as I was kidnapped too. I will have both criminal and civil kidnapping cases."

"We won't even have to test the prejudicial standard. We'll just let someone else handle it. Now, we will have to choose that person carefully, as we still do not know who the mole is in our office."

Rick asked, "You have a mole?"

Taylor replied, "We must because someone knew that I would be interviewing Crystal at the office on a particular day and at a particular time. This knowledge would be necessary to disable the cameras and have the car and hoods ready at the precise time and place necessary to carry out the kidnapping. They would also need to know at what time the Marshals would go on break, that is, presuming that the Marshals were not incompetent, complicit, paid off, or all three."

Rick asked, "Do you have any idea who the mole might be?"

Taylor replied, "Besides me, only my boss, Mr. Drake, knew when and where the interview would take place. I may have said something to Sharon, a new hire and my friend at the office, which means that she may have known. Unknown to me at the time, Sharon was sleeping with Rob, so Rob may have found out. Rob was set to have this case and some other important cases before I came along, so he may have a personal motive in addition to receiving money. Also, Rob seems to spend more money than he makes. It would not surprise me that he was selling information. This is why we need to keep Crystal here at the Reservation.

"The good thing about the RICO case is that it will allow the government to, in a manner of speaking, confiscate all of Franco's businesses, both illegitimate and legitimate, in addition to attaching his assets pre-trial. This I believe was the reason he was so set on blocking the indictment by kidnapping Crystal, the star witness.

"With Crystal's testimony, the indictment will probably go through, and the U S Attorney can seek a pre-trial restraining order or injunction to seize Franco's assets and to prevent the transfer of property before the trial.

177

Chapter 35
The Indictment

Taylor decided that among the various people at her office, she would choose to trust her boss, Mr. Drake. Sharon was young, and though educated, she was not very smart in the ways of the world. Her impression of Rob was that at best he was a low-level hustler and at worst a felon selling information. She thought that she might find out one day, but that day was not today.

She arranged with Mr. Drake to meet him at the Grand Jury hearing with Crystal. She would be escorted by the Marshal, whose work protecting Crystal had not been very good so far.

She also arranged a shadow escort by the Indians. She was later asked whether she should be criticized for having an Indian escort. She replied that if an attempt were made to kidnap Crystal, the Indians would prevent it. Otherwise, you will never know that they were there. The Indians are like the wind, you never know that they are watching.

Mr. Drake did a masterful job with the indictment. Crystal gave her testimony as she had practiced it with Taylor.

The grand jury issued an indictment against the defendants for sex trafficking, labor trafficking, drug trafficking, slavery, embezzlement, and money laundering. Our office, the prosecutor, drafted the indictment listing the charges we would file. The grand jury agreed, and the final version of the indictment or the "true bill" was handed over to the court.

The indictment is the formal legal document charging an individual with a crime. After the indictment, the defendant is arraigned. The arraignment is a court hearing in which the indictment is presented to the court, and the defendant pleads to the charges. An indictment does not require a plea. However, an arraignment does, and it ushers in a steady march towards trial.

At the arraignment hearing, a defendant may plead guilty. Sentencing would then follow. If he pleads not guilty, which is usually the case, the defendant may either be placed in custody, remain in custody, or remain not in custody pending a bail decision at the arraignment or at a bail hearing. A defendant is entitled to a trial within 70 days of the indictment.

Franco and the other defendants pleaded not guilty, and bail was arranged for all three of them, pending the trial.

Mr. Drake moved swiftly to tie-up Franco's property and prevent property from being transferred before it could be seized, if the U S won at trial.

Taylor and Mr. Drake met after the arraignment.

Taylor asked, "Did everything go okay at the indictment and arraignment?"

Mr. Drake replied, "Yes. Franco seemed to have cooled down a bit, probably at the stern advise of his attorney. I really think you did the right thing handing this case back to me. You really push his buttons, maybe a little too much."

Taylor replied, "That is true."

Mr. Drake said, "Even though Franco has been indicted and is now pending trial on the RICO charges, I worry about your safety. This guy is a real loose cannon, and he could do or order to have something done that could create a dangerous situation for you."

Taylor replied, "I know. But I don't know what I can do about it. To get away from him, I would have to move far away, change my name, and get a different job, and so would my husband. It's really unfair to everyone."

Mr. Drake said, "Even locking the guy up does not guarantee anything. He can reach out from the darkest corners of jail and get to just about anybody."

Taylor ended the conversation with, "Too true."

Chapter 36
The After Effect

The indictment was in, the arraignment was over, and the RICO case was marching towards trial. Taylor and Rick thought that they were in the clear and could get back to their normal lives. They even moved from the Reservation to their home, with Isabel.

But it was not to be.

Taylor and Rick each returned to his or her respective job hoping to get back to business as usual closing out their chapter with Bobbie Franco.

Just after lunch, Taylor was in a meeting with Mr. Drake to talk about some of the pending cases. Mr. Drake's intercom buzzed. It was Margo, Taylor's secretary.

Margo spoke with Mr. Drake over the intercom, "Mr. Drake, is Taylor with you?"

Mr. Drake responded, "Yes, she is."

Margo asked, "May I speak with her? Her husband is on the phone, and he says that it is quite urgent that he speak with her."

Margo connected Rick to Mr. Drake's phone line.

Mr. Drake handed the phone to Taylor, she said, "This is Taylor Shaw, how may I help you?"

Taylor heard Rick's voice. Rick said, "Hi honey, it's me. We need to talk."

Taylor replied, "Honey, I'm in a meeting with my boss, can it wait?"

Rick said, "No. And he should also hear what I have to say. If there is no one else in the room, can you put this call on speaker?"

Taylor asked Mr. Drake to put the call on speaker, which he did.

Rick asked over the speaker, "I'm afraid I have some bad news for both of you. I would prefer to tell you both in person, unless Mr. Drake is absolutely certain that this phone is secure."

Mr. Drake said, "I am only fairly certain that the phone is secure.

Maybe we should meet."

Rick responded, "Good idea. Can we meet at the Café Four down the street? I am sort of in the area and could be there in 10 minutes."

Mr. Drake replied, "We will see you there then."

Mr. Drake and Taylor left the suite and headed downstairs in the elevator. They exited the building and made their way, on foot, to the Café. About 10 minutes later, Mr. Drake, Taylor, and Rick all met. They were shown to a table on the outside patio.

Once seated, Mr. Drake asked what was so important that it could not be shared over a phone line.

Rick responded, "One of my friends in the police department told me today that one of his confidential informants told him that Mr. Franco is very upset with your office, and with Taylor in particular, for the efforts made in the RICO case against him. He says he also has a scar where she threw the letter opener at his throat and that the blade grazed his vocal cords leaving him with a slight speech impediment. The informant said that he has a plan to take Taylor out. As a side benefit, she will not be able to testify against him if she presses kidnapping or assault charges in State court. His lawyer has already told him that State charges could be filed and prosecuted against him even though he is under indictment for federal charges and that a civil case is available to her."

Taylor said, jokingly, "I guess I'll have to scratch him off of my dance card. Shucks."

Rick was not amused and said, "This is serious business. I've been with the DA for almost 25 years, and in that time, you get in pretty tight with the police who make the arrests, and you come to appreciate the information that they gather from their many sources. I'm just glad he told me."

Mr. Drake asked, "Do you have any ideas?"

Rick said, "My plan would be to put someone in his inner circle with a wire. At least in this way we can find out when and where his attempt will be made."

Mr. Drake replied, "We have been trying to get someone into his inner circle for years, but he has been too smart."

Taylor said, "It's funny, we have been trying to get someone into his inner circle but have been unsuccessful while he appears to have successfully gotten someone into ours. There is no way that Franco knew that Crystal would be having a meeting with the U S Attorney and that she would be finished and in the parking garage at the precise time necessary for his men to grab her, and me too for that matter. They seem to be better at dirty tricks than we are."

Rick asked, "Who was the mole in your department?"

Mr. Drake replied, "We still don't know. But, as Taylor says, they must have had one to pull off the kidnaping."

Taylor said, "I have my opinion."

Mr. Drake asked, "And what is your opinion."

Taylor replied, "No offense, but I think it is Rob."

Mr. Drake replied, "Rob? How did you get that idea?"

Taylor replied, "Only two people knew the time and place of the interview with Crystal, you and me. I know that you believe that Rob is your friend and that you feel as if you can trust him. I feel the same about Sharon because she is my friend.

"If we are willing to be honest with ourselves, I confess that I may have said something to Sharon, as we talk all of the time about many things, including our schedules. However, even by Franco's standards, Sharon would appear to be too new and too green to have any really worthwhile information.

"It would be more likely that Franco would be seek out someone in our office who is a little more savvy, fast cars, flashy clothes. Someone who appears to be spending more than he has; someone buying things that he cannot afford for from his salary. For Rob, this would be the perfect side hustle, selling information to criminals about criminal prosecutions, the very information he has anyway.

"Franco is no genius, but he knows the soft spots. Also, he knows that Rob, unlike Sharon, has been around long enough to be in the inner circle in our office. He also knows that Rob's advancement through normal channels will be long and arduous, particularly since I joined the department. When Franco heard that someone would be coming in above Rob, he knew that Rob would be desperate and vulnerable to the suggestion of impropriety.

"Rob is more enlightened about all things criminal than Sharon. Rob has been around long enough to gain some real inside information. Sharon has not. Rob is cocky and would be the type of guy who would be a pretty good fit with a gangster. Sharon, on the other hand, would not know where to begin.

"Now, I cannot rule out the possibility that Sharon learned the information and passed it along to Rob as talk among people who are

182

romantically involved. I think they call that 'pillow talk.' This seem to me to be more likely, unless Rob learned something directly, which I doubt."

Mr. Drake replied, "If this is true, it is a really terrible thought. Rob has been with the office a long time. He has worked his way up to second in command. I rely on him for administrative help. I cannot burden someone with your skills with such pedestrian tasks. I need you to be investigating and trying cases. It's going to be difficult to run the office when I can't talk to Rob about everything. I mean Rob would have been my first choice as someone to infiltrate Franco's operation. Guess that will not be happening."

Taylor said, "Frankly, finding anyone on our end to infiltrate a gangster's operation would probably not be possible. It would be way too dangerous, and we might spend the rest of our lives making up back stories. Perhaps we should rely on the police for police work."

Rick chimed in, "I agree with that. Undercover work tears people apart."

Mr. Drake said, "I guess for the time being I will be a little more careful about the information I share with everyone at the office, particularly Rob. Ben, Lisa, and Howard, the new hires, don't get inside information anyway. I hope Rick that you can put in a word with the police to watch Franco to see if he has anything planned. I'm thinking that under RICO he will probably get his 20 years, but even from prison, he will be running his operation.

"His trial should be coming along shortly as he has a right to a trial within 70 days of his indictment. Hopefully, he will be so busy with his own case between now and his trial that he won't be an immediate concern with respect to Taylor, but she will have to be vigilant. We might want to assign a small detail to her, at least for a while."

Taylor said, "Even I think that might be a good idea, and I never like anything even remotely like that."

Chapter 37
Returning to Work

After the indictment and arraignment, Taylor and Rick returned to work. Taylor had a small protective detail that watched after her when she was at the office and at night when she was home. Bobbie Franco was so busy with his trial that she was not in the forefront of his mind at this time. Besides, he knew that he would have plenty of time to deal with her later.

The U S Attorney fought to tie-up Franco's businesses, both legitimate and illegitimate, as was allowed under the RICO laws. This made Franco scramble to obtain money for his own defense. As encumbered as he was, with his vast criminal skills and resources, he was able to get around some of the government's road blocks and get his hands on enough to pay at least part of what would become significant legal fees. (His lawyers were convinced that even with a RICO conviction, he would be able to raise enough money to pay them.)

The work at the office was different. Prior to the kidnapping of Taylor, the atmosphere at the office was collegial and friendly. After the kidnapping, things became much more serious.

As a mole was suspected, Mr. Drake was much more guarded. Before the kidnapping, he shared information readily with co-workers. Now, he imparted only the information absolutely necessary for the handling of the case.

Also, there was much less socializing among the staff. Sharon and Rob continued their romance without much interruption. Taylor remained friendly with Sharon, and Sharon continued to confide in Taylor. The personal aspect of their relationship remained about the same, but the business aspect diminished. This was too bad for Sharon, as she could learn much from Taylor.

The fact that Pamela took a leave of absence to have her baby worked out to be good timing. One less person to worry about.

Taylor remained friendly with Mr. Drake and was fairly certain that he did nothing intentional to harm her. However, she continued to dislike Rob and was very suspicious of him and what she perceived to be his agenda.

Ben, Lisa, and Howard, the new hires, were essentially out of the loop, but it had been that way from the beginning.

Chapter 38
Rob and Sharon's Budding Relationship

Even after the kidnapping, the relationship between Rob and Sharon continued on an upwards trajectory.

As a girl smitten, Sharon would never believe that Rob would give out confidential information to the other side, particularly information that could get someone kidnapped or killed. She was pretty naïve.

Though Rob acted as if he had legitimate feelings for Sharon, he really did not. This made it easy for him to manipulate the situation. This made it easy for him to convince her that he would never do anything against the interests of the Office, even while he was doing just that.

Rob and Sharon arranged to meet at Café Four. They clearly were not concerned that they would be seen by someone from the office as the Café was very close.

They were taken to a table inside in the back. Sharon was dressed in a navy-blue business suit with a skirt down to her knees and low black pumps. Rob was dressed in a light grey suit with no tie accessorized with a gold chain, gold bracelet, two gold rings, very expensive Cole Hahn shoes, and a gold Rolex watch. The watch alone would be about two month's salary.

As Sharon moved in front of her chair, Rob moved behind it to guide the chair to the table. Rob sat on the side of the table next to her.

They exchanged pleasantries, water and menus were brought to the table, and they settled in for some conversation.

Rob asked, "How are you doing since all of the commotion? I know that you and Taylor are close, so you must have been worried, at least more worried than some of us?"

Sharon asked, "What does that mean?"

Rob replied, "Most people in the office don't like Taylor."

Sharon replied, "You mean that you don't like her. She has been great to me. She is very supportive and helps me out whenever she can, expecting nothing in return."

Rob replied, "She came in much later and took the best cases."

Sharon said, "Yes she came in later, but she did not take the best cases; they, like all cases in the office, were assigned to her by our boss."

Rob replied, "But why her?"

Sharon said, "If you are implying that she offered something to Mr. Drake for those cases, you would be wrong. She's not like that. She doesn't have to be. She doesn't have to offer or hold out the possibility of sex to get what she wants.

"Rob, I think you are, or at least could be, a great lawyer, but, in point of fact, she is a better lawyer than you, and that is why she gets the cases she gets."

Rob interjected, "I have a side gig which will make me more money than she will ever see at this office."

Sharon replied, "I don't doubt it. Your clothes, accessories, car, and apartment are all more than you could afford on your salary. So good for you. As long as it is legal and no one gets hurt, the more power to you. But your side hustle is not going to change things at the office unless you think you can bribe Mr. Drake with money."

Rob said, "No, I don't think that."

Sharon said, "Let's drop it then and get about eating and making small talk. We will just have to agree to disagree about Taylor. I like her. You don't. No big thing."

Rob said, "You're right as usual. Let's drop it."

What started out as a brawl settled into business as usual. It appears as if the relationship meant more to Sharon than going all of the way to the mat for Taylor, which Rob probably did not want anyway.

Even though Rob hated Taylor, he needed his close connection with Sharon to get confidential information that only Taylor has. It worked before when Taylor let slip to Sharon when and where the interview of the witness would take place.

Rob was in some ways disappointed in himself that he expressed to Sharon how he felt about Taylor. But on the other hand, since everyone already knew how he felt to pretend differently would look silly.

Rob and Sharon finished their nice meal and went on their separate ways. Sharon would come over to Rob's place later for the sex she apparently so desperately needed from him; the tool he used to keep her off balance and willing to talk about things that she learned around the office, including what she learned from Taylor.

Chapter 39
Taylor and Rick Before the RICO Trial

Rick was the one thing constant in Taylor's life. Ever since she met him as a 19-year old farm girl, he has always been there for her. With the birth of their child, he showed again the kind of man he was. He was so loving and nurturing. She thanked her lucky stars every day that she passed on the bad boys and went straight to a man.

She had a little glitch when it came to Chuck, call it a girl's version of a mid-life crisis. She was infatuated by his physicality, but Rick never even suspected anything. In fact, Rick thought that she barely knew Chuck. Pamela never mentioned any of her discussions on the subject with anyone. Hard to say whether this was because she liked and respected Taylor so much or whether she felt that she won out in the end, even if by default, so why dwell on it.

After her kidnapping, in addition to her regular work and her protection detail, she had to begin preparing for her acceptance speech for her Woman of the Year award, which was only a short time away.

She had her last meeting with Marlene which was postponed because of the kidnapping. They spoke on the telephone and decided that Marlene really had no more questions for Taylor, but that she would like to see a copy of her speech before she gives it, if that would be possible. Taylor agreed.

Taylor and Rick decided to take a two weeks' vacation with Izzy in San Diego. It was hot in Palm Springs, and San Diego, being next to the ocean, would be a welcome relief.

They opted to take the 74 from Palm Desert, through the mountains, to San Juan Capistrano. From San Juan Capistrano, they took the 5, along the coast, south to Del Mar. The hotel is in Del Mar. It has a beautiful pool, a small gym, two tennis courts, a couple of restaurants, and is a short walk, down to the beach.

They arrived, parked, checked in, and were taken to their room. A roll-away bed was arranged for Izzy.

They put their bags away and headed for the beach. They went down the path, past the duck pond, to the stairs, past the now defunct train station, across the street, across a large grass area, down another path, and onto the sand.

They took off their shoes, walked along the edge of the water, and felt the cool breeze. They returned to their room, got cleaned up for dinner, and walked down to a restaurant that was at the water's edge below their building.

Izzy was worn out from all of the excitement. Taylor and Rick were alone.

Rick asked, "Are you sure you still want to go through with this very public speech for the Woman of the Year Award? You understand that putting yourself in front of a large audience like that could be very dangerous?"

Taylor replied, "Yes, I understand the risks, but I still think that doing it outweighs not doing it. What kind of woman, or person for that matter, would I be if I chickened out whenever the situation appeared as if it could be dangerous?

Rick responded, "No one would call you a chicken for not voluntarily putting yourself in the line of fire."

Taylor replied, "Maybe not; but it's not for me."

Rick and Taylor spent two glorious weeks in Del Mar enjoying the sand, the surf, the pools, and Izzy. They took day trips to the zoo and Sea World. They went into downtown San Diego and the Gas Light District. They visited Point Loma. They went down the coast and visited La Jolla. Taylor even did a little shopping.

They went out onto Coronado and had lunch at the Hotel Del Coronado, the backdrop used for the famous movie Some Like It Hot.

They went north up the coast to Solano Beach and inland from there to Fairbanks Ranch and Rancho Santa Fe. The stopped at the race track in north Del Mar. They continued north as far as Carlsbad.

During the two weeks, Rick tried several times, and in several ways, to convince Taylor to not give a speech in such a public place where everyone in the world would know her whereabouts. He failed miserably.

He finally played his last card when he said, "Okay. I understand that you are bound and determined to give this speech. I will be good with it on one condition."

Taylor asked, "And what would that one condition be?"

Rick replied, "Before you positively decide to give the speech, we take the Chief to the location, and if he feels that you can be protected, I will be okay with it."

Taylor replied, "What kind of deal is that?"

Rick replied, "We both trust the Chief, don't we? If he says it is too unsafe, I think you should give the speech in another place or in another way, perhaps video."

Taylor answered, "Okay. We will take John to the location. If he is against it, we will have to make other arrangements, but those arrangements will have to be made with the awards committee and the magazine. I am not really in control, regardless of what John says. Of course, if John is good with it, it will be all systems go."

This was the best that Rick could do in a discussion with his wife.

They went back to their room. They had one more night left. They went down to the beach to their restaurant. They sat and watched the ocean as the food was served and consumed. It was sunset, and the ocean looked very beautiful.

After dinner, they took one more-short walk around the beach and the hotel property. It was such a beautiful place that they hated to leave, as they would be leaving the cool breezes of the ocean and returning to the desert heat. Taylor wondered if they could ever transfer their jobs and move to a place like this.

They returned to their room, put Izzy to bed, and went out onto their private balcony to take a last look. They had a nice chat. They went inside. When they saw that Izzy was sound asleep, they made love like two teenagers. They had a truly idyllic life.

The next day they headed back up the 5, over the 74, into Palm Desert, and up Highway 111 to their home in West Palm Springs.

As nice as it was to get away, it felt good to be home.

Vacation time was over. They would both return to work on Monday. They would have to arrange to pick up John to take him to the speech location on Saturday, when they were not working.

Taylor hoped that she could spend some time at the Reservation to practice her knife throwing and bow and arrow shooting. She was planning on working both knife throwing and bow and arrow shooting into her speech, as things women could do both as a hobby for fun and as a method of self-protection. She hoped that John would be able to help her with a target that could be set up on the day of the speech which would allow her to demonstrate throwing and shooting as part of her speech.

Taylor and Rick unpacked, got Izzy unpacked and situated, had dinner, and went to bed to be ready for a new week of work in the morning.

Chapter 40
Back to Work and Off to the Reservation

Taylor returned to work. Mr. Drake had his secretary ask Taylor to join him in his office.

Mr. Drake said, "I trust that your vacation went well? It seems as if Mr. Franco is not moving on you or Crystal as aggressively as we thought he might."

Taylor replied, "I wouldn't count on that continuing. It has only been two weeks during which we have been tying up his property and business interests. I am sure that he has been busy trying to un-tie what we've done, to the extent possible. Also, he knows that if he moves now, he will be the number one suspect. Additionally, both of our protection details are new and are probably as efficient as they will ever be. As protection goes on, the more-lax it seems to become. I say this not to criticize the protection people, but only to point out human nature."

Mr. Drake replied, "I don't disagree with you. I only wish it wasn't so."

Taylor advised, "I presume that you know that I won the Woman of the Year award this year from National Woman Magazine. I'm not certain that it has been made public, but it seems as if many people already know.

"There is going to be an awards ceremony in Riverside in about a month, and I may need to take a day or two vacation time. In addition to receiving the award, I will have to give a speech at the ceremony. I understand that the next edition of the magazine will feature me on the cover and have an extensive article about the selection process, the ceremony, and the speech.

"I'm telling you this because I don't want you finding out at the last minute from someone else. Also, you may need to have someone cover for me around the time of the ceremony. This is not something that I thought out. It just happened. At this point, I wish I had never received the award. It's been a lot of trouble."

Mr. Drake replied, "I have heard about it. All in all, I think that it will be good for the office. They are always pressing me to hire more women and minorities. This might be a good way to introduce the job to young female lawyers who are starting out. I'm sure that with some of your stories, the job might seem more interesting than it actually is."

Taylor replied, "I doubt that, but it might introduce the prospect of working for the government to young women lawyers which, in the final analysis, would be a good thing."

Mr. Drake said, "It appears as if it is going to happen now, so let's go with it. I trust your judgment, and I know that you, of all people, would not use an opportunity such as this to get out of working hard. I know that you will work hard anyway, even if it's on your own time."

Taylor said, "That is true. I would never take advantage of a situation to get out of working, and I appreciate the fact that you recognize that."

Mr. Drake concluded, "I think we understand each other. You go get your award, and we'll hold down the fort here.

Taylor concluded, "Good."

Taylor left the office and went home to Rick and Izzy.

Chapter 41
Rob Busted

Taylor came into the office at 8:30, which was her custom. She expected to see the receptionist and an empty reception seating area. This was not the case.

When she came in, she did see the receptionist, but she also saw three large, rather serious looking men sitting in the reception seating area. They were wearing dark suits. Each appeared to be armed.

She leaned over the receptionist's desk and asked in a whisper, "Who are the three men?"

The receptionist, also whispering, replied, "They are FBI agents waiting to see Mr. Drake. I'm sure that Mr. Drake will want to see you too. Either he or I will buzz you when the time comes."

Taylor walked through the suite's inner door, down the hall, and to her private office. She began arranging her paperwork for the day. A few minutes later, her intercom buzzed, and she was asked to join Mr. Drake in his office.

She moved down the hallway to the corner of the building where Mr. Drake's private office was located. She knocked gently on his office door. He asked her to come in.

When she entered Mr. Drake's office, she saw Mr. Drake, his boss, Earl Crenshaw, who had come down from Los Angeles, and the three men who she was told were FBI agents. They were all seated in chairs around the office. They chose Mr. Drake's office rather than the conference room because his office had been recently swept for bugs.

Mr. Drake asked her to take a seat. One chair had been left vacant for her. She sat. Mr. Drake started, "Firstly, allow me to thank you all for coming down. We have a situation which needs attention, and meeting face to face seems to me to be the best way to handle it.

"Recently, while conducting a routine interview of a witness for a grand jury hearing, Ms. Shaw here was kidnapped along with the witness. From what we can gather, Ms. Shaw's kidnapping was just fortuitous. The actual subject of the kidnapping was the witness, and Ms. Shaw just happened to be with her. The kidnapping took place after hours, around 9 p.m., from the parking garage under the building.

"This particular kidnapping, if successful, would result in the principal defendant not being indicted, which would have left him free to carry on both his illegal and harmful businesses, along with a couple of small legal businesses. On the other hand, if the witness was able to testify, an indictment would be almost certain. Further, as it is with RICO cases, prior to the trial, the government would be able to tie up all of the defendant's business interests, both illegal and legal. This would cripple his entire criminal enterprise.

"The tying up of his businesses would give him a clear motive to kidnap the witness. As I said before, Ms. Shaw's kidnapping was probably just a fortuity, and disposing of Ms. Shaw would be more difficult than disposing of the witness where he could contend that she just ran away as she was afraid to testify.

"Our concerns here are two-fold. Firstly, we need to better protect our attorneys when they are questioning witnesses who pose a threat to organized crime. Secondly, we appear to have a mole in our office.

"The first concern may be addressed by doing such things as arming our attorneys, supplying our attorneys with protection details, creating a more secure location for witness interviews, and other measures which are within our ability to accomplish.

"Our second concern is a little more complex. As we all know, the office handles some delicate matters as we deal with not just criminals but with operators of significant criminal enterprises who are equipped to protect themselves, provided that they have access to inside information, which they might obtain from a mole.

"In this case, the witness was under the protection of the Federal Marshal and was living with the Marshals at a safe house. The only time prior to the hearing that the witness would be out of the immediate control of the Marshals was before, during, and just after her interview for the indictment hearing with our attorney, Ms. Shaw.

"Arranging the kidnapping of a witness at the precise day, time, and place that she would be leaving an interview and returning to the custody of the Marshals, would be impossible to do without inside information from a mole, at least in my opinion.

"To this end, we contacted the FBI to ask for assistance. The FBI had some of its undercover people surveil some of our people, particularly the ones who might have knowledge of the time and place of the interview with our witness.

"After determining some likely candidates, phone records were obtained. Calls to and from one of our staff attorneys to Mr. Franco were found. As no other phone contact between any of our other employees and Mr. Franco were uncovered, we began to focus our investigation on the one employee who seemed to most likely be the mole, a Mr. Rob Fulton.

"We began to surveil Mr. Fulton and found that after hours he had several suspicious meetings. We feel that we have sufficient evidence for an arrest and conviction.

"The reason for our meeting today is to discuss some of our possible alternatives. It is our opinion that once we confront Mr. Fulton with this, he will be amenable to any suggestion we might have to better his position. We are of the opinion that we might make a deal with him to wear a wire during his subsequent meetings with Mr. Franco in exchange for a much lesser sentence.

"We need to bear in mind that what he did put two lives in danger, the life of the witness and the life of Ms. Shaw. Ms. Shaw saved herself with quick thinking and abilities she learned away from her job. She was invited to this meeting so that she may be heard in this matter and perhaps shed some light on the situation. If she is not prepared, that is my fault. I chose to not tell her prior to right now.

"So, Ms. Shaw, what do you think of Rob Fulton being our mole?"

Taylor, a little startled, answered, "Presuming that Mr. Fulton is our mole, and it appears as if he is, I think we should offer him a deal. He will be so frightened at the prospect of going to prison that I believe that he would agree to almost anything. Also, the real criminal here is Franco. Even if Rob is allowed to plead to a lesser offense and even if he doesn't do any time, his life will be effectively ruined. He will never be able to practice law. He will never be able to get a decent job. I believe he would receive punishment enough."

Taylor continued, "I am not really surprised. I never liked him anyway. I warned my friend Sharon to stay away from him. She is just lucky that she was not swept up in this net. But I know that she has never had any contact with Franco, and, apparently, the phone records indicate the same. She could easily have been privy to sensitive information and may have even given it to Rob inadvertently.

"In short, I'm okay with whatever you want to do."

Mr. Drake replied, "Good. We are all on the same page then. I would say this to you Taylor, please be careful. This Franco is a very bad guy and he can reach out even from jail."

Taylor replied, "I know."

Mr. Drake asked the three FBI Agents what they thought. They seemed to agree that sending Rob into Franco's meetings wearing a wire was a good idea. They agreed, as did Mr. Crenshaw, that the case against Rob was a little flimsy anyway. They might get more by having him turn State's witness than trying to prosecute him separately, where they might lose.

Mr. Drake asked his secretary to buzz Rob and ask him to come to his office. Rob knocked on the door and entered. He had several sets of eyes on him. Mr. Drake explained that they found that he was working with Mr. Franco and that unless he wanted to go to jail, he would have to wear a wire during his meetings with Mr. Franco. Rob was not stupid. He realized that he was getting a lucky break and agreed to wear the wire at their next meeting which the assembled group learned was just the next day.

Taylor would have to deal with Sharon privately.

Chapter 42
A Vindictive Bobbie Franco

Bobbie Franco was not a happy person. He spent years building up a criminal enterprise, and it was over in a flash. RICO allowed the government to tie-up his legitimate as well as his illegitimate businesses to the point where he barely had enough money left to keep himself afloat.

He was particularly mad at Taylor Shaw. Her lofty sense of good versus evil was abhorrent to the criminal types, and Bobbie was no exception.

Bobbie called a meeting of his various confederates. They all met at Bobbie's Indio office. Rob, unknown to Bobbie and his friends, was wearing a wire. He was a little nervous because if Bobbie learned that he was wired, his death would be certain and swift.

Hans was present along with Hank and Dan. Sully and Steven were still missing. No one knew that they were still in the cave on the Indian Reservation. Rob was at the meeting.

Bobbie addressed the assembled group, "I cannot tell you all how pissed off I am at how things went down. By not keeping Crystal from testifying, I got indicted, and most of my businesses have been tied-up or shut down. I have suffered a terrible financial setback.

"I am primarily upset with this Taylor Shaw character. Rob works with her. Hans had a little brush with her in the form of a letter opener to his neck.

"My plan is to kill her, her whipped husband, and her brat kid. The last time I needed to get near somebody, I had to get the information from Rob. Unfortunately, it turned out that Taylor Shaw was with her and had to be kidnapped too, which spoiled my whole plan. She got away this time, but she will not get away again.

"This time, she will be easy to find. She will be getting an award, and she will be out in the open in broad daylight for everyone to see as she gives her acceptance speech. It's almost too easy. Imagine that this bitch will be getting an award. They must be really hard-up. But it will put her out in the open where she will be an easy target, which is all I care about.

"I have seen the site of the speech. It could not be better for my purposes if I had built it myself. There is a street on one side. The area itself is a large concrete slab with a few trees and a stone-looking memorial in the middle. The vision is unobstructed.

"At the rear of the slab facing the street, there is a large semi-circular multi-story building with glass walls with an unobstructed view to the location where I presume the stage will be set up.

"I intend to have no screw-ups this time, and to do that, I intend to have three assassins tasked with finally getting this job done.

"One assassin will be in one of the offices with the glass wall directly facing the stage. This assassin will be a sniper. A hole to accommodate the snipper's rifle barrel will be made in the glass, and the table for the snipper's rifle stand will be set up behind the hole. The hole will be covered with dark plastic to match the window tint so it cannot be seen from the stage side. The plastic will be removed just before the shot, and no sooner. The distance is so short that it will be impossible to miss.

"I am not too concerned about the rifle chosen, Remington, Springfield, etc., or whether it is bolt action or semi-automatic. I am not concerned with what ammunition is used; however, I am concerned with how the ammunition is obtained.

"If pre-made ammunition is used, it may be possible to trace it back to the store and the purchaser, which could lead to the identity of the shooter. If the shooter packs his own ammo, the material might be traceable. We will need someone who packs his own cartridges with untraceable material.

"This covers the sniper. However, just to be certain, we will have two additional assassins. One of the additional assassins will be in the crowd and will be able to maneuver his way to within 20 or 30 feet of the stage. In other words, to a place from which the stage will be an easy shot. If the sniper fails, this person will have a clear shot during the commotion.

"Presuming that both of these efforts fail, we will have a hand to hand specialist right up next to the stage. I need someone really brutal for this job. I plan on using an MMA fighter. Someone who is able to kill with his bare hands because it will be very difficult for a man with a gun to get this close to the stage."

Franco finished his long-winded plan. Rob could not believe his ears. He's an idiot, but he's not a killer. He was actually relieved that his participation would not be necessary and was told as much by Bobbie. He bid his farewell to Bobbie and his guys and happily exited.

Over the next few days, Bobbie and his inner circle set about finding a sniper, a mid-range guy, and an MMA fighter for the close work. They settled on Rex Watson as the sniper. Rex was a well know expert. They selected Les Baker as the crowd guy. The more difficult decision was the up-close guy. They chose Larry Davies, a retired MMA fighter, who was politely asked to leave the business after killing two fighters in the ring. Need we add that he is a very strong and a very bad guy.

Chapter 43
Inspection of the Site of Taylor's Speech

Taylor and Rick drove over to the Reservation and picked up John and Chuck. Izzy was left with a sitter. She would also be left with the sitter on the day of the speech to keep her out of harm's way. The group drove out to Riverside where the speech would be given to see if the site could be protected.

Chuck was now a married man. Even though his relationship with Taylor over the years has been complicated, those complications were behind them now. Taylor was very supportive of his marriage to Pamela, who, as we know, was initially her friend.

Pamela wanted to preserve her relationship with Taylor because she genuinely liked her and because she wanted to keep as many connections to the U S Attorney's Office as she could as she hoped that she could return to her job when the time was right.

As to Chuck involvement with Taylor's protection, a heard of wild buffalo could not drag him away from the opportunity. The relationship was too strong and, perhaps, a little too real, to be disregarded. John felt similarly.

When they arrived at the speech site, they drove into Taylor's parking spot for work, as her office building with its underground parking was just across the street from the site.

Taylor remarked, "It was very nice of the magazine to choose a location for the acceptance speech which is so close to my office. It makes it much more convenient for me."

They exited the car and crossed the street. Beyond the street, there was the large flat slab and the semi-circular glass building looking down onto the slab. Assuming that the stage was erected on the street side of the site, from glass building, one would be looking down over the slab directly to the stage. There were a few trees for shade and the memorial in the center of the slab, but there were almost no other obstructions between the building and the proposed stage.

Once at the site, Taylor, Rick, and Chuck watched as John silently looked over the proposed area.

After 30 minutes of looking and examining everything from the street to the building, John made his assessment. John said, "There is no way that you can give this speech here."

Taylor, who liked the shaded spot, said, "No. And why not?"

John replied crisply, "Because I cannot protect you here."

When John made his proclamation, Rick became afraid to say anything, and Chuck knew better than to say anything; so, both remained silent.

Taylor asked, "Why not?"

John replied, "For too many reasons to state."

Taylor, relentless, said, "But then how will I know?"

John started, "If you must know, I will tell you. Firstly, the stage faces a glass building. Placing a sniper in that building would be so easy that even a dim-witted person could arrange it. Secondly, the sides bordering the audience seating will be open, and anyone may make his way to within 30 feet of the stage from where he would have an easy shot. Thirdly, a strong man properly dressed could appear to be a body guard and could work his way next to the stage from where he could attack you directly. Do I really need any more reasons? This location is so horrible that one might think that it was designed by someone seeking to attack and kill you.

"You need to move this inside in a large room of one story and no high windows. I can then place braves around the perimeter both at floor level and on lifts, with two at each door."

Taylor replied, "I cannot arrange that. Is there anything you can do with the present set-up?"

John replied, "If we must, I will make a plan."

Taylor said, "Also, it would be great if you could lend me a target and a bow and a couple of arrows. During my speech, I want to show everyone how handy it is to have a knife and bow and arrow always at the ready."

John said, "Sounds like a good idea. People should be more willing to look at some alternative weapons. Also, it will mean that there will be some weapons around if we need to use them."

Taylor said, "I doubt that. But I would like to have them for show, if that is possible?"

John said, "I will arrange it."

Taylor said, "Thank you so much. You have been such a great help."

John said, "I might as well show you my defensive plan for this place while we are here. It will be much easier than trying to explain it at the Reservation."

Taylor replied, "Okay."

John started, "With the sniper, the hole in the glass will probably not be drilled until just before it is needed. Something will be placed over the hole so that light cannot shine through it making it visible. I will plan on being near the stage so I can watch. When light comes through the hole, I will signal Chuck to breach the correct window. Chuck who will be tied to the roof by a rope and will jump from the roof and through the window. Another brave will enter the particular room from the hallway. This way, they will have the sniper boxed in. This will be the easiest and most organized part of the operation."

"As to the attack by a person within several feet of the stage, we will need a brave roaming the crowd. We can use Roger. He can put on white man's clothes and blend in."

Taylor asked, "What if they send someone directly to the stage?"

John answered, "If they send someone to the stage, I will remain as your last line of defense. I will be there posing as a body guard. That should do it, unless you can be persuaded to move the speech somewhere else."

Chapter 44
The FBI at the Site of the Speech

Taylor and Rick returned John and Chuck to the Reservation. Chuck drove home from there. Once home, Taylor and Rick dismissed the sitter, and, along with Izzy, had dinner. They both worked the rest of the week as usual. The speech was scheduled for Saturday at 2 p.m.

When Saturday arrived, Taylor spent the morning getting dressed in her best outfit. She wore a dark blue skirt, knee length, a matching dark blue jacket, and a frilly white blouse. She accessorized with a gold bracelet, a gold pin, and a gold necklace. She wore black translucent stockings and low black heals. In other words, she was walking the fine line between conservative and sexy. She was practicing her speech as she dressed.

On the morning of the speech, Rick drove himself and Taylor to the Reservation where they would pick up John and Chuck. Michael and Roger would drive separately so that they could transport the target and some knives and a bow and arrow set for Taylor's demonstration.

When they arrived at the Reservation, Taylor was flabbergasted with how good John and Chuck looked. Each was dressed in a dark suit, white shirt, string tie, and cowboy boots polished to a black sheen. Each had his black hair tied back into a pony tail. Michael and Roger were dressed similarly, as it was their intent to blend in rather than stand out.

When they arrived at the venue, they were all favorably impressed with the job done by the stage hands. The area looked very festive with red, white, and blue banners placed around the stage and entry.

A light-weight fence was constructed around the perimeter of the speech area. Inside of the fence line, there were nice white wooden folding chairs, the type that one might see at an upscale wedding, set up facing the stage where the audience would sit. There was a large opening in the fence which would serve as the entrance. It was equipped with a metal detector. The fence starts and ends at either side of the stage. The stage is 25 feet long. It is elevated six feet above the ground. It is 12 feet deep. In the center of the stage, there is a lectern with a microphone. Long tables extend from either side of the lectern.

The stage faces directly into the courtyard and back to the glass building which looks into the courtyard, as John suspected.

Upon arrival, Michael and Roger went their separate way to set up the target and the knives and the bow and arrow near the stage.

Taylor's party, which included Taylor, Rick, John, and Chuck, made its way into the speech area. The FBI set up a small restricted area for its agents adjacent to the entrance to the speech area.

Technically, the FBI was supposed to act as the protection detail for Taylor. Three agents, Special Agent Norman Reeves, Special Agent Harry Chandler, and Special Agent Brock Meyers, were on hand for this task. They were similarly attired in department store suits.

With curiosity, two of the FBI agents came over to Taylor's group for, we presume, a chat. The apparent leader, SA Reeves, asked Taylor, "Who are these guys?" He was referring to Rick, Chuck, and the Chief.

Taylor replied, "This gentleman is my husband, and the other two gentlemen are my friends who have come to watch."

The SA Reeves said, "They look like Indians."

Taylor responded, as only she can, "That would be because they are Indians. Is that a problem?"

SA Reeves replied, "No."

Taylor said, "You gentlemen will have to excuse me. I am supposed to meet with Ms. Hawthorne from National Woman Magazine, our sponsor, to talk about my speech. I will be back shortly."

When Taylor left, SA Reeves separated Chuck from John indicating that he wanted a private conversation. He said, "If you guys are here to provide protection, allow me to remind you that providing protection is our job. You have no training and no weapons, and your other guy is too old. Who is this other guy anyway, the medicine man?"

Chuck replied, "Oh no. He is the Chief. And I promise you that if anyone makes a move against Taylor, it will be the last move he ever makes on this earth. I have seen him paralyze a full- grown mountain lion with one hand, open the jaws of an alligator to save a child, and enter a burning building to bring out an elderly couple without receiving so much as a sunburn. Believe me when I tell you that this is a person with whom you do not want to tangle. So, my promise to you is this: After the speech is over and we all go our separate ways, I promise that I will never tell the Chief about this conversation. You may not know why now, but you will thank me later."

SA Reeves said, "Whatever. But what is he supposed to do here?"

Chuck replied, "If you must know, he told me that he is here as Taylor's last line of defense, and trust me when I tell you that this is a line that will not be crossed."

SA Reeves concluded, "Okay. Just as long as you guys stay out of our way, we're good."

Chuck closed with, "Fair enough."

Chapter 45
Taylor's Speech

People began filing into the speech area passing through the monitored entrance. Everyone was dressed in business attire, with no one looking out of place. Roger blended in with the crowd to keep an eye out for anyone who might take a shot at Taylor from the first several rows.

Michael went into the glass building, the building facing the stage where it was suspected the sniper would be located. His job would be to break down the door of the sniper's unit and take him down, once it was established in which unit he is located.

A lectern was set up in the center of the stage with two long tables, one extending from either side. Seated at the table to the right of the lectern, from left to right, would be Mr. Walters, the master of ceremonies, Ms. Hawthorne, the CEO of National Woman Magazine, and Ms. Hoffman, the editor of National Woman Magazine.

Seated at the table to the left of the lectern, from left to right, there would be Taylor, Mr. Johnson of the FBI, and Mr. Crenshaw of the US Attorney's Office.

The seats began to fill quickly. Everyone was dressed well. The ladies wore dresses and the men wore either a suit or at least a sports coat. They all passed through the entrance and took their seats. There were around 200 people.

After everyone was seated, Mr. Walters, the MC, moved behind the lectern to the microphone. He took up the mic and began, "Ladies and Gentlemen, my name is Mr. Walter. I am from the office of Patricia Dawson, the Mayor of the City of Riverside. I have the privilege of introducing to you Ms. Abigail Hawthorne, the CEO of National Woman Magazine who will present the 7th Annual Woman of the Year Award to this year's recipient. So, please extend a warm welcome to Ms. Abigail Hawthorne." The audience clapped as she rose.

Mr. Walters replaced the microphone in its stand and left the lectern. As he returned to his seat, Ms. Hawthorne moved behind the lectern. She addressed the crowd saying, "Ladies and Gentlemen, it is my honor to present this year's Woman of the Year Award to Ms. Taylor Shaw. Each year, this award is given to the woman who the committee feels best exemplifies the strides that women have made in the world of business or law. Woman have had a long and sometimes difficult road in the business world and have often had to out-perform their male counterparts just to break even. I don't want to take all of the wind out of Ms. Shaw's sails, so I will leave it there and allow her to impart what she has learned from her journey here."

Directed at Taylor, she said, "Ms. Shaw will you come up?"

Taylor left her seat and moved to the side of the lectern. She stopped opposite Ms. Hawthorne. The award itself, which consisted of a glass trophy, was sitting next to the lectern. It was inscribed with the words Woman of the Year 2023, under which was inscribed Taylor Shaw, Recipient.

Ms. Hawthorne remarked, "Ms. Shaw, please allow me to present to you the Woman of the Year award." She handed Taylor the award and continued, "I'm sure you will have a few words for us."

Taylor's began:

"Yes, I do. Let me start by saying thank you to Ms. Hawthorne and to everyone at National Woman Magazine who have made this award possible.

"I appreciate the fact that such a prestigious award is being given to someone working in the trenches such as I and not to someone who works exclusively in the Board Room.

"The U S Attorney's Office is constantly honing its skills to better serve the people of this great nation, and we believe that innovations in our pursuit of law breakers has contributed greatly to our success.

"For many years, when a single perpetrator committed a crime, he was arrested and tried for that criminal act. When a single perpetrator was arrested, he was incarcerated where he was essentially isolated from his confederates. Back then, he lacked the resources and the ability to communicate freely with the outside world. As a result, the victim, who is also generally the principal witness, would be relatively safe from retaliation, until the perpetrator was released from prison, which might be many years down the road.

"Unfortunately, with time, the criminals have become much more-savvy, and this has made it necessary for crime fighting to adapt.

"As time has progressed, criminals are no longer single perpetrators. The single crime is not sufficiently remunerative to justify the risk. Following the lead of corporate America, a criminal, rather than committing a single crime, would be more likely to form an enterprise with which he may commit several crimes using several low-level criminal associates to do the actual work.

"This form of organization has two effects. Firstly, by committing more crimes, the enterprise will realize more money. Secondly, because the crimes are being committed by low-level associates, the upper level actors are often insulated from arrest and prosecution.

"Even with the relatively broad application of Anglo-American accessory liability, the connection between the low-level perpetrator and the primary crime boss may be too ethereal to prove.

"The additional problem with the criminal enterprise is that through their illegal activities, the crime bosses become rich. They have money and may purchase additional legal businesses.

"Further, because our culture places so much emphasis on having money, the crime boss, because he is rich, garners respect and accolades from regular people. He is revered as a rich man. This is a deep-seated psychological problem which now exists in our universe.

"In our office, we have solved some of these problems by extending the use of the Federal Influenced and Corrupt Organizations Act, more commonly known as RICO, to other criminal conduct, such as sex trafficking.

"To violate RICO, a person must engage in a pattern of racketeering which consists of committing two specified crimes, also known as predicate crimes, within a 10-year period. The predicate crimes must be related. Predicate crimes include murder, kidnapping, arson, drug dealing, bribery, mail and wire fraud, and money laundering.

"The use of RICO provides distinct advantages. Firstly, it allows the government to go after the crime boss and not just the associates. Secondly, it allows the government to obtain a pre-trial restraining order or injunction to seize a defendant's assets to prevent the transfer of those assets so that there will be something to seize in the event of a favorable decision. Thirdly, the penalties are quite stiff including fines up to $25,000 and 20 years in prison per count. Fourthly, if convicted, the defendant must forfeit all ill-gotten gains. Fifthly, RICO allows a private citizen damaged by the defendant to file a civil suit in State or federal court for those damages. Sixthly, a RICO case is easier to prove since it focuses on patterns of behavior as opposed to criminal acts. Lastly, if an underlying crime carries a greater penalty than the RICO crime, the greater penalty may be used.

"So, you ask what is the problem?

"I have a one-word answer for you – the victim.

"Allow me to relate my own recent experience. The government was seeking a RICO indictment against a crime boss. He found out that the government intended to impose a pre-trial restraining order against both his legitimate and illegitimate businesses. The victim was scheduled to testify at the indictment hearing. To prevent the indictment from issuing, he had the victim kidnapped. Because I was co-incidentally with the victim interviewing her for the indictment hearing at the time, I too was kidnapped.

"We were locked in a jail cell. The next day they came to present us to the crime boss. Because of the skills I learned from my Native American friends, I was able to stab the two people in the room with a letter opener, jump on a horse, and beat the people chasing me across a national park to the Reservation. We were then able to return to rescue the victim.

"Our culture, with its emphasis on money, treated the crime boss as a respected business person.

"However, he had no alternative but to kidnap the witness because with her testimony, his assets could be seized pre-trial, taking away his precious money, without which he would truly be nothing.

"Not to blow my own horn but to just state the facts as they present themselves, if I had not been accidently kidnapped with the victim, she would probably be dead now. As a result, the case would have been dropped, and the crime boss would be left with his money and his freedom to commit more crime.

"Just after high school, while trying to rescue the little girl for whom I babysat, I was falsely imprisoned and tortured. Only my now husband and my motorcycle club friends were able to save me.

"After that when I witnessed a toxic waste dump and a resulting murder, I was kidnapped and thrown from a 15-story building. I was again saved by my husband and my motorcycle club friends when my husband scaled the outside of a glass high-rise building and jumped off of the roof tied to nothing but a bungee cord which allowed him to catch me in mid-air to keep me from falling to my certain death.

"Next, while pursuing a water rights case for the Native Americans in the Coachella Valley, the drug dealer posing as a food grower, feeling that kidnapping me would not be sufficient to slow down my pursuit of him, did the unthinkable. He kidnapped my four and a half-year-old daughter. With the help of my Native American friends, we were able to extricate her and bring the drug dealer to justice.

"Women have made great strides in this country. Many women are doctors and lawyers, and I have heard that many medical and law school students are women. Still as of March, 2022, there are only 74 women CEOs at Fortune 500 companies, about 15 percent. In 2002, there were only 7.

"As a point of interest, the other night on a radio talk show, the host, who I happen to actually like, pronounced that women made the same amount of money as men. He then qualified his statement by maintaining that though their pay is equal, a woman's pay might become unequal due to her need to perform child rearing services to her own child. Wow. Is child rearing really a valid excuse to reduce a woman's pay?

"Please, allow me to be so bold as to instruct you about how things are in the real world - without children, we have nothing - no business, no profits, nothing.

"The 19th Amendment granting women the right to vote did not go into effect until 1920, just a little over 100 years ago, when we were already 131 years into our new government.

"This reminds me of the first lecture I heard given by my now husband on the subject when I was a 19-year-old junior college freshman. Among other things, he opined that the United States Constitution freed no slaves and gave no woman the right to vote.

"As much as I believe and want to believe that things have changed in America, I hope against hope that we, as a country, can understand that the Founders were operating within the mores of their time, a time when women were, at best, second class citizens.

"One area where I fear that we have not progressed is the protection of women witnesses. If a woman witnesses a crime, she is subject to being stalked, intimidated, or even killed to prevent her from testifying. And this terrorizing can go on for as long as the perpetrator wishes, as there is no punishment for what a criminal might do in the future, even if everyone is certain that he is going to do it.

"My own experience alone shows this. I was tortured, thrown from a building, had my daughter kidnapped, and was kidnapped myself

211

because I was with a potential witness, and I am not even 40.

"If I had not been able to escape and go back to rescue my last witness, she would have been killed, and the crime boss would be free. As it worked out, the crime boss is still out and about on bail, so he is free to attack me again at any time.

"And a woman, due to her comparatively smaller size, cannot protect herself at the time that she is attacked, and as a result, she must suffer through life being pursued by criminals either to be disposed of as a witness or for revenge.

"Take, for example, sex trafficking cases. There are many cases across the country where women who have killed their trafficker now face life sentences or extended jail time for doing so. The favored defense to murder is self-defense. However, self-defense can only be asserted if the defensive killing was done in the same transaction as the initial the attempt.

"A look at the pre-printed jury instruction drives this point home. It states that with self-defense, the defendant must reasonably believe that he is in imminent danger of being killed or suffer great bodily harm. After that danger passes, self-defense is no longer available. The precise words of the instruction are, 'Belief in future harm is not sufficient, no matter how great or how likely the harm is believed to be.'

"Generally speaking, a woman is not physically able to square off against a man in a fight to even be in a position in which she might be able to assert self-defense.

"Additionally, a woman is prohibited from applying her cunning such as sneaking up on her predator and attacking him, even if he tells the world that he is planning to kill her in the future.

"Perhaps as time progresses, some jurisdictions might allow victims who kill their attackers to argue that their actions are the direct result of being trafficked. But this does not appear likely.

"So, it boils down to this. In our supposedly enlightened country with all of its protections and legal niceties, if a woman has been attacked or raped and seeks to protect herself from future attacks threatened by the same perpetrator, she is without legal recourse. She may only wait until she is actually attacked or killed before she may assert her rights, which, I would point out, is far too late.

"In sharp contrast, in 16th Century in Elizabethan England, the law stated, and I quote, 'In cases of felony, manslaughter, robbery, murder, rape, piracy, and such capital crimes as are not reputed for treason or hurt of the estate, our sentence pronounced upon the offender is to be [hanged until] he be dead.'

"In the 16th Century, a woman who was raped would not need to worry about being raped again by the same person because once caught, he would be hanged and gone.

"In our country, we lack judicial violence. Somehow the law makers believe that if they show compassion, the criminal will respond with compassion and will not commit more crimes. In places such as Los Angeles, the District Attorney barely prosecutes known criminals and barely keeps people in jail.

"In Elizabethan England people were kept in jail only while they were awaiting their actual punishment, such as hanging.

"Do we need more judicial violence now?"

John was sitting next to the stage throughout the speech. Somehow, with super human vision he has which has been preserved by a lifetime of using primarily natural light, he saw a spot on one of the glass panels of the building. The sniper must have removed the dark paper or film that covered the hole to keep light from shining through it, as it just did.

Chuck was on the roof above the glass wall. John gave Chuck a hand signal indicating which floor and through which panel he saw the now exposed hole.

Chuck leaped out from the roof and swung back towards the glass wall on a rope. He went feet first through the glass and into the poised sniper rifle that was on its stand on a table a few feet from the window.

At exactly the same time, Michael breached the hallway door for the particular unit. He grabbed the sniper from behind, and Chuck grabbed him from the front. The sniper was so taken aback by the two-pronged attack that he did not know what to do. Though either of the boys could have made short work of him, they gave him a quick beating and tied his legs and arms. The boys had much experience at tying up huge wild animals so the sniper was not much of a match for them. They replaced the film over the hole to signal to the Chief that they were finished and that the operation was a success.

After hearing the commotion and seeing the glass wall break, Bobbie's group knew that the sniper failed and that they would have to activate phase 2 of their plan, the part where their rover in the crowd, Les Baker, would work his way to a location from which he could take a shot at Taylor from a relatively short distance.

From the stage, Taylor could see him. Unfortunately, the FBI agent, Norman Reeves, in a sincere effort to apprehend him, ended up in the wrong place at the wrong time and was shot by Baker. Before Baker could shoot anyone else, Taylor grabbed the bow and arrow from the table and sent two arrows, both of which struck Baker, causing him to go down. Roger could not get to SA Reeves before he died from his gunshot wound. Fortunately, Taylor's two arrow shots took Baker down, and Roger was there to tie him up.

The next move was to be made by the MMA fighter. As he was on his way towards Taylor, he was accosted by the other two FBI Agents, Harry Chandler and Brock Meyers. He quickly beat both of them nearly to death.

After basically brushing the two of them off like flies, a clear path to Taylor opened up. She was out of arrows. The MMA fighter moved towards her.

Then, from nowhere, like the wind, a hand cut through the air and grabbed the MMA fighter by the throat nearly crushing his windpipe. It was the Chief. The Chief, grabbed the MMA fighter, picked him up by the scruff of his neck, and threw him like a rag doll 10 feet and onto the ground.

While this fight was going on, everyone cleared the area for fear that they might get struck by accident, as both men were huge.

A fight then ensued which would make a grown man cry. The Chief beat this guy up so badly that one almost felt sorry for him. He smashed his face with his open hand breaking his nose and jaw. He threw him to the ground and then bounced his head on the concrete. He was bleeding everywhere.

But the MMA fighter would not give up. He managed to get up and stagger back in the Chief's direction. He flailed at the Chief with some errant punches. The Chief hit this fellow in the jaw with such force that it was thought that his head might come off of his body. While the man was still standing, the Chief reared back and hit the poor fellow in the small of the back causing him to cry out in pain and fall to the ground, unconscious.

Taylor was bewildered. This was a side of the Chief that she did not know existed.

Chuck and Michael took the sniper back to the FBI containment area. They then went to Roger's location to help him take Baker to the containment area. Roger felt it was his duty to return SA Reeves to the containment area. He was, unfortunately, dead.

Chuck, Michael, and Roger went to the area adjacent to the stage. It took everything that they had to even move the unconscious MMA fighter, as he was so huge. The three of them somehow muscled him back to the containment area.

An ambulance had been summoned to take the sniper, Baker, and the MMA fighter to the hospital. The coroner came for SA Reeves.

Taylor and the Chief walked from the stage towards the containment area. Everyone moved away clearing a wide path for the Chief out of a combination of great respect and, in equal part, great fear.

The FBI agent who overheard the conversation between Chuck and his colleague about the Chief's his role in today's proceedings said the following: "I guess the kid was right. The Chief would be the last line of defense."

Taylor, Rick, Chuck, Michael, Roger, and the Chief were in the containment area. One of the medics who was left after the ambulance returned to the hospital was heard saying that someone from the hospital called to find out how the MMA fighter was injured so they would know how to treat him. It was initially thought that he had been hit by a car, as he was so badly damaged. The person from the hospital said that they took an ex-ray and found that the MMA fighter suffered a broken transverse process, something done by Joe Louis to Max Schmeling in a prize fight around the time of World War II.

Chapter 46
The Various Prosecutions

When Bobbie Franco, Luis Foley, and Sergio Marks were in the process of being indicted for the RICO violations of slavery, trafficking, and prostitution, in an effort to derail the indictment and prevent the government from being able to tie-up their property pre-trial, Bobbie purchased the information concerning the whereabouts of the witness, Crystal Covington, from Rob Fulton, Taylor's co-worker and Sharon's boyfriend.

With this information, Franco was able to kidnap Crystal so that she could not testify at the indictment hearing. As a result, no indictment would issue, and his property would not be tied up. Franco paid Rob for the information, and no one knew.

When Franco did have Crystal kidnapped, his man, by mistake, also kidnapped Taylor. Taylor was able to escape from the kidnappers by stabbing Bobbie's henchman with a letter opener and then throwing the letter opener at Bobbie. While they were seeking medical attention, she had time to get to the Reservation and then return to Eagle Mountain with a contingent of braves to rescue Crystal.

With Crystal able to testify, the government was able to get the indictment and tie-up Bobbie's property pending the trial. This made Bobbie very mad.

Bobbie arranged to take another run at Taylor at her awards ceremony. Because he knew where Taylor would be, he would not need Rob's services; however, Rob would attend the meeting to plan Taylor's killing. Unknown to Franco, Rob was wearing a wire. When Rob was advised that he would be prosecuted for telling Franco about Crystal's whereabouts, Rob agreed to wear a wire in exchange for leniency.

During the awards ceremony, the efforts of a sniper, a shooter, and an MMA fighter were foiled, and the killer of SA Reeves, an FBI agent, was apprehended. This required Chuck to jump through a glass wall, Taylor to shoot the man who shot SA Reeves with a bow and arrow, and the Chief to stage one of the most epic fights of all time against the MMA fighter.

After the awards ceremony, a meeting was set for the next day at the U S Attorney's Office in Riverside, just across the street from the ceremony location itself, at 10 a.m.

Chuck, Michael, Roger, and the Chief returned to the Reservation. It was everyone's hope that their part would be finished.

The next day arrived. Taylor asked Rick to drive her. For as brave as she is generally, she was still a little shaken. Also, Rick, as a local prosecutor, might have some ideas about the case.

Taylor and Rick arrived early. As this was her office, she was greeted by a small welcoming party consisting of the receptionist, her secretary Margo, Sharon, and a few other people from the office. They were all quite solicitous asking about her ordeal and wishing her well. Margo told her that it was all over the news including the daring deeds by the Indians and her shooting one of the perpetrators with a bow and arrow. She thanked everyone for their wishes and introduced Rick to the collected group.

The receptionist told them that the others had already arrived for the meeting and were in the conference room.

Taylor excused herself, and she and Rick walked towards the conference room. She lightly tapped on the door, and she and Rick entered.

In the conference room there was her immediate boss, Daryl Drake, his boss, Earl Crenshaw, who was at the acceptance speech, and his boss, David Stanley, who came down from Los Angeles. The other man was Dan Wallace. He was from the DAs office. He and Rick were acquainted, as he was one of Rick's remote bosses.

Taylor asked, "I hope that you don't mind that I brought my husband. I was a little shaken from yesterday so he volunteered to drive. He is with the Haven DAs office. I can have him wait for me in my office if you prefer."

Mr. Stanley, the highest-ranking person from the U S Attorney's Office, took over the meeting.

He fielded Taylor's question, "I think it will be okay if your husband stays."

Mr. Stanley continued, "Perhaps we should call the meeting to order. I believe that we are all here. We have me, Mr. Crenshaw, Mr.

217

Drake, and Taylor from the U S Attorney's Office and Mr. Wallace from the DAs office. Mr. Rick Miller of the DAs office is also present as an observer.

"As we know, yesterday, an elaborate attempt was made on the life of Assistant United States Attorney Taylor Shaw. The purpose of this meeting is to determine how we will share jurisdiction between our office and the District Attorney's Office in the apprehension and punishment of the perpetrators.

"As we all know, murder is typically considered a local crime and is typically handled by local law enforcement and local prosecutors, typically the local DAs office.

"However, as the deceased was a federal agent, we have other options.

"I understand that presently the defendant, one Bobbie Franco, is under indictment for RICO violations most notably sex trafficking, prostitution, and money laundering. His case is in the federal court as it would be with RICO. We now have a local case. We would be within our rights to have Mr. Franco face federal charges for RICO and, at the same time, local charges for murder.

"On the other hand, if he was first tried in State court and acquitted, he could again be tried in federal court for the same offense and could not plead double jeopardy as he would technically be being tried by two sovereigns, the State and the federal governments.

"Because the present murder involves the killing of a federal agent, the case would become a federal murder case under US Code, Section 1114. Another way to make it a federal crime would be to frame it as an attempted killing of a witness, Ms. Shaw. This avenue is a little more difficult to traverse. Either way, the case can be federal.

"If we had a choice of law problem, things might be different. Before 2019 and the passage of SB 1437, California had a very liberal felony murder rule law under which someone could be convicted of felony murder simply because a victim died during the commission of a felony even if the defendant did not intend to kill anyone, didn't know a homicide took place, or the homicide was an accident.

"Presently, under SB 1437, one may be charged with felony murder only if he actually kills the victim, aids or abets murder in the first degree with intent to kill, was a major participant in the felony and acted with reckless indifference to human life, or the victim was a peace officer killed in the performance of his duties.

218

"I believe that we would be well within California's more restrictive law as the on-scene perpetrators killed the victim or were major participants in the crime and acted with reckless indifference to human life. The off-scene perpetrator, Mr. Franco, aided and abetted in first degree murder with intent to kill. Further, a peace officer was killed in the line of duty.

"Under SB 1437, to get a first-degree murder conviction under the felony murder rule, the homicide would have to take place during the commission of one of the felonies listed in Penal Code Section 189.

"The federal code is clear that a federal murder charge includes the killing of a law enforcement agent, such as an FBI agent, which occurred in this case."

Taylor was in awe as to the breadth of knowledge Mr. Stanley had in these matters, and she wasn't done.

Mr. Stanley went on, "This has been a nice discussion of the law as it relates to murder, but now we need to get down to action. How will we round up this Bobbie Franco? This is not my first rodeo, and I have my own ideas as to how I would proceed from here. You may have some ideas of your own which I hope you will share.

"It is my opinion that we should act as swiftly as possible. As we all know, under the U S Constitution, a criminal defendant would be entitled to an indictment. But it might take us some time to assemble a grand jury and, once assembled, present enough of a case to get a true bill."

Mr. Wallace, who was the representative of the DAs Office, asked, "What do you think we should do?"

Mr. Stanley replied, "If it was up to me, I would say that instead of going the grand jury route, we file a written criminal complaint together with an affidavit by an agent familiar with the case. I believe the other two agents who saw the whole thing thankfully survived the incident. We will then submit the complaint and the affidavit to a judge or magistrate who will review both documents. Once the judge or magistrate reviews the documents, presuming that he or she finds probable cause, he or she will issue an arrest warrant.

"Once an arrest warrant is issued on the criminal complaint, federal law requires that the defendant, in the case of a felony, be charged by indictment within 30 days, which we will, of course, do.

"That is what I believe we should do. Does anyone have another or better idea?"

Everyone in the room, Mr. Wallace, Mr. Crenshaw, Mr. Drake, Taylor, and Rick were almost too impressed to speak.

Finally, Mr. Wallace, the senior representative from the DAs office, and Mr. Crenshaw, the senior representative from the U S Attorney's Office, both stated that they agreed with Mr. Stanley's plan of seeking a criminal complaint and then an indictment.

This would speed up the process and let Bobbie know sooner rather than later that he was considered the master mind of a murder, a crime which carries awesome penalties.

Mr. Stanley said, "It's settled then, we will continue on with the RICO case. We will treat the kidnapping, false imprisonment, and attempted murder by Mr. Franco of Taylor and the Crystal as State cases, criminal and civil.

"We will treat the murder case at Taylor's acceptance speech as a federal murder case as the victim was a federal law enforcement officer, an FBI agent. As to the federal murder case, we will file a criminal complaint, secure an arrest warrant, and have some unhappy campers from the FBI field office pick up this prick and put him in jail where he belongs."

Everyone in the room was in-agreement. It was coming up on noon at this point. Mr. Stanley, Mr. Wallace, Mr. Crenshaw, and Mr. Drake decided to take lunch. Taylor and Rick decided to skip lunch with the group and go get lunch by themselves.

After lunch, Mr. Stanley, Mr. Wallace, and Mr. Crenshaw left the building headed for their respective offices. Mr. Drake retired to his office. Taylor returned to her office. And Rick went home.

Chapter 47
The Legal Shakeout for the Rico Case and the Kidnapping

The RICO case turned out better than anyone could imagine. Elizabeth Ann Forrester, aka Crystal Covington, turned out to be a sensational witness. She had much more information than we thought about the slavery, sex trafficking, prostitution, and money laundering. As inquiry by the prosecution before an indictment is limited as an indictment is theoretically neutral, we were not in a position to find out exactly what she had.

Bobbie, Luis, and Sergio were found guilty on all counts. They were required to pay $25,000 for each count, sentenced to 20 years in prison for each count, and had to forfeit all ill-gotten gains.

Crystal's testimony was something to behold. She went through how the men used the women for their purposes and then threw them out like trash. The men would make the women perform heinous acts and then say that it was the woman's idea. The conditions in the sweat shops were outlined in tragic detail.

Crystal not only helped with her testimony, but she also helped out the women with social services. She convinced social services to allow the women to return to Mexico, if they wished, and to find good jobs if they wanted to stay. There were only a few prostitutes in the group. They all opted to return home. Crystal had a contact with the owner of a legitimate clothing manufacturer who was able to get decent paying jobs for the girls who opted to stay.

The trial for the State kidnapping and attempted murder came up. Rob was put on the stand as a false friend. He testified that Mr. Franco contacted him to find out where Crystal would be before the indictment so she could be kidnapped. Rob told him that she would be in the underground parking garage at the elevators, giving them the approximate time.

With this information, Franco was able to kidnap Crystal, but because Taylor was there, she also had to be kidnapped.

When Taylor and Crystal were kidnapped, they were thrown, hooded, into the trunk of a large town car. They were taken to Eagle Mountain, an old town once owned by Kaiser Steel. Franco used the town as a place to store drugs, people, and other contraband if he ran out of storage space in the valley. Eagle Mountain is located adjacent to Joshua Tree National Park.

The next morning after their kidnapping, Taylor and Crystal were taken to Franco's office to discuss their demise. Crystal was so hysterical that she had to be taken back to her cell. Bobbie's henchman Hans was also on hand. He has a personality which was about as welcoming as a dose of the black plague, but he is large and imposing.

Taylor saw a letter opener on the desk. She grabbed the opener and plunged it into Hans' shoulder near his carotid artery. As Bobbie was going for his gun in a desk drawer, Taylor withdrew the opener from Hans and threw it across the room causing it to stick in Bobbie's shoulder near his carotid artery. There was blood everywhere.

The direct examination went like this:

Defense Attorney: "Ms. Shaw, did you stab Hans with a letter opener?"

Ms. Shaw: "Yes."

Defense Attorney: "Ms. Shaw, did you throw a letter opener at Mr. Franco causing the opener to stick into his shoulder?"

Ms. Shaw: "Yes."

Defense Attorney: "So, you admit to stabbing both of these men with the letter opener?"

Ms. Shaw: "Yes."

Defense Attorney: "Why did you stab these men?"

Ms. Shaw: "As a general rule, when you are kidnapped and taken to a rural area by two men who are known to have questionable morals, if one draws his gun and the other goes for his, you better be throwing whatever you have or you will wind up dead very soon."

Defense Attorney: "I don't believe that you can throw a knife as far as you say. I have here a floor plan of the room showing Mr. Franco to be at least 30 feet from you at the time of the throw."

Ms. Shaw: "Are you suggesting that I am lying?"

Defense Attorney: "I don't have to suggest. I have had my young associate set up a target in the back of the room approximately 30 feet away. I would ask the bailiff to remove the exhibit tag and hand the letter opener to you for throwing."

Judge: "Where are we going with this?"

Defense Attorney: "We will be show that momentarily."

The bailiff removed the exhibit tag, walked over to Ms. Shaw, and stood behind her. Taylor turned her head so that she could see the letter opener in the Bailiff's hand.

Everyone in the courtroom was directed to move behind the bench. Taylor was taken to the far side wall of the room. The target was set up on the other side of the room. The doors were locked so that no one from the hallway could enter the courtroom where he or she might be in the path between Taylor and the target.

Taylor was standing approximately 30 feet from the target.

Ms. Shaw: "You want me to throw this opener at that target?"

Defense Attorney: "Yes."

Ms. Shaw: "The bailiff will have to hand me the opener as I cannot throw it unless I can hold it."

Judge: "Bailiff, please hand Ms. Shaw the opener."

Taylor held out her right hand. As the bailiff set the blade in her open hand, with one motion she threw the knife very hard across the room where it struck a perfect bull's eye on the target to the depth of the hilt.

Judge: "I think we have seen enough. But I have a question."

Ms. Shaw: "Please, that would be refreshing."

Judge: "Since you were so close to Hans and you have such accuracy from 30 feet, why didn't you severe the carotid artery?"

Ms. Shaw: "Your Honor, I may be resourceful and even well-schooled and trained in the art of knife throwing from years of practice, but I am not a killer. Neither of these penetrations were kill shots. I needed to make a bloody mess sufficient to cause Mr. Franco to think that he was scrambling for his life. If it had been the carotid, he would be dead. My intention was to put him in a position in which he had to gamble whether I knew the difference between a kill shot and a non-lethal shot. Presuming that he would not wish to take that gamble, he would have to leave the compound to find real medical attention very soon or die. This would give me time to lead everyone in the compound on a wild goose chase across Joshua Tree National Park, trap them in a box canyon, get my Native American friends, and return to Eagle Mountain to rescue Crystal."

Judge: "Did it work?"

Ms. Shaw: "It did. She testified the other day in the RICO case against Franco."

Judge: "How did you elude the compound full of men?"

Ms. Shaw: "That was the easy part. There was a horse tied up outside of Mr. Franco's office. I jumped on it and allowed them to chase me around in circles into the rocks of the mountain until they wound up in a box canyon. I then sealed the opening by starting a small avalanche."

Judge: "That's some riding."

Ms. Shaw: "Thank you your Honor. But I've been riding horses since I was 7 years old. Most people say that I ride better than I walk. Unlike most people in our profession, I grew up on an orange farm in the desert and not in Palo Alto or Beverly Hills."

Judge: (To the Defense Attorney) "Are you through with this witness? Or should I say is she through with you?"

Defense Attorney: "I have nothing else."

The jury brought back a guilty verdict in the criminal kidnapping case. As to the civil case, a criminal verdict can be used to establish liability. A criminal case requires proof beyond a reasonable doubt. A civil case requires only proof by the preponderance of the evidence. Here, the criminal verdict will establish liability in the civil case so settlement will swift.

Taylor reasoned that after the RICO and federal murder trials, between attorney's fees and recoupment of ill-gotten gains, Franco would be broke. So, she made a claim against Franco's landlord at Eagle Mountain. A landlord may be held liable for failing to protect people coming onto the property from being injured by the tenant. If the landlord had inspected the property, he would have seen that there was a jail with two cells and equipment for advanced interrogation. People coming onto the property were not protected by the landlord.

Taylor settled the case for $500,000, half of which she gave to Crystal and half of which she put into Izzy's college fund.

Chapter 48
The Murder Case

The first three cases were interesting, but the federal murder case was downright riotous.

The defendants, Rex Watson, the sniper, Les Baker, the mid-crowd guy, and Larry Davies, the MMA fighter, were present as was Bobbie Franco.

They were being defended by Stevie Wicks, a famous female attorney. When seeing this line up, Taylor was amused that four cave men would hire a woman to defend them.

The prosecution was represented by Assistant U S Attorney Carolyn Chu from the Los Angeles office. She was well known as a tough cookie who gave the appearance of being docile.

Taylor was not there in her capacity as a lawyer but as a victim and a witness.

For her opening shot across the bow, Ms. Wicks made a motion to dismiss as to defendant Bobbie Franco on the grounds that he was not present at the murder scene and did not order the murder.

The Judge pointed out that it is not necessary for someone to be present at a murder scene to be convicted of the murder if he aids or abets the crime. The judge said that he certainly was not going to dismiss the charge without at least hearing from the prosecution's witnesses.

The Judge went off the record and called the attorneys to the bench. The Judge admonished Ms. Wicks that though he could not tell her how to run her practice, each defendant should have his own attorney. The interests of the defendants are too different for all of them to be represented by a single attorney. Ms. Wicks said that she would consider his admonition.

Even before opening statements, we see how much the law has failed to keep up with sociology. Anglo-American law came into use around 1200. In older times, a criminal who committed a crime, was hunted down, arrested, tried, and hanged or otherwise punished. In other words, criminals themselves committed crimes and were punished.

As time progressed, so much money became involved, that criminal enterprises arose. Businessmen criminals ran criminal organizations where they did not commit crimes but hired others to do so.

As a result, when crimes were committed, only the low-level criminals hired to do the criminal acts would be caught and punished, and the businessmen running the criminal organizations became untouchable. In fact, because money is such an important factor in our present society, the businessman criminal often became elevated to the rank of successful businessperson with all of the rights and privileges that come with that designation.

In an effort to get to the leaders of the criminal enterprises, RICO was put into effect. With RICO, one could indict a non-participating businessman; however, it was necessary that he first commit two predicate offenses within 10 years of one another and that they be related.

The burden of proof is less with RICO. It is only necessary to show a pattern of criminal activity rather than proving guilt beyond a reasonable doubt with proof that the perpetrator aided and abetted the crime. The federal murder case here is not a RICO case. In the federal murder case, Bobbie Franco will have to be brought in as an aider and abettor.

When we came back from lunch, the judge sent us all home. We were told to return the next day at 10 a.m.

The next day we all returned at 10. At this time, each of the other three defendants had his own attorney, with Ms. Wicks staying on only as the attorney for Mr. Franco. On the record, Ms. Wicks substituted out as the attorney for Watson, Baker, and Davies. Bob Powers substituted in as the attorney for Watson. Bill Colvin substituted in as the attorney for Baker. And Gary Fields substituted in as the attorney for Larry Davies.

Ms. Wicks chose to listen to the Judge. That appears to be why we were let out early so that the trial would not start until everyone was properly represented.

The jury panel was brought in. The Judge made some remarks. From the panel, the Judge chose 12 jurors and two alternates. They were seated in the jury box. The Judge asked each juror a few basis questions.

The various attorneys began questioning the jurors. Attempts were made to excuse jurors for cause. They failed. Various attorneys made pre-emptory challenges. Finally, at the end of the day, after all of the pre-emptory challenges were used up, the jury was selected.

The actual trial would start the next day at 10 a.m. Everyone arrived at the appointed time. Ms. Chu would make her opening statement. Ms. Wicks could either make or waive her opening statement. She could make her opening statement after the prosecution completed its case in chief and before her defense.

Ms. Chu outlined how National Woman Magazine made an award for Woman of the Year each year, that Taylor received the award for this year, and that it was customary for the winner to be presented the award at a ceremony where she would give a short speech. This allowed the world to know the recipient's whereabouts on the day and time chosen.

She outlined how the ceremony was held at a small park across the street from the local U S Attorney's Office, where Taylor worked. She relayed how the park was decorated with a stage facing a glass building. She had some photos of how it looked.

She outlined that near the conclusion of Taylor's speech, someone jumped from the roof of the glass building, breaking the glass, and winding up in a room on the third floor in which there was a sniper and a sniper's rifle aimed through a hole in the glass.

She then went on to outline the killing of SA Reeves by Les Baker and the attempted attack on Taylor by the MMA Fighter, Larry Davies, which attack was foiled.

She then went into the connection between Bobbie Franco and the killers. At this point Ms. Wicks jumped up to object to the opening statement, which seldom happened. The opening statement is not evidence but is more like a wish list of what one intends to prove.

The Judge fielded the objection and asked Ms. Chu how she intended to make the connection between these events and Bobbie Franco. Ms. Chu responded that she had a witness who taped a meeting with Mr. Franco where he outlines the entire episode in detail.

The Judge overruled the objection. Ms. Wicks appeared bewildered.

Here we see the disconnect between the perpetrators and the bosses. Without a witness, a connection would be very difficult to make.

227

Warrants for phone records, bank records, phone taps, and other surveillance methods are very hard to get. This is why one may hire someone to kill someone else and may never get caught, unless someone informs on him.

Ms. Wicks reserved her opening statement until the prosecution's case was complete. She was working on the theory that if in its case in chief the prosecution could not produce a witness, she might get the case dismissed, at least as to her client, which is all she cared about.

Taylor was called as the first witness:

Judge: "Ms. Shaw, will you please state your full name and spell your last name."

Ms. Shaw: "Taylor Shaw Miller, MILLER."

Ms. Chu: "Ms. Shaw, how are you employed?"

Ms. Shaw: "I am an assistant United States Attorney. I work out of the Riverside office."

Ms. Chu: "How long have you been so employed?"

Ms. Shaw: "Approximately 6 years."

Ms. Chu: "And where did you work before that?"

Ms. Shaw: "I worked for the California State Attorney General in Fairview."

Ms. Chu: "And what were your duties?"

Ms. Shaw: "When I was with the California State Attorney General, I started out in Elder Abuse and was then promoted to White Collar Crimes. When I went to the U S Attorney's Office, I started out on the Native American Task force and was then moved to sex crimes."

Ms. Chu: "Did you recently receive the award for Woman of the Year?"

Ms. Shaw: "Yes."

Ms. Chu: "Where did you receive this award."

Ms. Shaw: "At a small park across the street from my office in Riverside which was decorated for the occasion."

Ms. Chu: "Can you tell us, in your own words, what happened that day?"

Ms. Shaw: "Near the end of my acceptance speech, I saw a man jump from the roof of the building opposite the stage and crash through the glass wall of the building. Inside of the room, which was then exposed, one could see a sniper's rifle and two men fighting with one man who appeared to be the sniper. In all of the commotion, someone from the audience pulled out a gun. One of the FBI agents

228

who I met earlier made a move to take the gun away from him and was shot. As part of my speech, I was going to shoot a bow and arrow that was brought in from a local Indian Reservation, at a target. I grabbed the bow and got off two shots, each hitting the shooter, one in one leg and one in the other. He went down, as the tips were specially prepared with curare. My Indian friend who was in the audience reached the audience shooter and tied him up. He was, unfortunately, unable to do anything for the FBI Agent who having been shot died.

My two friends who apprehended the sniper helped move the audience shooter to the FBI containment area.

My friend in the audience took the deceased FBI Agent to the FBI containment area.

I then looked to the side of the stage, and a huge man was coming my way. Two men tried to stop him, but he passed them with one or two punches each. The huge man was then coming towards me."

Ms. Chu: "And then what happened?

Ms. Shaw: "From out of nowhere, the Chief grabbed the huge man by the throat and threw him to the ground like a rag doll. The Chief then proceeded to bounce the man's head against the concrete and then beat him until he was almost unrecognizable. It was frightening."

Ms. Chu: "Was that it?"

Ms. Shaw: "No. The huge man got up to make yet another assault. As he moved forward, the Chief hit him so hard in his jaw that I thought his head would come off. He then finished him off by hitting him so hard in the body that his back must have been broken. The huge man literally could not move. He just collapsed. It took my other three friends just to move him to the containment area.

"The people in the crowd were so frightened that they moved away from the center of the infield to make a double wide path for the Chief. No one wanted to be mistaken, even by accident, for trying to mess with me. We walked together to the infield. The Chief and my other three friends, Chuck, Michael, and Roger, left in Roger's car and returned, I presume, to the Reservation."

Ms. Chu: "Anything else?"

Ms. Shaw: "No."

Ms. Chu: "I have nothing further at this time."

Judge: "Your witness."

Ms. Wicks: "Hello Ms. Shaw. My name is Stevie Wicks. I am the attorney for Bobbie Franco. Is everything you related to us here today all of the knowledge you have concerning the events of that day?"

Ms. Shaw: "No."

Ms. Wicks: "What else do you know?"

Ms. Shaw: "I have seen additional evidence about persons involved in the arranging of the various crimes committed on that day."

Ms. Wicks: "Where is this evidence?"

Ms. Shaw: "It is with my attorney and the witness who has first-hand knowledge of those facts."

Ms. Wicks: "Ms. Shaw, do you make it a habit to travel around with Indians?"

Ms. Shaw: "I am going to answer that question because I am required to do so. However, I find the question not only inappropriate but also repulsive."

Judge: "Ms. Wicks, I have to agree with Ms. Shaw. We are in a court room. Justice in this country, at least in this courtroom, is color blind. If you want to allege that someone in Ms. Shaw's circle did something wrong from a legal standpoint, I will entertain that. But being an Indian certainly does not qualify. From what I have heard, I would say that the Indians, as you call them, acquitted themselves quite well under the circumstances. Please continue Ms. Shaw."

Ms. Shaw: "I have a long-standing pleasant and productive relationship with many Indian people at the Reservation."

Ms. Wicks: "How did the relationship start?"

Ms. Shaw: "When I was appointed to the U S Attorney's Office, I was one of four people drafted to start an Indian Task Force. The Task Force was to investigate mishaps at Indian reservations and how justice and legal services might be better rendered at the reservation level. Most of the work is criminal in nature. The other three task force members are criminal-law specialists. I was selected because I am an environmental law specialist, and there are also environmental issues.

"The policy at office is for new assistant U S Attorneys to spend at least one day at an Indian reservation to see the conditions first hand. When the first day is over, we are offered the opportunity to stay one week. I was told that no one ever asked to do that. I went home and told my husband that I wanted to go and stay the rest of the week at the Reservation and that he and Izzy, our daughter, could come up on Saturday to take me home.

"I spent the week at the Reservation and fell in love with the place and the people, even though the living conditions were not only bad but were boarder-line inhumane. My husband and daughter came up that Saturday, we spent the rest of the day there, and then came home. Since then, I have returned many times.

"After this visit, I worked on the Indian water rights case. I won't bore you with it, but it is a rather important case involving the aquafer under the Coachella Valley. Later, about five and a half years ago when my daughter was kidnapped, the Indians helped me extricate her from her kidnapper who is a terrible gangster."

Ms. Wicks: "Yes, I see, you have spent quite a bit of time at the reservation. Is it a romantic thing?"

Ms. Shaw: "Again, inappropriate, but I guess that is all you have. No, 95 percent of the time I am at the Reservation with my husband of nearly 12 years and our 10-year old daughter."

Ms. Wicks: "Why would you spend so much time there?"

Ms. Shaw: "To learn."

Ms. Wicks: "To learn about what. They can't even read or write."

Ms. Shaw: "We go to the Reservation to learn about life. To learn about nature. To learn about animals. To learn about another culture. Indians are said to have no culture because they do not put the writings of their great thinkers into leather bound covers and place them on the shelves of great libraries, where they are never read. No, Indians sit by a fire and talk about their ancestors allowing their young people to learn from their elders. They do not hide their thoughts inside of bound books."

"You should go there sometime. I think you would be surprised at how much knowledge is available."

Ms. Wicks: "Aren't the living conditions at the Reservation terrible. How could you survive?"

Ms. Shaw: "Well Ms. Wicks, I grew up on a small orange farm. The conditions on my family farm were about the same as at the Reservation. We poor whites live at around the same level as the Indians. So, for me, it was not much different. My husband was there because for him learning is more important than being comfortable all of the time. At 10, my daughter doesn't know the difference, which is how I like it. Kids are not born with a sense of inequality; that is something which is learned."

Ms. Wicks: "Why did you have four Indians with you at your acceptance speech?"

231

Ms. Shaw: "They came to support me?"

Ms. Wicks: "Did you pay them as your personal protection detail?"

Ms. Shaw: "No."

Ms. Wicks: "If they weren't being paid, why would they come and why would they engage in the heroic efforts you outlined during your direct examination?"

Ms. Shaw: "Ms. Wicks, I'm afraid that I could sit here for the next year and never be able to explain to you how Indian people think. Indian people do not come and offer support for money. They come and offer support out of a sense of duty. Me and my girlfriend teach one day a week at the Reservation. We do not do it for money. We do it because it is the right thing to do, and it benefits the Indian children. Some people are motivated this way."

Ms. Wicks: "If this person they call the Chief is not professionally trained, how can he take down a huge professional MMA fighter with his bare hands?"

Ms. Shaw: "That is a simple question to answer. He can do this because he is the Chief. His training is far beyond the training that a white person receives as a professional fighter. His training goes back 3000 years and is handed down from generation to generation. His life's work is to protect all of those who live within his tribe. If a 300-pound mountain lion attacks a child, the Chief will wrestle the mountain lion with his bare hands because he is the Chief and that is his duty. I only have God to thank that he is so good at it."

Ms. Wicks: "Then how is it that the white man was able to take over the continent?"

Ms. Shaw: "Numbers and diseases. When the white man first came to north America around 1600, the Indians helped them survive the winters. Even so, by as early as 1620, many of the Indians knew that it was the white man's intention to take over the entire continent and to displace the Indians.

"By the middle 1800s, the white man began moving the Indians onto reservations where they took away their language, their culture, and their way of life, even requiring them to attend boarding schools. Why then could the Indians not remain self-sufficient? Because for the Indian, the land was his means of survival. When the Indians had control of the land, they had room to hunt, ground on which to grow, water for their crops, and everything necessary to survive.

"White men look at land differently. They fertilize, rotate, and

232

manipulate land for their use. The Indians, on the other hand, work with the land in its natural form. The Indians use a plot of land and then allow it to rest for a year or two before planting that area again. Once the reservation system was established, the Indians could no longer travel away from the reservation to find suitable land. They were confined to the reservation where the land might no longer be fertile."

Ms. Wicks: "During your direct examination, you state that after the glass was broken at the alleged sniper's den, you saw a man in the audience pull out a gun. You said that he had a brief encounter with one of the FBI men, Norman Reeves, and that he shot Mr. Reeves, at point blank range. Is this how you remember it?"

Mr. Colvin: "Objection your Honor. The man alleged to be the man in the audience, Les Baker, is my client. If Ms. Shaw testifies as to what she believes she saw, that is fine. However, I prefer to not have another attorney testify for my client. I need to cross-examine Ms. Shaw myself."

Judge: "I agree with that. In point of fact, Ms. Wicks does not even represent anyone who was physically present during the events. Ms. Wicks, I have given you pretty wide latitude because we need some of the background information anyway, and it appeared as if you were doing a pretty good job of eliciting it. Until we reach the aiding and abetting element, I believe that the questions for Les Baker and Ms. Shaw's recollections about his participation should be left to Mr. Baker's attorney, Mr. Colvin."

Ms. Wicks: "That is fine you honor."

Judge: "Ok. Mr. Colvin, since Ms. Shaw is on the stand and has been sworn in, would this be a convenient time to ask her about you client?"

Mr. Colvin: "Yes, your Honor."

Judge: "Go ahead then."

Mr. Colvin: "Ms. Shaw, after the episode with the sniper, what did you see?"

Ms. Shaw: "From the stage, I saw the man, the man sitting next to you, get up and move towards my right. He encountered the FBI man I met earlier, Norman Reeves. He shot Mr. Reeves from point blank range."

Mr. Colvin: "And then what happened?"

Ms. Shaw: "I saw that Roger was close by and that your client still had his gun drawn. When we were setting up for the speech, my friends kindly brought a bow and two arrows so I could give a demonstration of arrow shooting to the crowd. Seeing that Roger was in trouble, I grabbed the bow and got off two quick shots. Both arrows hit your client, one in each thigh. He went out as the tips were dipped in curare. He was taken for medical attention."

Mr. Colvin: "Do you mean to tell me that you got off two arrow shots from 30 feet. How did you do that?"

Ms. Shaw: "Like anything else, practice, practice, practice. Over the past nearly 10 years I have made hundreds of arrow shots and knife throws."

Mr. Colvin: "I have set up a target outside of the courtroom in a patio area. The bailiff has the bow and arrow set you used which has been entered into evidence. Would you be willing to demonstrate your shooting?"

Judge: "Mr. Colvin, that is all well and good, but many people witnessed the two bow and arrow shots that struck your client. Ms. Chu, do you have any information regarding Mr. Baker's injuries?"

Ms. Chu: "Yes, your Honor. I have the medical report from the hospital which confirms that Mr. Baker was struck with two arrows, each of which was dipped in curare. They were both removed in the emergency room on the day of Ms. Shaw's speech."

Judge: "Mr. Colvin, do you still think that the demonstration is necessary?"

Mr. Colvin: "Yes, your Honor. It is our contention that someone else must have shot the arrows as Ms. Shaw was too far away from Mr. Baker to land those shots."

Judge: "Very well. Ms. Shaw, are you prepared to do this demonstration now?"

Ms. Shaw: "Yes, your Honor. It would be my pleasure."

The entire courtroom, including all court personnel, the jury, the jury alternates, and all of the parties, attorneys, and witnesses adjourned from the courtroom and made their way to the patio outside of the court building under the supervision of the bailiff, who was also carrying the same bow and the same two arrows present at the site of the speech.

Upon arriving at the patio, it could be seen that a target had been set up approximately 35 feet away from a chalk line made on the concrete patio. All people were gathered 10 feet behind the chalk line.

Taylor was asked to proceed to a location just behind the chalk line and was asked to face the target.

Judge: "Bailiff would you be so kind as to hand the bow and arrow to Ms. Shaw after which she may shoot both arrows at the target."

As the bailiff handed the bow and then the two arrows to Ms. Shaw, she made two quick shots at the target with both arrows striking the dead center.

The entire group returned to the courtroom. The Judge resumed the bench and Taylor returned to the witness stand.

Judge: "Do you have anything else for Ms. Shaw?"

Mr. Colvin: "I have nothing else at this time."

Judge: "Ms. Shaw has done enough for today. I am inclined to allow the prosecution to bring forth its other evidence and witnesses. Then, if necessary, defense counsel may again question Ms. Shaw, though I fail to see any advantage there. She seems to remember things better than anyone else, as she was in the middle of it all. We will all meet back here at 10 a.m. tomorrow."

Court reconvened at 10 a.m. The Judge asked whether the prosecution had any other witnesses or evidence. Ms. Chu responded that she did. She called Rob Fulton to the stand. Rob was wearing an expensive dark grey suit with various gold accessories including a class ring and a Rolex watch. He looked appropriate.

Ms. Chu: "Please state your full name and spell your last name."

Mr. Fulton: "Robert David Fulton, FULTON. But my friends call me Rob."

Ms. Chu: "Thank you. Did you have occasion to meet with the four gentlemen sitting at counsel table in a private room at a club facility owned by one of these gentlemen?"

Mr. Fulton: "Yes."

Ms. Chu: "Which of these gentlemen owned the club facility?"

Mr. Fulton: "Bobbie Franco."

Ms. Chu: "Did you make a recording of what transpired at this meeting?"

Ms. Wicks: "Objection. Lacks foundation."

Judge: "Ms. Chu."

Ms. Chu: "Mr. Fulton, have you had occasion to hear the voice of Mr. Franco before?"

Mr. Fulton: "Yes. On several occasions concerning business, I spoke with Mr. Franco on the telephone. The meeting I had with Mr.

Franco and the other defendants was in person, and I heard Mr. Franco's voice, in person, on that occasion."

Ms. Chu: "How many times have you heard his voice?"

Mr. Fulton: "Dozens of times."

Ms. Chu: "Tell us how you are familiar with Mr. Franco's voice?"

Mr. Fulton: "On each occasion I spoke with Mr. Franco, he introduced himself as Bobbie Franco, and during our meeting, I saw that the voice belonged to him."

Ms. Chu: "Have you heard the recording marked as Exhibit A for identification?"

Mr. Fulton: "Yes."

Ms. Chu: "Do you recognize the voice on the recording?"

Mr. Fulton: "Yes."

Ms. Chu: "And to whom does the voice belong?"

Mr. Fulton: "Mr. Bobbie Franco."

Ms. Chu: "We move to have the recoding be admitted into evidence as Exhibit A."

Judge: "Any objections?"

Ms. Wicks: "Yes your Honor. The prosecution lacked consent to make the recording."

Judge: "We are in federal court, and the consent from one side is sufficient. Objection overruled. The recording marked Exhibit A shall be admitted into evidence."

Ms. Chu: "Due to the importance of the tape-recorded evidence, we submit the audio recording and a written transcript prepared by a qualified transcriptionist, Dr. Richard David along with his declaration that the recording device has been examined and was capable of making an accurate recording and that the device was not tampered with."

Judge: "Very well. Please continue on with your examination of Mr. Fulton."

Ms. Chu: "Thank you your Honor. Mr. Fulton, are you prepared to play the recording made of this meeting for us today?"

Ms. Wick: "Objection. Hearsay."

Judge: "Overruled."

Ms. Chu: "Will you play the tape for us?"

Mr. Fulton: "Yes. On the tape, the following was said by Bobbie Franco: 'Gentlemen, I have a problem that I need to get rid of. I need to get rid of Taylor Shaw. She is an assistant United States Attorney

236

in Riverside. She has caused me endless problems and thousands of dollars. She is a complete bitch, and she has to be killed. She is pretty clever and elusive for a woman. My plan includes using three people to kill her. If the three of you, Rex Watson, Les Baker, and Larry Davies work with me here and execute this plan, we will be successful, and I won't have to think about this bitch any longer.

'Firstly, a sniper will be dispatched to the glass-walled office building across the quad from the stage location. A hole will be drilled in the glass wall, and a sniper's rifle will be set up on a table behind the hole. The barrel of the gun will look into this hole. She will be giving her little speech in the quad in front of the glass-walled building. She'll be an easy target. Mr. Watson will man the sniper's post.

'I then want one man in the crowd maybe 30 feet from the stage. If the sniper misses, in the confusion, he will be able to shoot her and kill her. Les I thought you would handle this. If somehow Rex and Les fail, I am going to the big guns, the no-way-to-miss approach. I have retained an MMA fighter, Larry Davies, to bat cleanup. If all else fails, I will have him grab her and kill her with his bare hands. Up close and personal. You will each be paid $1,000,000 for your work. I will give you each $500,000 today and $500,000 tomorrow, when the job is complete. Let's meet here tomorrow at 11 a.m. to get going on it.'"

The court room was hushed. Everyone in the jury box, to a person, looked both sickened and disgusted.

Ms. Wick jumped up with a variety of wild objections all of which were overruled by the Judge.

The other three attorneys had a few questions for Rob. Rob was excused, and Taylor was re-called to the stand. All four attorneys had a few additional questions, which she answered. She was excused.

Closing arguments would commence the next day. On the next day, all of the parties convened at 10 a.m.

Ms. Chu's closing argument was succinct. In the law, if the facts are on your side, arguments tend to be direct and to the point. Also, there were multiple eye witnesses to everything that went on. The defendants who were present, Rex, Les, and Larry, included an obvious perpetrator, Les, who shot the FBI man, and two attempted acts, Rex the sniper, and Larry the MMA fighter.

The felony murder rule aspect was somewhat interesting. Rex and Larry could go down for felony murder as the murder of the FBI man

237

did occur during the commission of a felony or an attempted felony. One would question whether attempted murder would be merged into the murder and not form the basis for a separate felony. If the three had been robbing the place or were kidnapping victims, the lone murder might have been done during a felony.

The other four attorneys delivered their closing arguments. It was a circus of cross-finger pointing and protests of denial. Les, the man who actually pulled the trigger, offered to help authenticate the tape as being Bobbie's voice in exchange for 25 to life rather that life without the possibility of parole.

The MMA fighter made the case that he did not have a weapon so the worst crime for which he could be held liable was battery. His attorney pointed out that the fists of an MMA fighter are not considered weapons which need to be registered. Even so, his clear intention was murder.

Rex, the sniper, took the unusual position that he did not intend to go through with the assassination but that he was only pretending because of his fear of Bobbie Franco. His effort was foiled before he could get off a shot.

As to Franco, as he was not present at the site, his liability would be based on his role as an aider and abettor. The Judge's jury instruction will be of interest.

The federal jury instruction for the United States Courts for the Ninth Circuit for aiding and abetting states the following:

A defendant may be found guilty of murder, even if the defendant personally did not commit the act or acts constituting the crime but aided and abetted in its commission. To "aid and abet" means intentionally to help someone else commit a crime. To prove a defendant guilty of murder by aiding and abetting, the government must prove each of the following beyond a reasonable doubt:

First, someone else committed the murder.

Second, the defendant aided and abetted, counseled, commanded, induced or procured that person with respect to at least one element of the crime.

Third, the defendant acted before the crime was completed.

It is not enough that the defendant is merely associated with the persons committing the crime or that he was unintentionally helpful to that person. The evidence must show that the defendant acted with the knowledge and intention of helping that person commit murder.

The government is not required to prove precisely which defendant actually committed the crime and which defendant aided and abetted.

Both sides rested, and the jury deliberated.

Rex, the sniper, was convicted of attempted murder. Les, the shooter, was convicted of second-degree murder. Larry, the MMA fighter, was convicted of battery. Bobbie was convicted of murder in the first degree, as he arranged a pre-meditated murder.

The prosecution did not get the full punishment for Rex, Les, and Larry, but it got what it was really after, murder in the first degree for Bobbie. This would mean life without the possibility of parole. There would be no date in the future on which Bobbie would be able to get out and injure more people, a good thing. His inability to get out would mean that his business connections would eventually evaporate as well.

Rick was with Taylor in the court room when the sentences came in, and there was a sigh of relief. Now they could get back to their lives, all that they ever asked for in the first place.

Taylor and Rick drove home. It was Friday afternoon, and neither would have to work in the morning.

Taylor called John and told him the news. He was pleased. She called Chuck and spoke with him and Pamela. They were pleased. Chuck said that he would call Michael and Roger, as they had been such a great help throughout the whole affair. Chuck let out his two prisoners from their mountain cave jail cell and took them back to their car.

Izzy would remain with her sitter for the night as her parents were very involved with the trial.

This left Taylor and Rick alone, a condition with which they were not at all familiar. They decided to go to dinner. They went to a nice restaurant.

After eating Taylor said to Rick, "Honey, I'm glad this case is over. Having it over lets me know that now we can truly get back to our most beautiful life together."

Rick concluded, "That sounds like a great idea to me."

About the Author

Tighe Taylor is a graduate of Whittier College, School of Law, located in Los Angeles County. He lives and works in Los Angeles where he owns an insurance and property consulting business and practices law. His prior literary works include the book, The Tragic Death of Marina Habe, a true crime account of the most unfortunate kidnapping and murder of Marina Habe, a friend from junior high school, and the crime fiction books entitled The Kidnapping of Tammy Fitzgerald, The Kidnapping of Taylor Shaw, and the Kidnapping of Isabel Miller.

Milton Keynes UK
Ingram Content Group UK Ltd.
UKHW010242221123
432980UK00002B/214